FAT CHANCE

FAT CHANCE

a novel by

Aviva Orenstein

QUID PRO BOOKS
New Orleans, Louisiana

Published in 2016 by Quid Pro Books.

ISBN 978-1-61027-340-4 (pbk)
ISBN 978-1-61027-341-1 (cloth)
ISBN 978-1-61027-347-3 (ebk)

QUID PRO BOOKS
Quid Pro, LLC
5860 Citrus Blvd., suite D-101
New Orleans, Louisiana 70123
www.quidprobooks.com

Publisher's Cataloging-in-Publication

Orenstein, Aviva.

Fat chance / Aviva Orenstein.

p. cm.

ISBN 978-1-61027-340-4 (paperback)

1. Women lawyers—Fiction. 2. Jewish women—Fiction. 3. Jewish families—Fiction. I. Title.

PS3552.A487 O21 2016 817' .31.5—dc22

Front cover original artwork provided by Alison Stake, © 2016, used by permission. Author photograph on back cover inset provided courtesy of IU-B. Additional editorial consulting was generously provided by Lee Scheingold and Hannah de Keijzer

All characters, places and incidents are used fictitiously, and any resemblance to any person, living or dead, or to any place or incident, is entirely coincidental.

To my sons, David, Michael, and Ben
(Maybe skip chapters 47-48)

FAT CHANCE

1

Doughnuts," I said, as I passed by Molly's desk.

"Good morning to you, too. Glazed or jelly?"

"I'm wearing a white shirt, so let's go for broke."

"Coming up," Molly said. "I'll look for an extra gooey one."

"Make that two," I instructed. "I've got a meeting with Travis in twenty minutes."

Tuesday morning, and my day had started with an 8:00 a.m. email about Travis Jensen, the whiz-kid head of information technology. Apparently, Travis was wearing a T-shirt that read, "I need a hug, but I'll settle for a blow job," and the secretary whose machine he was repairing first thing this morning wasn't amused.

Travis was fabulous at his job—accurate and quick. He understood all the software and had tailored much of it for our company's use. I'd worked closely with him in generating user-friendly, online employee evaluations, and there was no doubt that the little twerp was capable. However, he had the maturity of a fourteen-year-old. I'd been having way too much first-hand experience with that demographic. I didn't need a teenager at work too. At least at work, I had a clue how to handle it.

When Molly ushered Travis into my office, he was still wearing the damned shirt. I threw him a T-shirt left over from the last company picnic, and pointed to my private bathroom. "We'll talk after you've changed," I said.

"This is ridiculous," Travis said as he emerged wearing our company logo. "I know my rights. There's such a thing as the First Amendment, you know."

"Please sit down, Travis," I said, pointing to two wing-backed chairs near a small table with fresh flowers.

"Have you ever read the First Amendment?" I inquired.

"Er. . ."

"Let me tell you how it goes. 'Congress shall make no law abridging the freedom of speech.' Do I look like Congress to you?" I asked.

"No," he said, quickly glancing at my 5′3″ frame stuffed into a 1X pantyhose and a size-16 navy blue suit. "But I don't see why everyone has to be so hypersensitive. A lot of people find my T-shirts hilarious."

"Maybe, but some people are deeply offended. It's hard for a woman to think she's being taken seriously when the guy working on her computer is wearing a T-shirt that reads 'no fat chicks.'"

Travis squirmed a little at that one, but remained undaunted.

"This is just political correctness. Has everyone lost their sense of humor? I don't see what the big deal is."

"I'm afraid there's only one way to handle this," I said with determination.

"You're not going to fire me over my T-shirt collection!" Travis exclaimed.

"You're right, that would be stupid. I'm going to address the underlying problem. Molly," I called, "would you come in here? I want a witness."

Molly bounded in. She can always tell when something good is about to happen.

"Molly, you saw Travis come in here with his T-shirt that announced that he needed—I'm sorry—would *settle* for a blow job, right?"

"Yes, I did."

"Well, I think I should just give him one; then maybe he won't feel the need to keep advertising his sexual desires on his sleeve, as it were."

"Sounds reasonable to me," Molly deadpanned.

"Drop your pants," I said as I stood up, maintaining eye contact.

The look of horror on his face was unmistakable and quite satisfying.

"Seriously, I'm good at this," I assured him with a confident smile, releasing my hair, which was desperately in need of coloring, from its bun at the nape of my neck. I gave my head what I hoped passed for a sexy toss.

Travis' eyes darted wildly and he looked a bit like a cornered animal as he shrunk back in the chair.

"You . . . you . . . you can't do that," Travis stammered.

"I wouldn't dream of forcing you, but isn't this what you want?"

"No!"

"Are you sure?" I asked in my most sultry tone.

"Cut it out. This isn't funny," Travis said in a low voice, backing the chair farther away from me.

"Am I making you uncomfortable?"

"Of course you are. Don't touch me," he said with what sounded like genuine repulsion.

"Well, you know what? I don't want to make you feel uncomfortable. I withdraw the offer. And I promise that I won't offer again."

"Are you insane?"

"No, I just wanted you to experience what it feels like when someone makes you feel sexually uncomfortable. It's really unpleasant, don't you think?"

Molly, to her credit, had kept a straight face throughout my little escapade.

"Since it's pretty clear that you won't settle for a blow job after all, let's cut out this crap for good, OK?"

"OK," Travis muttered.

"You're a talented guy, and a really valued employee. Don't hold yourself back. Making coworkers feel uncomfortable is unprofessional."

"I get it. You really had me going there," Travis said with a forced smile. He was still pretty pale. "Would you have really gone through with it?" he asked.

I just smiled. Let him wonder, I thought.

"I'm glad we've come to an understanding. Molly here is very discreet. She wouldn't dream of letting anyone know what happened. But, I do worry that if you wear another provocative T-shirt, she could slip up and tell folks about how you turned down my offer."

"I get it. I'd no idea you played so dirty."

"Don't ever cross her," Molly said gravely to Travis. "She seems nice, but Claire can be brutal when she has to be."

"Look," I said, turning to Travis, "I believe that you do get the message. And, you know, you're getting a little old for T-shirts anyway. Go buy some shirts with buttons on them. Your future is worth investing in."

"Thanks, Claire," he said with as much dignity as he could muster, then turned and high-tailed it out of my office.

"I can't believe you did that," Molly said once Travis had departed.

"Me, neither," I said, inordinately pleased with myself.

"Aren't you afraid he'll make a complaint?"

"To whom? All harassment charges have to go through me. Besides, Travis Jensen has been a walking billboard of sexual harassment for months. I don't think the guy who owns 'show me your tits' T-shirts in five separate colors is in a position to lodge any complaints. Corey would back me up on this."

"The look on his face was priceless," Molly said, chuckling.

"I know," I said conspiratorially. "But the story ends here. I don't want to embarrass the guy any further, and out of context, this incident could be misconstrued."

"I won't tell anyone. There are a lot of guys at this company who wouldn't turn down a blow job, and I couldn't handle all the foot traffic."

"Thanks, you're the best," I said.

"Remind me not to mess with you."

"Will do," I said.

I returned to less urgent matters, planning a training for middle management about our maternity and disability leave policy and reviewing a brochure about various retirement fund options for employees. I loved my job and was good at it. I marveled at how differently I felt about my life at home. I felt utterly incompetent at handling my son, Sam, who for the past year had been at best, sullen, and at worst, just plain mean. God knows what happened to that sweet little boy who used to let me read him stories and begged me to play superheroes. It was always the same scenario: I would be the little kitty stuck in a tree; Sam would play Superman to the rescue. I didn't appreciate it when I had it. The angry teen he was becoming would no doubt leave me in the tree to die of exposure without a second thought.

I looked up and saw Molly enter the room. Usually, we just bellowed for each other, or, on more formal occasions, she buzzed me.

"What's up?" I asked.

"Claire, I think there's some bad news."

"Is Sam all right?" I asked in a panic.

"Sam's fine, but there's a call from Florida. It's about your dad," Molly said with a hand on my shoulder.

Pop? I'd just spoken to him on Sunday. He was fine. He had gone for his daily swim and was taking some woman out for dinner.

Over the phone, a police officer explained that Pop had suffered a massive, fatal heart attack. He was in a revolving door when the attack came on and dead before he could make it through to exit the building.

I sat at my large desk, stunned. Molly brought me tea, cleared my calendar, purchased airline tickets for Sam and me, and phoned my neighbor and best friend Joan, who immediately invited us for dinner and offered to take me to the airport the next day. Throughout this bustle of activity I sat motionless at my desk.

2

The next few days were a blur, with little time for any true reflection. I found myself, post-funeral, seated on the balcony of Pop's West Boca condo with a view of a golf course manicured to within an inch of its life. I picked absentmindedly at a plate of strudel that a neighbor had brought by. In accordance with Jewish mourning ritual, I'd covered all the mirrors in the house. I was grateful that no reflection would indict me for the extra pounds I had put on, at least not any time soon.

I was jolted by a voice that had only recently hit a lower register.

"Mom, look at yourself," my son admonished. "That's so gross. I hope you weren't planning to give that strudel to anyone else."

"OK, Sam, you have permission to eat with your fingers when *I'm* dead."

"Why the hell are you so morbid?" he asked, casting me a contemptuous look.

Instead of responding—really, why was I so morbid?—I tried to focus on Sam's behavior at the funeral. He had hugged me, not one of his standard stiff-as-a-board, I'll-allow-you-to-drape-your-pathetic-self-over-me hugs, but a genuine embrace. Such gestures from the boy were rare and never offered without exceptionally good cause.

My attempts to focus on the positive were overwhelmed, however, by Sam's resumption of his campaign to return home early.

"I'm sick of this place. There's nothing to do but swim laps in the pool," Sam whined.

"But you haven't met all the little old ladies who had a crush on your grandfather," I protested with mock enthusiasm. "You clearly need to stay a little longer."

"Mom, please!" Sam was using his elementary-school-teacher-who-is-about-to-blow voice on me.

"Maybe I could stay with Dad," Sam proposed after I again nixed his suggestion that he stay home alone.

The mention of my ex made my stomach lurch. Someday soon I'd have to meet Jeremy's new wife, but I was damned sure I that my first contact with the newlyweds wasn't going to be to request a favor.

"Dad and Kimberly just left for their honeymoon. Ever heard that three's a crowd? It applies particularly to honeymoons."

"I could stay with Joanie," he suggested.

"Joanie is pregnant. There's no way you're staying with her," I said wearily.

"I won't get in Joanie's way. I'll even play with the twins."

"Ain't happening," I said, trying to summon up anything vaguely sounding like resolve.

"Can't you just ask Joanie?"

"No, babe, but. . . ."

"Don't call me babe!"

"No, Sam," I said, struggling to keep my tone even, "but I do have an idea."

"What?" Sam asked, his tone grudgingly hopeful.

"How about if I ask Marjorie if she'll take you for a few days?"

"I could stay with Ben?" Sam asked.

"And I could owe Marjorie big for the rest of my life. I'll never hear the end of it, ever. Every long-winded anecdote will begin, 'Claire, you remember the time I took Sam in after your father died?' My one solace is that by the end of the visit I'll be looking pretty darn good in the mother department," I said.

"That's not exactly hard," Sam pointed out. "She still makes Ben kiss her good night."

"Now that's an idea. Give mumsy a kiss."

"Don't be gross," he said with sincerity.

I phoned Marjorie, the mother of Sam's best friend, and for ten full minutes was treated to a lament of how the Hudsonville schools don't serve the truly gifted. I hung up and told Sam that he was going, and that Stuart, Ben's older brother, had learned absolutely nothing in science last year.

"Stuart's a nerd," Sam pronounced.

"He'd be OK if that woman could just let up a bit. Look, Sam, you're going to really have to clean up after yourself and be a considerate guest. . . ."

"I know. I'll turn out the lights and won't leave any water on the bathroom floor."

"And make the bed in the morning. Normal people do that, you know. Not everyone are slobs like us."

As he left the room, Sam mumbled, "Thanks, Mom," with studied casualness.

A knock came at the door, and I hurriedly swallowed a large chunk of strudel, acknowledging that I wasn't among those for whom a death in the family caused a lack of appetite. Opening the door, I met a very short woman holding a large Pyrex baking dish in two bright yellow oven mitts.

"Hello, Claire. I'm Mrs. Teitelbaum. You don't remember me, but I know all about you."

Yipes, I thought, what had she heard?

"Of course I remember you, Mrs. Teitelbaum," I assured her with what I hoped was the appropriate degree of warmth. "You're down the hall, right?"

"Yes, 4-C," Mrs. Teitelbaum confirmed, and then added in a somber voice, "We're all so sorry about your loss. Everyone in the complex will miss your father. He was a *marvelous* man."

I took another good look at Mrs. Teitelbaum (whom I always remembered by her full name, "You don't remember me, but I'm Mrs. Teitelbaum"). Mrs. T's thinning hair was a very bright orange. She sported matching orange lipstick and a creamy blue splash of color above each eye. She must have been at least seventy-five, but she had an hourglass figure, with some serious cleavage popping out of the front of her pale orange pantsuit. Who wears velour in the summer in Florida? I wondered whether Pops had ever gotten into Mrs. Teitelbaum's velour pants. "This is dairy. Your father used to like my kugels very much, but this one didn't come out so good. I don't know what's the matter with me. I put in too much sugar. I'm going to stick it in the oven to stay warm, and you can have it when I go. OK, darling?"

"This is so nice of you. Won't you join us?"

"*Gotinyu*. No, no, darling, I'm not a guest. This is for you and Sam, for the *shiva*."

"Well, Sam is going home tomorrow, and I won't be able to finish this all by myself."

Mrs. Teitelbaum shot me a look expressing her conviction that I could, and indeed too often did, eat whole noodle puddings on my own.

"Sam's going back? Darling, you can't be here alone."

"I'll be fine, besides, my cousin is coming tonight. Sam is very eager to get back to his friends."

"Sure, he'd rather be with his friends," Mrs. Teitelbaum said indignantly. She immediately became more animated, looking younger and fiercer. I wondered whether Mrs. Teitelbaum had been a natural redhead before she started hitting the bottle.

"Take it from an old lady, darling, you're not doing him a favor. He should stay. A son should be with his mother at a time like this. Honestly, darling, tell him to stay."

"Thank you so much for worrying about me, Mrs. Teitelbaum, but the arrangements have all been made," I explained in my sweetest voice of calm inevitability.

I invited her to have a slice of kugel, which she refused, and then offered her some tea, noting that I was just about to put on the kettle.

"Just some hot water and a few raisins, but only if it's not a bother."

"No problem at all," I said, digging through the cupboard.

"Golden raisins OK?"

"If that's all you've got," Mrs. Teitelbaum said, examining the portion of kugel I'd served myself. "You don't like it," she said pointedly.

"No, no, it's delicious," I protested and heaped on another, more generous, slice to accompany the half-eaten portion on my plate. As I ate, Sam walked in.

"Hi," he said, eying the food.

"Is this Sam?" Mrs. Teitelbaum asked in mock wonder. "What a big young man you are!" she exclaimed. "How tall are you, darling?"

"Five-seven," said Sam.

"Hoo hah, five-seven. What a handsome boy. Would you like some kugel? It's not up to my usual, but you children don't mind the extra sugar. Not like a dilapidated old lady, like me."

A brief look of panic crossed Sam's face.

"I hope I look half as good as you when *I'm* sixty," I said.

Mrs. Teitelbaum couldn't hide her pleasure. "Sixty! What's the matter with you?" she said with a wave of her hand. "Really, Claire, darling, it's not too sweet?"

Sam successfully avoided eye contact and managed to answer in one word or less questions about his age, grade, whether he had a young lady, whether she was Jewish, and how the kugel tasted, really.

After showing Mrs. Teitelbaum to the door, I walked back to the kitchen and asked Sam, "Well, *darling,* do you want some more kugel?"

"Nah, it wasn't sweet enough."

I laughed—my first laugh since Pop died—and told Sam to get packed.

I knew from experience that Sam's version of packing would be to roll most, but not all, of his clothes (including his new suit purchased for the funeral) in a ball and shove them into the suitcase, on top of which he would throw his shoes, at least one sock, and some dirty underwear. All his toiletries would inevitably be left behind. While he was engaging in this maneuver, I remained in the kitchen sipping Earl Grey tea. As I surveyed Pop's kitchen, I reflected how much like the man the apartment was—neat, well-appointed, and thoroughly unobjectionable. He'd stayed out of the kitchen except to grind and brew fresh coffee, a smell I'll always associate with him and that still lingered in the room.

What kind of a monster was I, feeling nothing at the loss of my father? Certainly, there must have been many good childhood memories I could conjure. We'd shared many meals together, but at the moment, all I could bring to mind were his constant comments about my table manners. When I was an adult, Pop and I had many visits over the years, but we'd never stayed in the same house together. He couldn't tolerate the chaotic mess at my place, where my chief decorator was Fisher Fischer Price. Sam and I were certainly not welcome to sleep at his condo, even though he had the room.

Again my thoughts were interrupted, this time by the rabbi and his wife, who stopped by to pay a *shiva* call. The rabbi, no more than fifty for sure, seemed stricken by Pop's sudden death at seventy-nine. I felt awkward in the face of the rabbi's effusive efforts to console me. Didn't this guy deal with death as a profession? I'd always assumed that, after a while, rabbis, like morticians, viewed death as just another day at the office. Sure, Pop was a nice guy and he helped make the *minyan*, but the rabbi's sense of loss didn't compute. On the other hand, the rabbi's wife, the *rebbetzin*, a compact woman with frosted hair and a personality to match, did look appropriately bored. How many dark suits did she own just for such occasions?

The rabbi embraced me as he departed, uttering the traditional phrase, "May the Lord comfort you along with all the other mourners of Zion and Jerusalem."

"Thank you for everything, Rabbi," I muttered, embarrassed by my own calm.

Why didn't I feel grief? Maybe it just hadn't hit me, I speculated. Maybe Pop's death would feel real when I was back in Hudsonville. But what would be different? Our regular Sunday phone conversations always seemed disjointed, as if Pop was distracted by something much more engaging on ESPN. Pop wasn't big on small talk. He did, however, repeatedly note that I hadn't inherited my mother's athletic build, but instead, was built like his father's side of the family. Even as a little girl, I realized this wasn't a compliment.

As Sam grew, Pop seemed more comfortable with Sam than with me, playing chess and watching sports. Pop even taught Sam to play golf. Sam's advantage wasn't only that he was a boy, but that he was an undemanding one who lived far away and had no claim to Pop other than an occasional gift on his birthday or Hanukkah. I knew better than to expect more from my father, whose disapproval was palpable. And now, the time to impress him had run out.

3

I hadn't seen Lydia for months and was looking forward to our time alone together.

"Hey, tubby," she greeted me, looking striking, as usual, with her long white hair setting off her all-black attire.

"Come on in. Leave it to you to hassle a mourner," I responded with a smile.

Lydia was here to babysit me, just like old times. As she went to shoot the breeze with the monster, I gathered some sheets from the linen closet and started opening the living room couch, feeling a little guilty at how pleased I was that Lydia was going to stay the next couple of days. I'll never get over that special thrill of getting attention from Lydia. The seven years that separate us didn't matter much in middle age, but it had seemed like an unbridgeable gap when we were young. How I puppy-dogged after my cousin and sometime babysitter! Lydia, the queen of cool, magnanimously tolerated my adoration.

Lydia emerged from Sam's bedroom. "Man, he's big! He's got a mustache for Christ's sake."

"Yep, we've passed that crucial mother-son point where his mustache is more pronounced than mine. Did you catch how deep his voice has gotten? This whole puberty thing creeps me out. Can I get you some tea?" I offered.

"Nah, I don't want any. Besides, you're sitting *shiva*; you shouldn't be serving anyone. I'll bring you some herb tea and I'll take some coffee."

Assuring me that the coffee wouldn't render her sleepless, Lydia began to grind the beans. She inhaled deeply and noted that my dad always had the good stuff. It was true, Pop made a point of living well.

"Did the man ever fly coach?" Lydia asked.

"Not to my knowledge," I replied. "It's funny, I've been thinking the past couple of days that he knew how to live, but he also knew how to die. It's tough that he died so suddenly, but it was the best thing, really."

"It was a heart attack, right? I know it's trite to say, but it's good that he didn't suffer," Lydia said, placing her hand on mine.

"No, you're right. I can't imagine Pop sick. In fact, I don't even remember seeing him with anything worse than a cold. Pop couldn't stand the least discomfort or deviation from routine. That's why I wasn't really ever part of his daily life, I guess."

"Bubbe whisked you off when your mother died," Lydia observed. "It's not like he was given much of a chance."

"True, but Pop didn't exactly make a fuss over it."

"Maybe he was in no condition to. He was a mess when your mother died. Remember the funeral?"

An image of my father, head in his hands, doubled over in grief, suddenly flashed through my mind. It was the only time I saw him cry. I remembered feeling scared and lost.

"You're right, but I think he was relieved that Bubbe and Grandpa Sam took me."

Lydia found the filter for the coffee maker, and the aroma of brewing coffee soon filled the room. I inhaled and recalled how when I was with Pop, every meal always ended with coffee, good coffee, and some wildly expensive and inappropriate dessert for me. My favorites were the flambés. It wasn't every six-year-old who regularly ordered bananas foster.

"You know," I told Lydia, "at restaurants, Pop would send back food and demand to speak to the chef."

"Were you mortified?"

"Not really, and it wouldn't have mattered if I had been. If nothing else, it was worth it because of the way his high living annoyed the hell out of Bubbe. She was furious when he brought me back late, and I mean late—eleven or midnight. Flaunting my pleasure at his company was the closest I ever came to defying her, at least that she knew about."

"You were an insufferable little goody-two-shoes," said Lydia as she searched for the mugs.

"It's true, I was," I conceded, "but I managed to have some fun."

"I'll bet you got away with murder."

"Nah," I replied, "I just protected Bubbe from some of my less savory activities. I don't know which would have mortified her more—that I lost my virginity in college or that I ate *treif* in Chinese restaurants."

"The *treif*, no contest. In her own way Bubbe was a pretty juicy lady. I wish I'd known about these infractions when she was alive; maybe I could have done a little revisionist history on the growth and maturity of my baby cousin, Saint Claire."

"What are you talking about? I could never measure up to you. I was just a dorky little kid."

"*We* both know that," Lydia agreed, "but Bubbe and Grandpa Sam saw it a bit differently. They were old school—and Bubbe honed the rhetorical question to a fucking art form. She would constantly ask me why little Claireleh had such good grades and I didn't."

"Wow, I never knew."

"And I used to envy those jaunts you took with your father," Lydia said as she poured the coffee into a cup labeled World's Greatest Dad.

"Really?" I felt a flood of pleasure, but it was quickly followed by a sense of unease. "It was kind of fun, but we were rarely alone. Even when I was a teenager, he'd always schlep some woman along. I could always tell how much the girlfriend du jour liked Pop by how much she would dote on me."

"Did your dad like it when they were nice to you?"

"If he noticed, he didn't let on. I actually felt kind of sorry for some of them."

"Still, staying up late and going to the theater and those sports events, it must have been exciting."

"It was, but don't forget that the rest of the time, I ate a steady diet of boiled chicken and overcooked vegetables."

"Ah, yes," said Lydia. "Bubbe's cuisine never varied, though she did make a mean chicken soup."

"Cuisine, my foot," I scoffed. "At least your mother could cook."

"So could your mother. You just hadn't graduated from macaroni and cheese yet. She died before you had a chance to appreciate it."

"She died before I had a chance to appreciate a lot of things," I said, and suddenly the mood shifted and the two of us were very still.

"You know," I said, my eyes welling with tears, "I still think about her all the time."

"I know, I know. Come. Sit down." Lydia led me by the hand to the opened couch. She rubbed my forearm and patted my back softly.

I began to sob, muffling my cries so that Sam wouldn't hear, not that I thought he would care. All I could think of was that I was an orphan now.

"Listen," Lydia commanded softly, "one thing's for sure, there are plenty of people who love you. It's natural for you to feel so low," she continued soothingly. "You just need to let yourself feel bad for a while. It's good for you to cry, babe. Let it out."

Lydia's admonition had the opposite effect, and I pulled myself together. As I calmed down and my breathing slowed, Lydia gently nudged my head onto a pillow. She patted my back gently. With some snorting and sniffling, I drifted off to sleep.

4

When I awoke my eyes wouldn't focus and my tongue felt like it had been bathed in lint. Through the blur I saw that Lydia and Sam were ready to depart. "My God, what time is it?" I croaked. Sam ignored me so I repeated the question. Twice. The kid literally wouldn't give me the time of day.

"Hey, Claire," Lydia interjected. "Sorry we woke you. Sam, give Sleeping Beauty a kiss goodbye," she directed.

"No way," Sam declared.

"We're out of here if we want to make the plane at 12:05. Bye, Claire."

"Wait! Sam did you have breakfast? Did you pack your toothbrush?" I asked.

"All set, go back to sleep." The suggestion was more than I could resist and my head sank back onto the pillow. I revived long enough to call out, "Sam, call me when you get to Marjorie's," and then heard the door slam.

When I next awoke, Lydia set down a cup of tea on the end table near my head. Morning was long gone. I felt scuzzy and before I ate, I desperately wanted to hop in the shower. I knew I wasn't supposed to. Traditionally, mourners sitting *shiva* aren't allowed to shower or have sex (little chance of the latter). I decided to shower anyway.

I stripped and stepped on the bathroom scale. Damn, I thought, 173. I showered quickly, omitting the tweezing, shaving, lotions, makeup, and all the other aspects of my regular morning ritual. I gathered my hair, squeezed out the excess water, and put it into a metal clip. I wrapped myself in a towel, or tried to, disgusted as I noticed one nipple protrude where the towel didn't quite cover me.

Pop's bedroom was well appointed and, despite my stay, still relatively neat. As I dressed, I looked around the room at the solid, dark wood furniture. I opened the walk-in closet and looked at the twelve pairs of shoes on the door and noticed more shoe-boxes on the top shelf. I ran my fingers through a clump of silken strands and wondered whether I should save some ties for Sam.

"Hey," Lydia said, and I jumped, accidentally dropping a rack of ties to the floor. "Didn't mean to startle you. Are you ready for some lunch? I bought bagels." I followed Lydia into the kitchen.

"Do you want cream cheese or butter?" Lydia asked.

"I really shouldn't have either," I replied.

"Shouldn't?" Lydia asked archly.

"Come on. I've gained four pounds since I've been in Florida." We sat quietly for an uncomfortable minute. Even I couldn't delude myself that the silence was companionable. But what followed was worse.

"Claire, how long have you been dieting?"

I thought for a moment and replied, "Since I was eleven, I guess. In sixth grade Bubbe started packing me low-cal yogurts instead of a sandwich for lunch."

"That would be twenty-nine years?"

"Actually, thirty."

"Well, what would it take for you to concede that maybe your approach isn't working?"

"It's not the approach that's wrong, it's me. It's just that I tend to eat a bit compulsively," I looked straight at Lydia, "especially at a stressful time like this."

"Has it ever occurred to you that it's not your eating, but your dieting, that's compulsive?"

"If I were a compulsive dieter, maybe I'd be a little thinner," I joked, but Lydia was having none of it. "For God's sake, do you know how much I weigh?"

"I couldn't care less what you weigh. You look great, Claire, I wish you could see that. You have beautiful brown eyes, big boobs, and good teeth. I don't think you're fat. You're *zaftig*." I cringed. Lydia noticed but continued, "You're a luscious, desirable woman. I hate to see you depriving yourself of a schmear of cream cheese."

"Thanks, you're so nice to say. . . ."

"You want to know what I think?" Lydia asked. The question was purely rhetorical.

"I think the reason you break all your diets," Lydia continued, "is because deep down you feel deprived. Eating for you is an act of resistance."

"Let me think about it," I said as I spread some butter on my bagel. Was this an act of resistance or acquiescence? To her credit, Lydia, who sometimes doesn't know when to shut up, didn't say a word.

5

Two days later, Lydia and I were preparing to part. "You know," I mused, "I'm almost sorry to see it end. Sounds like I'm talking about a party, not a *shiva*."

"Hell, if we were Irish, it would have been a party."

I told Lydia how much I looked forward to returning to work. I didn't tell her how much I dreaded returning to Sam. I also mentioned this guy, Doug, whom I met at a manager's workshop.

"We're going out to the movies, but I'm not sure whether it's a date," I said.

"Why aren't you sure?"

"Well, I invited him."

"I'm impressed that you asked him," Lydia said.

"It's amazing what desperation will do for a gal."

"Well, let's hope it's a date. What's he look like?" Lydia asked.

"Not bad looking. He's got a mustache, glasses, bald. . . ."

"Captain Picard bald or Captain Stubing bald?"

"More of a Danny DeVito bald," I said, smiling and realizing that Lydia and I had watched all the same TV shows.

Lydia reminded me that my pretty-boy ex was no bargain, so maybe it was time to branch out a bit.

"Speaking of Jeremy, didn't he recently get married?"

"Yep. To Kimberly."

"Kimberly? Really. Not a member of the tribe, I take it."

"I think she converted. I haven't met her yet and I'm dreading it. The plan is for Jeremy and her to take Sam every other weekend. We'll see how long that lasts. I can't think about it. Lyd, tell me about your work."

Lydia described her upcoming fellowship at an exclusive retreat for scholars and creative artists at Lake Como, Italy, where she'd be starting a new project, something that wouldn't require lugging half of Berkeley's library with her. Lydia was going to analyze the relationships among women in three Victorian novels written by women. When not hobnobbing with the great and near-great, Lydia was just going to read and reread the books. I commented on what a shamefully decadent life Lydia led, just sitting around and reading novels. She grinned.

"Suffice it to say that I have some pretty tough questions about what Jane Eyre was doing when she shared a bed at that awful boarding school she went to."

"You love making trouble."

"Hey, I've got tenure. I'm out. There's really nothing anybody can do to me now."

"Did you have a coming out party?"

"What? You mean like some goofy debutante? No, I didn't," Lydia said with a chuckle. "I wish I'd thought of that."

"Did Aunt Ida ever know?"

"Depends how you define 'know.' Ma was the queen—no, I'd better rephrase that—the empress of denial. But she must have suspected something, because after a while she stopped trying to set me up with all her friends' loser sons."

"Those dates must have been excruciating."

"Most of the time, but that's how I met Harold."

"Harold? Your gay friend Harold?!" I couldn't believe it.

"Yep, let's just say that his mom was just a little out of touch also."

"Aunt Ida never broached the subject?"

"Bill Clinton first developed his 'don't ask don't tell' policy by talking to my mother. You know, I think she kinda felt guilty. Her marriage to my father was not exactly an advertisement for heterosexuality. Ma believed in the trauma school of sexual preference. She thought my father had made me loathe all men."

"Well, I bet he helped. Sometimes I think I'd be better off with a woman."

"I'm sure there's a dance at your local gay bar, maybe you'll get lucky."

"No, I'm serious."

"So am I, Claire. Being a lesbian isn't just something you do because your father was a violent creep or because all the cute, eligible guys are married. It's not a choice. . . ."

Uh oh. It was too late to stop her.

"It's not a choice," Lydia continued. "At least for me it's not. It's a deep attraction."

"Oh, I know. . ." I tried to reply, but any attempt at interruption was futile when Lydia was on a tear.

"Hell," Lydia persisted, warming to her subject, "doesn't *everyone* like women better than men? Women are nicer, softer, and less competitive. We rarely have gross hair on our backs or in our ears."

"Speak for yourself," I interjected.

Lydia took no notice of the attempt to deflect her with my special brand of self-deprecating humor. "The tragedy of my life is that not only do I like the company of women, but I like to nibble on their ears, stick my tongue down their throats, and lick them in places that would make you blush."

"OK, OK, so I wouldn't make a good lesbian," I confessed in exasperation, strongly suspecting that I wasn't the first recipient of this soliloquy. "A person can dream, can't she?"

"More like being a big talker if you ask me."

The phone rang. It was Sam.

"Hey, Mom, you always say I never listen to you, but look, I'm calling you just like you said."

"Apparently, there's a first time for everything," I said. "Hang up and I'll call right back." Mercifully, Marjorie didn't pick up when I called. I issued my standard injunctions about behavior and consideration, which were greeted with Sam's usual disdain.

After I hung up, I realized that this would be my last opportunity to talk to Lydia alone before the visitors arrived to help me end the *shiva*. I tried, not altogether successfully, to set aside my annoyance, and hugged Lydia tight. She could be such a load. Even so, I did appreciate her babysitting me this one last time.

Lydia smiled and said, "You know, it's really only after your parents die that you become a full-fledged adult. And it's not like a wedding or a bar mitzvah where you can prepare yourself for the big event," she added. "It just befalls you one day. Boom! You're the leader of the next generation."

"It stinks."

"No shit. Welcome to the world of being a grown-up."

We promised to stay in touch and Lydia reminded me that I would have to e-mail her about how the date went.

"If it is a date," I sighed as I went to the door to greet Pop's friends who came to console me and help me mourn.

6

My grasp tightened on the armrest of my seat as I strained to hear any unusual sounds from the cockpit and tried to ignore that weird nauseating smell that all airplane cabins (at least in the economy section) seem to have. I listened attentively as the crew reviewed safety instructions and made sure I knew the exact location not only of the exits, but of my air-distress (read: barf) bag. Every little noise made my heart jump. I gasped when the wheels made a grinding sound as they were raised, and I looked at the pleasant, vacant face of the flight attendant, searching for some signs of covert panic. Seeing none didn't comfort me much. I've pretty much concluded that most of flight attendants' training, aside from memorizing all the beverages and pointing out exits and emergency floor lighting, consists of learning how to look calm in the face of an imminent, fiery death.

I was jammed between a hugely obese snoring man and a woman who chewed gum at a rate of one stick a minute. I was too nervous to be disgusted, almost. I craned my neck, looking around the plane, and focused on a cute little girl coloring pictures with her mom and chatting in a happy, sing-song voice. Certainly God wouldn't allow such an innocent child to go down. I scanned for nuns. Seeing none, I sort of settled for a Hasid who unfortunately looked like a diamond merchant. No special solicitude for that guy, no matter how often he prays, I thought.

Thumbing through the airline catalog of yuppified gadgets that no one could ever need but frequent fliers might lust after, I eyed a massage chair, very expensive but inviting. It used "wave action" and could target different muscle groups. I sat in one once and found it amazingly soothing. Seven thousand bucks. Well, maybe on my fiftieth birthday.

Meanwhile, a much cheaper investment in my happiness caught my eye—a full-sized male rubber doll. I was immediately smitten with this "male guardian," whom I could inflate and dress to taste (no duds included). According to the catalog, this "Man Around the House" simulated a 180-pound, six-foot male. The specimen in the photo needed a shave. He could be used to gain access to carpooling lanes or to discourage would-be intruders at home. The perfect boyfriend, I thought, particularly as I read on and discovered that the doll folded back into a convenient nylon carrying case as soon as he served his purpose. Wow, I thought, how many women wished they could stuff their men into a gym bag after they deflated? No longer would I have to look pathetic in restaurants; Mr. "Man Around the House" would accompany me everywhere. Between the massage chair and the "Man Around the House," who would need a real man at all? All I'd have to do is add a little recording, like those talking Barbies that say "Neat outfit!" and "Let's go to the mall." Except, my "Man About the House" would say stuff like: "But honey, you're not fat," "Please tell me about your day," and, if I were really lucky, "Let's make passionate love. I can't get enough of you!"

Would this guy be like those female rubber dolls I'd always heard jokes about, I wondered—anatomically correct? Dared I hope, enhanced? I couldn't wait to tell Joanie all about it. Ripping the "Man Around the House" ad out of the catalog, I briefly considered doing the same for the massage chair but thought better of it.

A sudden jolt reminded me where I was. The seatbelt light was illuminated and I heard a southern twang warning the passengers that they were going to "hit a few bumps" due to some "choppy air." That's probably code for wind shear, I thought. I recalled Bubbe's obsession with saying the traveler's prayer before getting on the plane. Bubbe was nuts, but hearing Grandpa Sam utter the words of *Tfilat HaDerech* immediately calmed her down. Oh, how I longed for that kind of comfort. Despite my panic as the plane began to sway and dip, I couldn't connect with faith. At least I'm consistent, I thought. I'm the atheist in the foxhole. My only sincere emotion was a terror of crashing.

The time had come to do the only two things that really could distract me—plan my funeral, and make resolutions (just in case the plane didn't crash). I closed my eyes and tried to concentrate on the funeral guest list. Naturally, Sam would be there. He'd be sad, but he'd make it. Jeremy and his new wife would take care of Sam—spoil him, in fact, to make up for his tragic loss. Lydia would fly in for sure. Joanie would be heartbroken. So would Joanie's husband, Aaron, and their kids, at least those old enough to understand what was going on. Mr. Huntington, the CEO, would send flowers, but my immediate boss, Corey, would know what to do. He would come to the funeral and bring food to the *shiva*. I bet a lot of the employees, my staff, and those whom I'd helped over the years would come too. Jeremy's wife would undoubtedly buy a new black mini for the occasion, but I'd have my revenge. Tootsie-girl would have to sit through the eulogy.

But wait! For the first time engaged in this airplane ritual, I was prompted to wonder who would perform the funeral. I had no rabbi. Pop had belonged to a *shul* and the rabbi did a beautiful job. Perhaps I should think about joining a synagogue in Hudsonville. Aha, I'd moved on to making resolutions. I glanced at the woman to my left. Resolution one: never chew gum. Resolution two: join a synagogue. No, I wouldn't over-promise. Resolution two: investigate joining a synagogue. The plane tilted to the right and a woman one row forward stifled a gasp. I was considering asking the man next to me, who had just woken up with a start, if he would hold my hand. I've done this before. It does make me feel better but I can never look the person in the eye after we land safely so I save it for truly desperate moments. I looked at his fleshy hands perched on a round mass that hung over his belt like a six-month pregnancy. Resolution three: I'll exercise, I promised myself. I'll join a gym.

Another bump interrupted my musings, but this time it was the wheels descending. One way or another, I thought, I'm going down.

7

When I got home, I listened to my voicemail messages as I went through the stack of accumulated mail. In a minute I would call Marjorie to find out what was happening with Sam. Separating the sympathy cards from the regular mail, I felt more drawn to the Land's End catalog than to the letters of condolence. What a shallow creep I am, I thought. For the first time in over a week I called my work number to check that voicemail too. I listened absently as I continued the triage: junk, condolence, bills. Most of the messages were insignificant by now—reminders for various meetings that had already happened, the library wondering what happened to the book I borrowed . . . but what was this? It was a message from the guy I met at the workshop.

"Hi Claire, it's Doug Green. Sorry I'm going to have to ask for a rain check for the movie on Saturday. My girlfriend will be in town. Normally, I'd just say that all three of us should go together, but I haven't seen her in a while and I kinda want to spend as much time with her as possible. You understand."

I snorted.

"Anyway, I'll give you a call. Bye."

Which would be worse, if he didn't call—which was usually what I'll give you a call meant—or if he did call, indicating that I wasn't even conceivable as girlfriend material? I could just imagine his explaining to his girlfriend, "Claire? Come on, she's in her forties, she's got a teenage kid, and she's fat for God's sake. She's just a friend."

My cell phone rang. I ignored it and a message from Joanie popped up, reading, "Hey girl, I know you're home," accompanied by some absurd and vaguely threatening emoticons. I called Joanie right back.

"You OK?" Joan asked, and I could hear the deep concern in her voice.

"A little tired, but OK," I said, and immediately felt ridiculous. How could I claim to be tired? Joanie had four little kids and another on the way, and I was complaining.

"Honestly, I could have picked you up from the airport. Why didn't you call me?"

"Why don't I come on over so you can yell at me in person?" I retorted.

She agreed and told me to hurry because the milk was already heating up. Joanie correctly assumed this was an occasion that called for her famous hot chocolate made with melted Swiss chocolate, hand-whipped cream, and peppermint garnish. As we were talking I heard a shriek in the background. "Gotta run," Joan announced. "Let yourself in."

I walked next door to Joanie's house, inhaling deeply as I walked through the flower, herb, and vegetable gardens. I called to her as I entered the kitchen from the back porch.

"Be right out," Joanie's voice echoed from the baby's room. On the plush Indian rug in the living room, I saw the five-year-old twins, Rachel and Zack, wet from their bath, pinching each other and crying. They should have been drying off and getting into their pajamas, and they certainly shouldn't have been in the living room. No kid was allowed in the living room, especially near Joanie's white couch. Who has four kids and a white couch, for God's sake? Somehow, Joanie managed to pull it off and even the two-year-old followed the rules of the house. In fact, all of Joanie's kids were better than Sam at remembering to put their dishes in the sink.

I offered to tell the twins a story as soon as they were in their pajamas. I looked at their clean, angelic faces. Both kids had wide green eyes and curly, bright orange hair. They looked so similar that an occasional idiot would ask Joanie if they were identical twins.

"What kind of story would you two like Auntie Claire to tell you?"

"Dinosaurs!" announced Zack.

"No, a Princess story," countered his sister.

I scooped a kid in each arm and headed for the playroom. I plopped down on the brown couch and cradled them, one on each side, surveying the room admiringly. A small oak kids' table and four chairs stood in a corner. Boxes marked "Lego" and "Lincoln Logs" filled the shelves alongside such classics of children's literature as the *Anne of Green Gables* series and *The Wizard of Oz* books. I gave each child a squeeze and said: "This story is called Princess visits the land of the Dinosaurs."

"Does she see a triceratops?" Zack inquired.

"And a Tyrannosaurus Rex," I answered, as I warmed to the task. Joan didn't walk in until the Princess had explained to a certain Brontosaurus how fond she'd been of her horse-drawn carriage, and could the dinosaur be more careful with his tail?

"Aunt Claire will finish your story when you're ready for bed. You two come with me and we'll brush teeth," Joan said, smiling in the doorway, and they trotted off. When was the last time Sam brushed his teeth? I wondered. I dreaded taking him to the dentist, but he was really overdue.

Joanie had my hot chocolate ready in the kitchen and soon returned to join me. The hot chocolate was thick and creamy. I took my first sip and liquid pleasure slid down my throat.

"How are you doing?" Joan asked.

"OK, I guess. It was an awful flight. How are you feeling?"

"I'm fine, really. It's not like I don't have a little experience being pregnant. I'm so sorry I couldn't make it to the funeral. The doctor was being overcautious, I'm sure."

"Oh, please. I didn't expect you to schlep out."

"I know," answered Joan, "but I wanted to be there. I remember how hard it was when my mother died." Her eyes filled with tears. "What can I do for you?"

"You're doing it," I replied as I took another sip and basked in the welcoming comfort of her kitchen. Though sparkling, the kitchen almost screamed cozy. The walls were painted deep forest green and the borders were stenciled with a pattern of colorful fruit. I sat at the long farmer's table. Above me was a large rectangular stained glass lamp, extending the fruit motif. I accepted a plate of cookies from Joan and remained in my padded oak chair. I knew better than to try to take any food out of Joan's kitchen.

"This has been a hard month for you," she observed. "You holding up OK?"

"I'm managing. In fact, I'm kind of looking forward to getting back to work. It will inject some normalcy into my life. I'm not done cleaning out Pop's apartment, but I needed to get back. You know, the rabbi was nice. He really seemed to have known Pop and cared that he was gone. It made me think that maybe I should join a *shul* here."

"Well, we have a really nice new rabbi, very down-to-earth," Joan said with what struck me as way too much enthusiasm. "Come with me sometime," she added.

Uh-oh, now I'm hooked, I thought. All those years Joanie had been trying to get me to go to *shul*, and now she had me. I changed the subject, telling Joanie about the "Man About the House" inflatable doll I'd seen on the plane and added: "As it happens I'm going to need the rubber doll because Doug called to cancel. He's got a girlfriend, and he called to tell me he has a hot weekend planned."

"Oh, no!"

"Worse yet, the guy didn't even have the courtesy to lie to me about it," I said. "I didn't even rate an excuse."

"That's awful," Joanie said, though I wished she would have contradicted me. Couldn't it be something less pathetic?

"I guess I'd better call Sam," I announced. "I'm hoping Marjorie will invite Sam to spend one more night over there."

"Do you want to stay here?"

"No thanks, I'm kind of looking forward to sleeping in my own bed," I answered. I offered to finish the kids' story while Joanie assembled my take-home package—lasagna for tomorrow's dinner and a homemade lunch. She issued the microwave instructions: four minutes on high for the rice and lentils. No more than thirty seconds for the banana pudding. The salad included tomatoes and cucumbers from the garden and I was sternly admonished not to waste them. I smiled at Joanie. This sort of loving bossiness reminded me of Bubbe, only Joanie was a good cook.

"Speaking of waste, will Rachel be upset if the Princess gets trampled? Or I could aim the stampede at Prince Charming—he's such a load."

"You're in charge, just don't give them nightmares."

After I finished the twins' story, I called Marjorie, who answered on the first ring. "Can you hold?" Marjorie asked, "It's my mother on the other line and she just can't stop talking."

I agreed and held the phone to my ear while listening to Joanie sing an old Yiddish lullaby. Joanie inserted the name of each twin as she crooned. She seemed to have gotten the baby—the soon-to-be-supplanted baby, two-year-old Jake—off to sleep as well.

My peaceful state was jolted by Marjorie's voice.

"Claire, you still there? Good. I can't really talk for long. My mother thinks the world revolves around her. So be it! I know she's lonely, but she lives across town and I have responsibilities here. I have to get Jack's dinner, Stuart has piano, and then I have to get Ben to his computer lesson. And, I have Sam here, as you know."

Was Marjorie's voice genuinely annoying, or did one have to develop a distaste for it? I wondered.

"By the way," Marjorie continued, "Sam loves those grilled cheese sandwiches I make. The trick is to use Colby, not cheddar. I can pick you up some at the store if you'd like. I have to go to the store again tomorrow anyway. Your Sam sure drinks a lot of milk! Where was I? Oh yes, well my mother acts as if I don't have anything to do, like I just eat bonbons all day and watch soap operas."

I managed to get a word in sledgewise, thanking Marjorie for letting Sam stay over.

"You're very welcome. Sam is hardly any trouble. It's really just the sheets to wash. You know, while I have you on the phone, I know that Sam is quite talented in science. I've been putting together a petition for AP Earth Science in the high school. Would you like to sign?"

"Let me talk to Sam; I don't know whether he's interested."

"But you'll sign the petition one way or the other, right?"

"Let me think about it."

"What's there to think about?" Marjorie challenged. "Don't you want advanced placement at the high school?"

"I guess so," I said, trying to sound noncommittal and aloof.

This isn't worth it, I thought. It was never worth it to let Marjorie take Sam. I can't take this, I said to myself, rolling my eyes for Joan's benefit.

"I really should pick up Sam; you've been so kind already."

"Let him sleep over tonight," Marjorie suggested. "They're keeping each other entertained."

Entertained? What was Sam, five years old? Nevertheless, whatever irritation I felt was outweighed by the chance of one more night without the angry one. I gave an enthusiastic thumbs-up to Joan, who was enjoying my side of the conversation.

"Can you pick him up by 7:30—a.m.?" Marjorie emphasized. "Ben has swim club."

I agreed. God forbid she'd let the kids sleep late. I asked Marjorie if I could talk to Sam.

"He's outside and I've got something cooking here. Have you ever made Chicken Paprikash? It's one of Jack's favorites. . . ."

I heard Joanie's doorbell ring. Thank God.

"That's the door. Got to run. See you tomorrow at 7:30."

"A.m.," Marjorie reminded.

"A.m.," I repeated, dutifully. "Bye."

I walked down the slate-covered hallway to thank my savior. I opened the front door and chirped in my best June Cleaver imitation, "Who is it?"

"It's the lasagna lady," said Joan, standing on her front porch with a finger on the doorbell. "I had *rachmanus* on you. Marjorie sure is persistent. I finally just took those math flashcards she gave me," Joan confessed.

"OK, but if I see you flashing any of those wonderful kids, I'm reporting you to the authorities."

Joanie entered the cavernous family room and went to the bar to make herself a drink of seltzer and lime. She sat in a leather wing chair and propped her feet on the ottoman.

"This is the life. The kids are in bed. I'm finally over being nauseated. Aaron's due home in twenty minutes. I have just enough time to cover myself in Saran wrap and answer the door in full frontal nudity."

"You got it, party girl. But hey, be careful."

"It's a little late for that advice. Besides, I like sex when I'm pregnant."

"For one thing," I pointed out, "you don't have to worry about getting pregnant."

"There are some other advantages as well. You must remember from when you had Sam."

"As far as I can recall, we had sex just that once." This wasn't literally true, of course—but closer to the truth than I would have wished.

"Jeremy is such a cold fish." Joan said with no attempt to hide her contempt. Joanie rarely spoke ill of anyone, but she did me the immense kindness of making my ex-husband an exception to her rule against malicious gossip.

"Maybe he's not so cold to his new wife," I suggested.

"What's her name? . . . Tiffany?"

"Kim-ber-ly," I replied, relishing every syllable. "Jeremy has absolutely no sense of irony. You know, in about fifty years all the blue haired ladies will be named Kimberly, Tiffany, Megan, and Krista. Give me a good solid name like Sarah or Rachel. Rose is making a comeback. Remember that for number five."

"I've tentatively pegged her as a Miriam—Mimi, after my mother. What do you think?"

"It's no Kimberly, but it could work. You know, I don't really know much about wife number two. Sam indicates—I never pump, mind you—that not-so-old Kimberly has her bitchy moments. As I like to say, she may be a trophy wife, but she's no prize."

"Jeremy lost the prize," Joanie said as she approached me and squeezed my arm.

Despite myself, my eyes filled with tears as I looked up at her. "Thanks for being so good to me," I said.

"You're easy to be good to. I just wish you could see that."

"I wonder if he *schtups* her much?" I mused.

The question was left hanging, interrupted by the entrance of a large figure with a loosened tie, a suit jacket hooked on his index finger, and sleeves rolled up to expose furry red arms. Aaron carefully returned his briefcase to its appointed spot, put away his keys, sunglasses, jacket and cell phone, and then joined us in the living room. Awkwardly, he leaned over the back of the white couch and kissed me on the cheek. I felt his scratchy face. Aaron's five o'clock shadow rivaled most men's three-day growth.

"Sorry to hear about your dad," Aaron said simply.

I thanked him and turned down Joanie's invitation to stay to dinner.

"I'm full on junk food," I explained. "Besides," I added looking up at Aaron, "Joanie has big plans for you tonight."

Joanie winked at Aaron. He looked vaguely uncomfortable, but by now the guy was used to our antics.

"Aren't you going to at least ask Aaron about his day?" I asked in mock dismay. "Is he nothing more than a hunk of meat to you, Joanie?"

"Wait, I'll get the steak sauce," she replied.

Clearly this was my cue to skedaddle. As I carried my care package through the garden, I heard her shout, "I'll call you." At least with Joanie, I knew she really would.

8

I looked around the locker room at the tanned, lithe twenty-year-olds and wondered how in the world this exercise gig was going to lower my stress. In five minutes I had an appointment with someone who was going to show me how the instruments of torture actually worked and tailor an exercise regime just for me. Yippee. Stealing surreptitious looks at the naked bodies in the locker room, I only wished I'd gone to the beauty parlor first or at least had purchased a form fitting exercise outfit, which seemed to be de rigueur. Who was I kidding? That look, with the exposed midriff, was definitely out for me, no matter how fashionable. I was dressed in a faded Cornell Law t-shirt and some gym shorts. I hadn't even realized there was fashion-wear for exercising. Wonderful. Yet another venue for me to appear dowdy.

What a way to spend a Sunday morning! Sam, no doubt, was having an elegant brunch with Jeremy and Kim. At the thought of Jeremy's new wife, I panicked. Oh my God, what if Kimberly goes to this gym? We hadn't met yet, and I didn't think I could face her in here. She probably does go to a gym, but this one wasn't particularly close to where they lived. I'd purposely chosen this place because it was close to work and because I was unlikely to run into anyone from Hudsonville. I swiftly transformed any anxiety I might have felt into self-righteousness, a coping mechanism if not an outright talent of mine. Damn it, I thought, I'm allowed in here too. I can't avoid her. I've lived in this area since she was in her fancy-pants diapers on the upper-east side—well not in diapers, maybe, but definitely in junior high. I have a right to be here. If I were in perfect shape and coming here I'd be nothing but a narcissist. I'm here for my health. With courage born of indignation, I marched out to meet Kurt, my wellness coach, the guy who would make sure I didn't break their equipment.

"Hi, you must be Claire," he said giving me a predictably firm handshake.

"Hi," I replied, noticing that Kurt was almost as wide as he was tall. Now that certainly could not be healthy.

"We'll have one more person joining us. He's a beginner, just like you, and you two will be using the same machines, only he'll be lifting heavier weights."

Great, I thought, my humiliation is complete now that I have a stranger watching. A minute later, I was introduced to Rob, who flashed me a bright, if slightly ironic, smile. I did not smile back.

"I'm really intimidated by all the equipment and all the people in such great shape," Rob confided. "It's not too late," he continued in a conspiratorial tone, "Let's ditch this place and go out for a malted."

I wasn't sure whether to be charmed or insulted. Did I, in particular, look like the kind of person who would turn (her ample) tail to go get a malted?

"Bob, buddy, you'll learn to love being in shape," Kurt said as he patted Rob's pot belly.

I looked for signs of annoyance from Rob but saw none. If Kurt touches my stomach, I swear I'll sue him, I thought. No, I'll punch him and then sue him.

"Let the wild rumpus start," Rob said.

"I recognize that quote, but I don't remember where it's from," I said.

"A children's book, *Where the Wild Things Are.*"

"I love that book!" I exclaimed. This time I smiled.

"Guys, this isn't library hour. We're here to get you into shape. Let me show you the circuit."

Rob and I dutifully followed Kurt as he demonstrated and calibrated the equipment. After showing us how to use the various weight machines and running us through some mat work, Kurt had us "hop" on the elliptical machine for fifteen minutes.

"Let's talk while we still have some breath," Rob said, flashing his crooked smile.

"Sure," I said. "How come you seem so cheerful?"

"I'm cheerful for someone with a cholesterol level of 346."

"Ouch."

"Why are *you* here?" Rob asked.

Was he blind? Was he mocking me? Or just being nice? I looked at Rob's wavy black hair, which was becoming matted with perspiration, and noted that his exercise clothes were even rattier than mine.

"I'm here because I promised myself I would get into shape," I replied sounding more prissy than I'd intended to.

"I made that same promise to myself last New Year's."

"But this is August," I pointed out.

"It's worse than that. It was a *Jewish* New Year's resolution. I made it last September. I just couldn't face another Yom Kippur knowing I'd done nothing. Besides, the doctor said it's exercise or drugs to lower my cholesterol. You know," Rob huffed, "on Yom Kippur, there's a special confessional you say for too much eating and drinking."

"Yes," I said, "I know—the *al-chait* prayer."

"I thought you might be Jewish," Rob said.

"Oh," I said without thinking, "I *knew* you were." I was mortified, but Rob didn't miss a beat.

"Oh yeah, what tipped you off—besides my Semitic good looks, I mean?" Rob asked, panting.

"You offered me a malted, rather than a milkshake. Besides you've been muttering '*Ich hulush*' under your breath," I answered, touched by his good cheer.

Rob sputtered and nearly missed a step. "I never said that! Don't make me laugh, my stomach hurts from the crunches Kurt made us do. And it's true, I could faint at any time," Rob added in mock earnestness.

The stepping was getting harder. Despite the obvious effort, Rob resumed talking. "Tell me, what do you do when you aren't on this existential walk to nowhere?"

"I work in human resources. And I hang out with my incredibly surly fourteen-year-old," I said, looking for a reaction to the mention of a child. None was forthcoming, other than what seemed to be genuine interest. I told him about the little ingrate, describing Sam's temper, foul mouth, and addiction to video games.

"Hard age," Rob remarked between heavy breaths. "What's his name?"

"Sam, after my grandfather. I was raised by my grandparents." Why the hell had I disclosed something so personal so soon? This was so damn typical of me, doling out private information as a sort of freak-show entertainment. And I didn't know more than the guy's first name and the obvious fact that he was Jewish.

If Rob noticed my discomfort, he didn't let on. Each word punctuated by a gasp, he persisted, "But aside from hanging out with Sam, what do you do for *fun*?"

"Fun, what's that?" I responded, vaguely annoyed at myself for sounding so cynical.

"I'll tell you what it isn't," Rob said as he wiped his forehead with his shirt, exposing little man-breasts and a chest-full of thick, black curls. "This machine isn't fun. How—gasp—much longer?"

"Four more minutes," I answered, noticing that my breath was getting awfully heavy and hoping that Rob didn't think I was panting over him.

"I'm not going to make it."

"Of course you are. You're more than two-thirds of the way there. Just think how great you'll feel when you stop."

"Yeah, and I can crawl to the car," Rob wheezed.

Kurt came by and reduced the pace, announcing that it was time to "cool down."

"Thanks for the pep talk. What a *michaiya!*" Rob said, and winked at me.

"What a what?" Kurt inquired.

"Rob's just saying it feels good to slow down," I explained.

"Yeah," Rob said, smiling at me again—what a nice smile—"I like taking it slow."

9

On Monday morning I entered my office suite greeted first by the receptionist, then by Molly. "Hi. Welcome back. There's a mountain of mail for you and Corey wants to see you," Molly said.

"Great," I said, rolling my eyes, and then added with sincerity, "Thanks for all your help getting out of here."

"Of course, Claire. I'm so sorry about your dad."

"What's the news?" I asked. Molly knew the dirt on just about everyone in the company.

"There was a fight in the cafeteria with some racial element, and there's a serious problem with the assistant manager in purchasing and supplies."

"What's the matter?"

"Seems she's just stopped coming in on Mondays altogether."

"You know, I think I need a cup of tea and a doughnut to listen to this. Go flag down the cart, will you, Molly?"

I began sorting through my various mails—e, voice, and snail. As I perused, a bald, elderly man in horn-rimmed glasses knocked, and before I could say anything, flopped down on my leather couch, propping his feet up on the coffee table.

"Hi, Bill, are you visiting today?" I asked.

"Yes, ma'am, I am. Just like to make sure that the place is running smooth since I retired. I notice you have a new girl down there in accounting."

"Do you mean Julie Hecht, the new accounts manager? She's not a girl. We follow all the child labor laws."

"Julie Hecht. What kind of a name is Hecht?"

"Well, it's a Jewish name, a German-Jewish name."

"Jewish?" he repeated, repositioning his girth on the couch. "You know, I had a very good friend who was Jewish—Al Bernstein, do you know him? He and I grew up together in Toms River. His family owned a department store."

I resumed sorting mail, trying to avoid eye contact.

"Come to think of it, all my Jewish acquaintances from there were in retail. Why is it, do you suppose, that the Jews have been so successful in business?"

"I don't know," I said without looking up.

"Do you have an idea why the Jews have done so well financially in America, especially in Hollywood?"

"Maybe because they were thrown out of all the other countries."

"Well, Hitler sure didn't like the Jews, not one little bit, there's no denying that. My theory—actually I got this from my friend Al that I was just telling you about—my theory is that it's genetic. The rabbis—they were the smartest ones—all had big families. . . ."

"I'm working on a deadline here, Bill. I'll have to excuse myself," I said, staring directly at him with the most pleasant smile I could manage.

He met my glance. "Sure thing, just like to stop by and say hi."

"Best of luck to you."

As soon as he left, I beeped for Molly. "I'm never in for Bill," I told her. "Never."

"Sorry. He must have slipped in while I was out fetching your tea. I'll bring it in with the doughnuts. Also, don't forget to call Corey."

I left a message on Corey's voicemail and spent the rest of the morning putting out fires and chomping on doughnuts. At lunch I sat in the company cafeteria with Corey, who greeted each employee by name. We never talked business in the cafeteria, just put in an appearance. Corey, a six-five black man who had played basketball in college, always cut a dashing figure in double breasted suits, expensive shoes, and a Rolex watch.

"It's the only way I don't get mistaken for the cleaning staff," he once explained to me. I understood perfectly. My so-called power suits and pearls were the only thing that kept me from being confused with the secretaries.

Once we were reconvened in his office, Corey dropped two antacids into a glass of water and began to fill me in on the fight in the cafeteria.

"It seems that, with the backlash against political correctness, the n-word is back in vogue. In my book, anyone using racial epithets should be fired. But if we fire either one of them, we'll have the union on our ass," Corey grumbled.

"Let me do some investigating. Also, we probably need to do another seminar for middle management on racism and sexism."

"What, another how-to?" Corey asked. "I have to wonder. Does the guy who throws the word 'nigger' around in the cafeteria think of me that way too?"

"I think part of the rehabilitation plan I have in mind might just allow you to ask him that question, but let me check into it. As long as you're in such a great mood, let's talk about Jensen."

"What now?" Corey groaned, sinking his head into his massive hands.

"I think I made some headway with him. But I have to warn you that my methods were a little unorthodox."

"I don't want to know, do I?"

"Nope, you don't want details. Why don't you relax a bit?" I asked. "I'll give you the ultimate Jewish compliment: You look terrible."

Back at my office—which, thanks to Molly, was cleaner and more welcoming than any room in my own house—I scanned my surroundings. On the walls was framed artwork from Sam's elementary school and my diplomas. On my desk sat a photo of Sam and one of me and my mother from when I was five. As I looked at them, I made appointments to talk to the racist and the misogynist. That's what I love about this job, I thought, it's the people you get to meet.

10

I relaxed during my twenty-minute drive home, a period of time I could count on for a measure of tranquility. When I arrived home I found Sam navigating outer space on his computer while eating (and dropping all over the family room floor) his microwaved popcorn.

"Want to watch a movie?" I asked. In the face of silence I repeated the question three more times, each time more irritated than the last, until Sam responded.

"Nah," he replied distractedly.

"Want to call up a friend?"

No answer.

"Can I heat you up some lasagna?"

"Thanks a lot, Mom," Sam snapped. "You made me mess up my game."

"Sam, you've been on that thing for hours."

"Yeah, and you wrecked up all my progress. What's the matter with you? Do you live just to ruin my fun?"

"Yes, I apologize," I said, my voice dripping with sarcasm. "How silly of me to offer you some dinner. What was I thinking?"

I went to my room to change and a few minutes later heard a yelp.

"Yes! I beat the level!"

The lasagna was predictably delicious—three different gooey cheeses surrounding vegetables fresh from Joanie's garden and perfectly cooked lasagna noodles. When I handed a heaping plate to Sam he didn't look up from the computer.

"I'm going over to Joanie's, want to come?"

"Want to come?" I persisted, louder and more annoyed. "Suit yourself, punk," I murmured under my breath and left the house. I cut through the fragrant garden and rapped on Joanie's door.

"Hey there, where's Sam?" Joan asked as she balanced Jake on her hip.

"Oh, he's re-bonding with his computer games. Right about now he should be crushing the rebellion, the little fascist."

I thanked Joanie for the wonderful lasagna and told her about my hectic first day back at the office. Then I smiled and said with immense satisfaction, "You'll never guess how I started the day."

She went on SUNDAY p. 34

"Egg McMuffin?" Joan had a strictly kosher home and regularly needled me about eating *treif*.

"The gym."

"Jim who?"

"You know what I mean," I said with mild irritation. I detailed my thirty minutes on the circuit, the crunches on the mat, and my fifteen minutes on the elliptical.

"Kurt, my wellness coach, said it was a good workout."

"You're joking!" Joan exclaimed, sounding more astonished than necessary.

"Nope, I really did it," I said.

Joan deposited Jake on the floor and gave me a hug. "Sweetie, I'm so proud of you. I'm going to buy you a workout outfit. Do you have an exercise partner?"

"No . . ." I said hesitantly.

"What? What?" Joanie said, gauging from my expression that that I was holding something back.

"If you'd told me I would meet men at the gym, I'd have started this exercise routine a long time ago," I said.

"Really, what was I thinking? I've been trying for years to get you to go to the gym, I just didn't realize how to package it. My, my, you're full of surprises. Tell me everything. Don't omit a single detail."

I described how Rob and I worked out together, getting initiated into the functions of the various weight machines and how he seemed . . . I don't know . . . really nice and funny. I told Joanie how he seemed pretty Jewishly knowledgeable, and how he quoted from *Where the Wild Things Are*."

"The day Max wore his wolf suit. . ." Joan commenced.

"That's the one."

In response to more questioning, I described Rob. "He's about five-eight, glasses, curly black hair, great smile, penetrating green eyes." Anticipating the next question, I added, "No ring." I told Joanie that he wasn't in great shape, but he was like a furry teddy bear with an ironic, knowing smile.

"Did he ask for your phone number?" Joanie asked and then immediately corrected herself, noting that if he had asked me for my phone number, I'd, of course, have brought over my cell phone.

I decided that I would just go to exercise often and try to bump into him. I planned to go every morning. If he was there, I'd find him easily. He and I would stick out like sore thumbs, pudgy mortals among the gods and goddesses.

11

I did see Rob again and quickly learned his schedule—Sundays, Tuesdays, Wednesdays, and occasional Fridays. There was no need to be coy. Over the ensuing weeks he sought me out and made small talk as we used the various machines. He was complimentary—of both of us. "Look how much we've improved!" he'd exclaim. And it was true; we were going further, faster. I'd started firming up and he was definitely losing his belly. Our conversations seemed unforced and oddly intimate, even if they mainly addressed the pace of our fitness progress, the weather, or current events.

Once in while, though, our conversations took a deeply personal turn.

"Claire, can I ask you a question?"

"Shoot."

"You seem to know a whole lot about *Yiddishkeit,* but you don't seem at all into it," Rob said.

"That's for sure. Sam didn't even have a bar mitzvah."

"But you know an awful lot," Rob observed.

"I went to Jewish day school from third to eighth grade."

"Third?"

"Yeah, after my mother died, my grandparents took over. So I got to go to a school where I thanked God for making me 'according to his will,' while all the boys thanked God for 'not making me a woman.'"

"Ouch," Rob said without losing his stride. "You know, that *shelo asani isha* isn't in the Conservative prayer book anymore."

"Well, it doesn't matter. I didn't stop being observant because of some high-minded feminist objections, I just o.d.'ed on all the rituals and rules," I explained.

"What was Shabbes like at your grandparents' house?"

"A lot of sitting around. Some singing. I read a lot. We ate rubbery chicken, overcooked vegetables, dry potato kugel. I remember being bored a lot. There wasn't much I could do on Shabbes. No TV, no writing, no talking on the phone, no music. According to family lore, I once asked if it was OK to breathe on Shabbes."

"Where was your father in all this?"

"As far away as he could get. He'd grown up in a very assimilated household. The only reason my parents' house was kosher was to please my grandparents. Even as a kid I could tell that Pop thought the whole thing was stupid."

"So he was OK with your living with your grandparents?"

"My mom had been sick for over three years. Bubbe came every morning at 6:30 to take care of the house, help Mom, take care of me, and get me off to school. Dad was busy and traveled a lot. I guess it just seemed natural that she would continue caring for me after my mom died."

"And your dad didn't object?"

"He pretty much shut down after Mom died. I doubt Pop would have be able to care for me."

"Did you see him much?"

"It was complicated. The relationship with my grandparents was very tense. They didn't exactly blame him for her breast cancer, but they were incredibly angry that he didn't let her rest enough. According to them, he ran her ragged."

"What did he do?" Rob asked.

"Well, I remember just months before she died, the three of us went to a baseball game at Shea Stadium. Getting the tickets was a big deal. Pop only got them because he worked with one of the players."

"What did your father do?"

"He was an accountant and a financial manager for professional athletes."

"Do you remember who his client was?"

"Art Shmancy?"

"Shamsky!" Rob said excitedly. "Could it be Shamsky?"

"Yeah, that's it."

"He was my hero growing up. You know he refused to play on Yom Kippur, just like Koufax. Shamsky later went on to manage a team in Israel. Did you get to meet him?" Rob asked eagerly.

"I think so. I ended up meeting a lot of guys Pop worked with. Most of his clients were either baseball or football players."

"Anyone else I would know?"

"I don't know. I didn't really pay much attention to that stuff. Pop loved sports and he loved the athletes."

"Did he play?"

"He played baseball in high school and spent one season in the minors before realizing that college was a better bet. Later in life he played a lot of golf."

"What kind of things did he do for his clients?"

"He helped them invest and manage their money. He advised them on all sorts of matters and got to know their whole families. He really cared about his clients. I got a condolence card from someone Pop helped—the wife of a football player who has Parkinson's. She wrote that her family couldn't have made it without Pop's planning and help."

"Sounds like a real mensch."

"He was," I agreed. Pop was a good guy, I thought, he just didn't connect with me. Maybe I served as a painful reminder of all he had lost. I'm a squatter, plainer version of my mom. I inherited her facial features, but not her height, grace, or sense of fashion. I think it pained Pop to see this inferior copy of his adored original. Mom shared his love of sports and his love of fine things. Either I inherited or became acculturated to my grandparents' more sedentary ways and plebian sensibilities.

As Rob and I continued to tread on the machines, my thoughts returned to that day at Shea Stadium. Even though it was warm outside, Mom was wrapped in blankets. She was wearing her wig—not the pretty fall she sometimes wore on nights out on the town with Pop but the one she wore once she'd lost her hair. She was really pale and had deep, dark circles under her eyes. Bubbe was furious that we went out, and I remember a screaming match between Bubbe and Pop before we left, but Mom settled it, telling Bubbe that she really wanted to go. She couldn't spend the rest of her life in the house. At the ballpark, Mom sat between me and Pop and held both our hands. She kept on kissing our hands, too. Pop bought me an ice cream and himself a beer. Mom didn't eat anything. I rarely saw her eat. That outing may have been the last time she left the house before she went into the hospital. Once she was in the hospital that final time, I never saw her again.

12

The next time I saw Rob at the gym, I arrived with puffy eyes, blotched cheeks, and a red nose.

"What's the matter? Are you OK?" Rob asked, sounding genuinely concerned.

I mumbled something about felonious teenagers.

"I used to be one of those. Maybe I can give you some insight."

Thus began an informal counseling session, in which Rob was both helpful and kind. It was comforting to hear that someone that sweet had given his mother such a hard time.

"I found her mere existence irritating, and any hint of sexuality, well, that was intolerable," Rob explained. Somehow listening to how Rob's flesh would crawl when his mother tried to hug him made me feel better about Sam.

"I was such a little jerk," Rob recalled without pride but also without self-blame. Now, there is no one, no one, I care about more. A hug from my mother is . . . a delight. I just don't see her often enough."

"Why don't you visit her more?"

"Well, she lives in Florida and has an active life down there. I can't get to her on weekends because I'm busy with work . . . but you're right, I should make more of an effort. I'll call her tonight. Thanks." He flashed me a megawatt smile, crooked and warm.

It made me feel better to know that my rotten kid's rudeness ("these eggs taste like crap"), my predictable over-reaction (grabbing the plate of eggs and angrily throwing them on the floor, shattering the plate), and his rejoinder (icy stare and audible mutter of "psycho-woman"), had prompted Rob to call. At least his mother would get some *nachas*.

Rob and I spoke at length and I was more honest than I'd ever been with anyone about the shameful scenes that go on in my house. I didn't feel judged by Rob, just listened to. When had that happened last? Joanie, with her brood, was always so busy and so in control. I was ashamed to admit how bad things had become between Sam and me. I certainly couldn't talk to my ex, Jeremy, Mr. Aloof Superiority, married to his not-so-sweet young thing. Lydia was already in Italy, and besides, she didn't really understand kids. Yet, here was this schlumpy guy with a great smile and an open heart to whom I could talk without reservation or artifice.

Rob reminded me that it's a teenager's job to be obnoxious. He encouraged me not to take it personally and just think of Sam as a teenager dedicated to his craft—driving his mother crazy. In a few years Sam and I would be very close, Rob assured me. Rob's comments were truly comforting. I was going to ask him what he did for a living that made him work on weekends, but his cell phone began to vibrate. He glanced at it announced, "Got to run!" and darted off.

My suspicion that Rob was a doctor was confirmed during our next conversation the following Friday when I invited him out to breakfast after the gym.

"I'd love to, really I would. I'm so happy you asked, but I'm due at the hospital as soon as I'm done here. This is a crazy time of year. Please, let me take a rain check."

He left me to muse as I continued on the treadmill.

Even though I understood and believed his reason for not accepting my invitation, the rejection stung. I hated putting myself on the line and hearing a no, even if it was polite and thoroughly reasonable. My experiences with men had been, upon analysis—and one didn't have to be overly analytical here—dismal. Naturally, each relationship (I'd slept with seven guys, four before my ex, Jeremy, and two after) had its own set of idiosyncratic mistakes, but some troubling patterns did emerge. I moved too fast. I was committed way before I should have been. Also, I was too impressed by what men did for a living, too invested in the professional accomplishments of the potential Nobel laureate or the mogul. This served to set up barriers to getting to know the real men behind the professional masks.

I trudged on and continued to think, appreciative of this time on the machine to sort things out. In an effort to at least make new mistakes, rather than just repeating the same old ones, I promised myself to go slow with Rob, painfully slow if necessary. No more invitations, I swore to myself. Let *him* make the first move. Let dating be the guy's idea for a change.

Also, I was determined not to talk to him about his work. I simply wouldn't discuss his profession until he chose to bring it up. I'd always resented the American obsession with "what do you do?" even when it wasn't merely a more polite way of asking "how much money do you make?" I hated it when people suddenly treated me with more respect just because they found out I was an attorney and a director of human relations for a large corporation and not just a frumpy suburban mom. Something told me that, in the same fashion, Rob enjoyed our conversations precisely because I wasn't part of his work life. I inhabited space outside the stress of the hospital. My respect for him didn't depend on his professional status.

He was clearly some fancy-pants doctor—maybe head of a practice group. So what? I was increasingly impressed by Rob's genuineness and equanimity. What I liked about him was the fact that he would recite Lewis Carroll, and tell me, in a way that was neither smarmy nor fake, that I was looking great.

Still, I did wonder. I doubted he was a surgeon. Rob didn't have the hands for it (or the obsessive protection of his hands that I'd heard was common among surgeons and violin players). Not a gynecologist, though if I was very lucky, maybe I'd have a chance to find out whether he had the hands for *that*. If I had to guess—and I was committed to not asking, so guessing was my only option—I'd put my money on a pediatric oncologist. He fit the bill—kind, knew a lot about kids, and could quote the children's classics. Besides, there was something wise about Rob. It seemed as if he'd seen enough death and heartache to truly appreciate life.

13

Although I could try to delude myself that it was my newfound appetite for exercise, it was really the thought of seeing Rob that was getting me up and to the gym, particularly on the days when I knew he would be there. We'd been meeting at the gym for over six weeks and I never tired of talking with him. More amazing than my continued attendance at the gym was my adherence to my resolve not to push things with Rob. We chatted and huffed and puffed but I didn't invite him to breakfast again and I steadfastly refused to ask him any personal questions.

An added bonus on this particular Tuesday morning was that going to the gym minimized interaction with the Angry One, who had pitched a fit because his favorite jeans weren't clean.

"I put them in the laundry two days ago," Sam indicted. "I only have one pair I really like."

"Sorry I didn't get to it," I said, trying to stay calm. "Why don't we just buy you a few more pairs of the same kind, so you won't run out?"

"Sure, waste all of Dad's money buying clothes because you can't be bothered to do the wash. Ben's mother does the fucking laundry every day."

"Do you want the deal that Ben Greenberg has? Really? I bet Ben helps around the house, and doesn't curse at his mother."

"There you go, changing the subject. The point is I need clean laundry. I don't ask you for all that much. There are a lot of kids doing drugs and getting bad grades. You just don't appreciate what you have."

"You're right, I just don't appreciate how respectful and wonderful you are. It's amazing how blind I am to my very good luck that you aren't some junkie, and that all you do is scream, curse, and criticize me all the damn time."

"Look who's talking!" Sam yelled with genuine umbrage.

I gathered my gym clothes and stomped out the door without eating the breakfast I'd made for us. Doubtless the food would still be on the stove when I came back that evening.

As Rob and I worked out next to one another on our steppers, I told him about my morning. He was remarkably tough on both me and Sam.

"Shouldn't Sam be doing his own laundry by now?" Rob asked.

My admittedly lame explanations—he's only fourteen, he'd mix up the light and dark so that he'd have an entire wardrobe in pink, it's easier just to do it myself—were totally unpersuasive to Rob. He actually got me thinking about the role I play in the pathetic morning dynamic that goes on at my house.

"Sam's entitled to be moody, but not abusive." Rob stated as he continued his stepping. I noticed his breath wasn't labored at all. I also noticed that he was in need of a good shave.

"You need to take care of yourself and make him step up to the plate a bit."

"I'm here at seven, isn't that taking care of myself?"

"Oh," Rob said, "I thought you were here to take care of *me*. With your encouragement, I've lost ten pounds. I'll bet my cholesterol has gone down too."

"I'm just good for your heart," I said, and then immediately regretted it.

"More than you know, Claireleh," Rob said softly, "more than you know."

Suddenly, despite the hum of machines, the grunts of the weightlifters, and the giggles of the pretty twenty-somethings gossiping while they ran on adjoining treadmills, everything seemed to go very quiet. The room was getting darker and I felt cold. I must have looked the way I felt because Rob exclaimed, "Oh, no," and immediately rushed over to me, asking if I was OK. I told him I was just a little winded and that I needed to rest for a second. Rob persisted and helped me off the machine. He took my pulse, which did nothing to slow it down. His face was full of concern as he escorted me to the juice bar and insisted that I drink the fresh-squeezed orange juice that he ordered. He encouraged me to sit awhile. He was clearly troubled that I'd suddenly become so pale and my pulse was racing beyond anything the elliptical machine could explain.

As I was trying to assure Rob that I was fine, and I had just neglected to eat breakfast, Kurt came by and started to schmooze us up in his dim, gung-ho fashion. He asked about our progress, but didn't wait for a reply and instead, patted Rob's stomach, professing to be impressed.

"Good going, Bob my man. You're really working it. I see a lot less of that gut of yours," Kurt said.

Then he turned to me. "Claire, you're doing great too. Your butt was much bigger when you first started, but I really see a difference. You've tightened up and have more definition. Keep it up, but lay off the juice: you don't need the calories. Stick to water."

I felt revived enough to slug him but Rob intervened, thanking Kurt for the encouragement.

"Claire does look fabulous," Rob said and he gave me a little pat.

Rob's touch on my back, even through my sweaty tee shirt, sent a jolt through me. Even Kurt seemed to notice and he looked at us quizzically. I guess it never occurred to him that people of our size and age could have attractions or sexual feelings. But if we did, it made sense that we were attracted to our own kind. Awkwardly, Kurt announced that he was going to take a quick run and jumped on a nearby treadmill.

"Ignore him," Rob whispered. "The wheel is spinning but the hamster is dead."

I let out a rather unladylike noise in between a snort and a guffaw. So much for being sultry.

"So, are you saying that my ass is still huge?" I asked.

"No, I'm saying that your heart is huge, and your tuchus, well, I can't comment because anything I say would be an admission that I've been admiring it."

"OK," I said, happy beyond reason. "Where'd you learn that hamster phrase?"

"From some of the kids I work with," Rob said. "It just seemed apt. Are you feeling up to breakfast, or should we try for it another day?"

14

Breakfast was at the Sage Diner. It's the kind of place where the waitress is sure to be middle-aged, wear sensible shoes, have a bad dye job, and call you "hon." We attacked the food like wolves; whatever nervousness I may have felt didn't translate into demure table manners. Rob had pancakes and slathered them in syrup. My eggs didn't disappoint and the bacon was crispy. I offered Rob some but he declined. He did take my strawberry when I explained that I was allergic. I thought how admirable it was that he was watching his cholesterol. But then, I was thinking that everything about this remarkable, if slightly unkempt man was admirable. Usually, I only got to look at Rob in profile as he climbed on the machine next to me. Full frontal Rob (fully clothed in a charcoal grey suit and red striped tie) was a joy to look at. Beneath his bushy eyebrows that grew in all directions were very bright green eyes framed by lots of laugh lines. The tea was bitter and had a weird metallic aftertaste, but I would gladly have drunk cup after cup to remain across the booth from Rob.

Rob reached across the table and held my hand. Again I felt a jolt but tried to keep my reaction under wraps. "I feel that I owe you an explanation," he began.

Uh oh, I thought, this doesn't sound good.

"I've been acting like some goofy man of mystery, while you have been so open about your life."

This was certainly true. Rob and I talked about everything and nothing—teenagers and bosses, the weather and religion—but he never revealed much about himself or what happened in his life outside the gym. I could have let him continue but didn't. Instead, I told him that I *did* understand. I knew he had a pressure-filled job and that the gym and our friendship were respites from the emotional drain of his work. I didn't need to know who he was outside the gym. He was precious to me because he was Rob. No honorific, no title, just Rob. As I finished, I was amazed to see tears in his eyes.

"Your friendship is valuable to me beyond anything you can imagine," Rob said, his voice low and trembling a little. "You're the only person, the *only* person with whom I have a true, unencumbered friendship. If you like me, it's because you like the true me, not some pillar of the community."

Rob heaved a great sigh and forced himself to look me in the eye. I braced myself, knowing that I wouldn't like what was coming.

"I do have to tell you one thing about me," he continued. "It's been nagging at me, and I have to tell you. I guess I don't feel you can fully know me until you know."

There was a long silence. Rob was still holding my hand. His voice was tight and his face was very white. "I don't have any children. I can't have them," he confessed. "All that advice I've been giving you . . . well, I'm a bit of a phony. It's so easy to pontificate about other people's parenting. The truth is, God never blessed me that way. It's the sorrow of my life. I try to compensate and surround myself with kids, work to help kids and nurture them, but it isn't the same. Family is everything to me and I can't give my mother a grandchild."

His voice began to quiver and I dreaded what I knew would come next. "I can't give my wife a baby," he said with eyes downcast, "and she'll never forgive me for it."

Had I suspected he was married? He didn't wear a ring. He never, not once, mentioned a wife. Yet, I can't say it was a total surprise. A man that kind, fun, and funny couldn't be unattached. He was so incredibly warm, but to be fair, he'd never been overtly sexual with me—just open, friendly, and a tad flirtatious. Besides, I believed what he was telling me. Despite his being married, I was the only one who knew and appreciated him for who he truly was. I realized that the wife thing might have occupied center stage had our relationship been different, but I knew that the deepest revelation was about his inability to have children. He, who quoted at length from Lewis Carroll and Dr. Seuss, didn't have a child of his own to read to. What a tragedy. How unfair. And how stupid and petty my daily complaints about Sam seemed to me at that moment. My eyes welled with tears. I couldn't think what to say. He'd comforted me many times, and I couldn't find the right words for him. Finally, I said the only thing that struck me as unequivocally true. I held his hand and thanked him for telling me. He'd trusted me with his sorrowful secret, and I would love him forever.

15

"Do you ever believe that adultery can be justified? I mean, is it always wrong?" I asked Joanie.

"Oh my God, gym-guy is married!" Joanie howled with more volume than I would have liked, given that we were walking down the aisles of Trader Joe's. I felt ridiculous even raising the question, but I didn't know who else to ask. Lydia believed that all marriage was patriarchal and wouldn't have had a moment's qualm about seducing a married woman. Joanie, though no prude, was religious and grounded and I thought might have some insight. So despite her glee at being able to read me like a book—the large print, easy-vocabulary variety—I decided to pursue my question. Somehow, I didn't think Rob was very close to his wife. She probably was among the ladies-who-lunch doctors' wives set. I'd bet she spent all her spare time at Neiman Marcus, that is, when she wasn't ordering the maid around. Could I ignore the deep connection I felt for Rob? If he didn't value his marriage, why should I? Besides, it wasn't entirely clear that he was interested in me that way. I just wanted to think it through, just in case the spark I felt was mutual.

"Well, two things," Joanie began. She was a consummate list-maker and organizer. Every drawer in her house was labeled and inventoried, she had a catalog for all their books and movies, and even Joanie's speech was infected by her desire to impose order.

"First, you might be surprised to learn that I don't think it's always wrong. Especially if the spouse is just sticking around for the kids." I tried not to wince. One thing I wouldn't disclose to anyone was Rob's childless state and his grief and guilt about it.

"But to put it into perspective—and this is point number two—" Joanie continued, "I'd kill anyone who messed around with Aaron, and I don't mean that metaphorically. I'd really kill the woman."

I went on the record as finding Aaron charming, but entirely off-limits. I reminded Joanie to keep my question and implied confession quiet, admonishing her to tell no one.

"Tell no one what?" said a voice that was gratingly familiar. My cart barely avoided hitting Marjorie's as we rounded the corner. Joanie, who never seemed to have that deer-in-the-headlights look that I sport with regularity, supplied the answer:

"Hi, Marjorie. Claire was just begging me not to tell anyone how much she spent on the organic mangos. Oops," she continued in mock mortification, "now I've told you. You won't spread it around, will you?"

Marjorie eyed me suspiciously. "You buy organic mangos? They're $3.65 each."

"Hence her deep embarrassment, Marjorie, come on, don't tell anyone, OK?" Joanie was practically pleading.

"You know, if you peel the mangos there's no pesticide residue," Marjorie said. "I can't imagine why you'd choose such an expensive item. So be it. I only come here because Stuart has a sensitivity to wheat—all gluten products really—and there's a brand of gluten-free cracker they sell here that he really enjoys. Come I'll show you. They come in onion and vegetable flavors."

No amount of polite demurring, not even the obvious fact that neither of us had to shop for anyone with a gluten sensitivity, could deter Marjorie from leading us down the aisle stocking shelf after shelf of salt-free, wheat-free, hydrogenated-oil-free, and, probably, taste-free crackers. Marjorie had launched into her lecture on allergens and was just segueing into her petition for Earth Science AP when Joanie clutched her stomach and announced that she wasn't feeling well. Even Marjorie had to take notice, and we left our carts in the middle of the store and headed for the parking lot.

"Good going," I said approvingly. "It's a shame to lose the groceries, but we had to get out of there. I think she really believed you aren't well."

"Something's really wrong," Joanie said with a look of panic on her face. "Can you get me home and call Aaron and Dr. Lewis?"

16

I sat next to Joan on her king-sized bed as she lay there on her back with her feet propped up. The kids were still with the sitter and Aaron was on his way home. We were waiting for a call from the doctor.

I surveyed the bedroom. It was painted pale yellow. The bedspread was a deep gold with red brocade. Everything was neat, color-coordinated, and calming without being boring. No television in the bedroom, just this huge bed and various dressers, fresh flowers, kiddy art, and pictures of the kids. The look was French countryside meets the Brady bunch. On the night table lay a paperback entitled *The Far Euphrates.*

"Any good?" I asked.

"Tragic, but wonderful," she answered. "We're reading it for our Sisterhood group at the synagogue. Any chance you'd come? It's Thursday night. It would really cheer me up."

How could I deny Joanie as she lay there in obvious distress? Of course I agreed to attend the Sisterhood book club. There would probably be some good eats, and it was a chance to escape from the monster for an evening. I'd been meaning to check out the synagogue, and this seemed like a painless first step.

At the sound of male voices, I looked up and at the door was Aaron, and Joan's obstetrician, Dr. Lewis. Dr. Lewis was a huge man, taller even than Aaron, with a gentle, weather-worn face and gigantic hands, probably larger than some of the babies he delivered.

"Wow," I said in disbelief, "you make house calls?"

"Only for my very special patients," he answered warmly.

"Dr. Lewis's just counting on us for some more repeat business," Joan quipped.

"You keep it up, Joan, and I'll be able to retire early. We already have the pool house named after you," he added with a smile.

I excused myself and waited in the kitchen as Dr. Lewis examined Joanie, trying to think of what I could make for dinner. I decided on pizza. Without bragging, I must confess that I excel at ordering pizza, which I'm willing to do even without the assistance of a coupon. I did so with glee, knowing it would be a treat for the kids, who are normally subjected to Joanie's wholesome, balanced fare. Besides, I could run a pie over to Sam later in the evening.

Joanie was put on bed rest, to which she was entirely temperamentally unsuited. Now, I'm the sort of person who would relish medical orders to lie around and do nothing. I'd be thrilled, apart, of course, from the concern over the baby's welfare. Joanie was itching to get up and was trying to manage things from her bedroom. She was constantly shouting orders and reminding me about everything from where I could find the kids' pajamas to making sure Aaron took his evening vitamins. The twins kept on sneaking in, and finally we just shut the door. Aaron and I muddled through the evening rituals somehow.

By the time I left, the kids were in bed, all was relatively quiet, and I crawled home bone tired. Four kids, even cute well-behaved ones, can really wear a girl out. True, I was spared commentary on my eating habits, nobody glared menacingly at me, and the kids actually seemed to enjoy talking to me. Nevertheless, I was beat. How did Joanie do it every day? Furthermore, how did she keep the house spotless, have time to garden, exercise, and make so many fabulous meals?

I checked my cell phone for messages. Though rationally I should have learned by now to associate the voicemail icon with bad news—or, at the very best, requests for charitable donations—I still had an immoderate measure of girlish hope. Could Rob have called? Outwardly, nothing had changed between us at the gym, but I could sense that we had somehow become more intimate. He was no longer just counseling me about the spawn of Satan; we were supportive friends who knew each other's deepest challenges. We had leapfrogged all the trappings of acquaintanceship and had gotten down to the core of friendship. He knew that I was a lawyer. He knew that I was divorced from Sam's dad, but probably didn't realize that I'd been married to a handsome, hot-shot corporate litigator who now had a new, barely-legal tootsie. The details didn't matter. He knew *me*, and it was thrilling, if a little intense.

I tapped the phone to speaker: the first message was from Dr. Braunstein, Sam's principal, asking me to make an appointment with his office first thing in the morning. This couldn't be good, I thought.

"Sam," I bellowed. Again I called him, more irritated. The third time I yelled his name, I rated an annoyed, "What?"

"Is there any reason Dr. Braunstein should be calling me?"

"Not that I can think of," he replied.

"Are you sure you aren't in trouble?" This question also had to be repeated and finally elicited a disdainful reply, "Why, yes, I knifed a teacher. Sorry I forgot to mention it."

Well, I'd find out the next day. The next message was even more upsetting.

"Claire, this is Marjorie. I need to talk to you. Also, I was wondering how Joan's feeling. I can't imagine how she's going to manage with five. I find two kids exhausting with all their activities and lessons, and working with the school system. So be it. I really need to talk with you. Please call me as soon as you get this."

I knew that the smartest thing to do would be to call Marjorie back immediately and discuss the latest emergency. Had Sam left some towels on her bathroom floor again? Was there another meeting to attend or petition to sign?

"So be it," I said to myself as I dished out some pistachio ice cream, and plopped down in front of the TV.

17

First thing in the morning (after waking a snarling Sam three separate times), I checked in on Joanie, who was still on bed rest. Aaron was taking the day off from work at his engineering firm and I agreed to stay with Jake while Aaron drove Sarah, Rachel, and Zack to school. This would mean missing the gym on a Tuesday when Rob would undoubtedly be there, but there was no question—Joanie needed me.

Joanie was clearly frustrated at the prospect of our making the kids' lunches so she tried to do it by proxy. Rather than yelling, they'd set up the baby monitor so Joanie could talk and Aaron and I could hear her in the kitchen.

"No junk," Joanie commanded. I gave Aaron a conspiratorial wink as I deposited into each lunchbox Yodels I had sneaked over. Let them eat cake, I thought. Aaron confirmed that the milk money was enclosed. And napkins. And a note. All of which were indeed in there.

Joanie was going nuts with the enforced bed rest, but seemed in good spirits otherwise. When I entered the room she motioned for me to sit next to her on the bed.

"At least I'll be sure to finish reading the book for the book group," she said. "They're moving the discussion to my house. The rabbi's wife, Beverly, is handling everything. She's a real tornado. I swear, she makes me look laid back!"

I widened my eyes in disbelief. Who could make Joanie look laid back? I had to meet this woman. Joanie explained that Beverly had called all the Sisterhood members and arranged for everyone to bring something, so starting Thursday night there'd be home-cooked meals. Dr. Lewis gave Joanie special permission to sit in the living room

Thursday night for the book group as long as she didn't move around and kept her feet up.

"How's the house looking?" Joanie asked.

"Good," I lied. Well, it was good by my standards, and I couldn't help it if it wasn't up to its usual sparkle. It's enough that I did the laundry and put it in the kids' rooms. I couldn't be expected to vacuum every five minutes. Joan's house was still ten times neater and cleaner than my own so, really, "good" was a reasonable response, I assured myself.

I told Joanie about the call from the principal and she suggested that it might be something wonderful, a science prize or something. Fat chance. No one gets summoned to the principal's office for good news. But the sooner I made the call the better. Reluctantly, I said goodbye to Joanie. I checked to make sure that Sam had made the bus, and then I headed off to work.

When Molly connected me to the principal, he wouldn't discuss the matter over the phone. That struck me as ominous. We set an appointment for later that afternoon and I was filled with dread. Meanwhile, Marjorie had called three times. Molly knew not to put her through, but I reluctantly decided to return the call before the little pink phone slips accumulated into a big accusatory stack on my desk.

When I returned Marjorie's call, she, too, was evasive. Why all the secrecy? Rather than tell me what was up or even harangue me, she just asked me to come over at seven with Sam. I tried to beg off and let her know that I'd be happy to sign any petition without actually attending the meeting, but Marjorie was insistent. She repeated her request that Sam and I come over at seven and reiterated that she wouldn't ask me to come unless it was important.

Maybe it was having missed my morning exercise, but the day seemed endless—full of hassles, boring but with an undercurrent of trouble brewing. The absolute low point was realizing that I'd have to deal with Teresa Williams, who had pulled another Monday morning no-show the day before. I was immensely irritated. If everyone else at this stupid place could make it into the office on Monday mornings, why couldn't she?

18

I parked in visitors' parking and pasted one of the guest passes required of all visitors to Hudsonville High School on my lapel. Security had been enhanced, but as far as I was concerned, anyone who wanted to kidnap Sam was welcome to him. I just hoped they didn't have any expectation that I'd pay the ransom. I made my way through the warren of musty-smelling administrative offices. I was directed by the secretary to sit in the waiting area, which consisted of three chairs with desks attached. I was barely able to squeeze myself in. Above my head were the teachers' mailboxes, and every once in a while a teacher would come by and reach over me to get mail.

Dr. Braunstein kept me waiting for twenty-five minutes, but I'd brought work with me and spent the time reviewing Teresa Williams' file. How could anyone call in sick so many Mondays? Also, the woman was positively accident prone. In the past six months alone she had dislocated her elbow, smashed her thumb, and tripped, bumping her head. Maybe, it dawned on me, Teresa had a drinking problem. On the job, she seemed perfectly competent. Aside from her absenteeism, she always behaved professionally, if a bit coldly, towards her fellow workers. She dressed very fashionably and always wore a ton of makeup. I marveled at these women who considered their faces canvases on which to paint a beautiful, flawless, but to me, eerily inhuman, mask. That wasn't my style—I got by with a little lip gloss and mascara—but since I was still, despite my recent exercise, pretty much of a dowdy fatso sans any identifiable style whatsoever, I was hardly in a position to criticize the appearance or fashion choices of others. As I was tabulating Teresa's absences, Dr. Braunstein greeted me and ushered me into his office.

"Hello, Mrs. Schiff. Thanks for coming." The only people who called me Mrs. Schiff (Jeremy's surname, a name that I never formally adopted) were Sam's doctors and teachers. It's not a name I associate with good times.

Dr. Braunstein was a short, paunchy man with aviator glasses that used to be fashionable circa 1972. He had more dandruff than I'd ever before seen on one person's shoulders. He was not a smiler.

"I'm sorry Mr. Schiff can't make it," he said pointedly.

I informed Dr. Braunstein that Mr. Schiff and I were divorced, and that Mr. Schiff had just returned from his honeymoon, double-daring Braunstein to say another word about it. I promised to convey any important information to Sam's father. Frankly, I thought to myself, Jeremy had never attended any school conferences when we were married or after we divorced. Why should things change now?

"I'll get straight to the point. Your son Sam and his friend, Ben Greenberg, have been abusing their computer privileges here at the school. They disabled certain controls set to prevent students from connecting to adult websites and have been going to web pages that contain pornographic images."

"Oh." That's all I said, and I'm pretty sure it came out as a squeak.

"We take this issue very seriously, Mrs. Schiff. Your son and his friend disabled a program that was protecting the entire student body from lewd and inappropriate material. We first discovered the problem when a student looking for information on baby animals did a search that led her to a pornographic site. She was quite upset. As were her parents. After our computer technician did some investigating, he reported that it's clear the boys entered the computer system posing as administrators and intentionally disabled the restrictions. They have also visited various pornographic sites repeatedly when they were supposed to be doing research in the library. I have the list of sites here."

Oh God, I thought. All that time Sam has been on the computer at home! I thought he was just developing anti-social habits and fascist tendencies. I had no idea he was interested in girls or sex. Video carnage? Undoubtedly. Computer hacking? Maybe. But looking at naked women? It had never occurred to me. But then, who knew what transpired in his head? Certainly not I. The kid was so angry and closed off all the time. My entire interaction with him was restricted to feeding, nagging, and snarling.

"I have talked to Mr. and Mrs. Greenberg about this and they said they would be in contact with you about how the families would handle the matter. Meanwhile, each boy will receive a three-day suspension from school and be prohibited from using the school's computers for the rest of the semester."

"That sounds fair," I said, because it sort of did once I was able to wrap my mind around what Sam had done. I wasn't overly upset, more mystified than anything else, and, of course, irritated that I would have to find something for Sam to do for the next three days of school.

"I hope I'm not prying, but does Sam get to see his father regularly? Sometimes, if boys don't have adequate male role-models, they get confused about how to behave, particularly around sexual matters."

I bit my tongue so as not to tell Dr. Braunstein that there was absolutely nothing I wanted Jeremy to teach Sam about sexual matters. Instead, I told him that Sam had been extremely difficult this past year, something I'd chalked up to Sam's budding adolescence. I thanked Dr. Braunstein again for his time. Thanks for nothing, I thought. Stunned, I returned to work, dreading the conversation I would have to have with Sam about this. I decided to be there when he returned home from school.

19

"What the hell?" Sam yelled as he stomped into the living room, after discovering that his new 21-inch flat screen color monitor was gone. Sam demanded to know where it was and what had happened. He railed at me, reminding me that he had repeatedly told me not to touch his stuff. What was I doing in his room anyway, he wanted to know, and when was the monitor going to be replaced?

Calmly, I informed Sam that I'd confiscated the monitor and that he was done playing with the computer for quite a while. He was incredulous and white with fury.

"I took away the monitor because of what Dr. Braunstein told me today at school." Sam looked confused.

"According to Dr. Braunstein, you and Ben disabled the filters on the school's internet access and looked at various porn sites."

Sam just continued to stare at me.

"Here's one: 'Big busty blondes take it up the ass.' Some sixth grader really needs access to that website."

Sam couldn't continue to look me in the eye, but everything else about his body language indicated that he was still fuming. "This is fucking ridiculous," Sam exclaimed to his shoes, seething.

"Here's what is going to happen," I said with what I hoped was steely calm. "You're going to do your homework, eat dinner at the kitchen table, not in front of the television, not in your room, and then accompany me to Ben's house. From my perspective, having to listen to Marjorie rant on and on about this will be ten times worse than talking to Dr. Braunstein, which, by the way, was pretty awful. I suppose it would be too much to expect that you would give any thought to how this must be for me. I'm furious with you and I expect you to behave yourself. OK?"

Sam didn't respond.

"*OK?*" I said more loudly. "Fine, don't answer me. You'll have no television or computer as long as you're suspended from school. That's going to be three days."

"This is bullshit!" Sam yelled.

"I'll tell you what's bullshit," I shouted. "My having to miss work to see the principal, that's bullshit. My having to go to Marjorie's house, that's really bullshit. Just try me, Sam," I said, losing whatever calm I'd mustered. "Just try defying me on this and I'll take a bat to your precious monitor."

"You're so fucking crazy you just might do it."

"Damn right," I screamed. "Go to your room and don't come out until I call you for dinner."

I was wondering how Joanie was doing and wished I could call her, but I was sure I'd give away what was going on and I couldn't bear talking about this with her. I thought of writing to Lydia, but somehow the sexual content of the pages might get her going. I supposed I should tell Jeremy, but I didn't have the heart to just yet. Instead, I made some mac 'n' cheese and waited for the dreaded rendezvous at Marjorie's house.

As we ate a sullen dinner and took a silent—I mean totally silent—car ride, I was thinking that things could be worse. Sam and I could be screaming and cursing at each other; I could be driving like a maniac, which I'm wont to do when I'm really upset. Also, with Marjorie on the case, I was confident that I couldn't be labeled the worst mother in the world.

We entered Marjorie's house, as always, through the side kitchen door. The kitchen was the center of everything at Marjorie's house—the locus for all sorts of hectoring about the school system, unsolicited advice about cooking, and complaints about everything under the sun. A huge calendar was affixed to the refrigerator listing the kids' various lessons, appointments, clubs, and competitions. On the wall next to it hung a bulletin board with various store circulars, coupons, and announcements from school. Finally, there was a white board with a grocery list and a list of chores for each boy to do. Ben took out the garbage, washed the deck furniture, and unloaded the dishwasher? Amazing.

I expected that Marjorie would sit us around the kitchen table with some cookies purchased by the gross at some awful chain store that locked in its workers and didn't give them health insurance. The moms would drink watery decaf with skim milk, the boys, 2% milk with their cookies, and Marjorie would lecture about rules, and honesty, and somehow make this all Sam's fault.

Imagine my surprise to be ushered into the living room where Jack, Marjorie's husband, was sitting with Ben. Jack rose and politely directed me to a plush armchair. Marjorie's living room was painted white and the furniture was all browns and rusts. A Rembrandt reproduction hung above the brown couch, where Jack indicated that Sam should sit next to Ben. No one would ever call this place cozy, but the throw pillows and art all came together to create a stark but not unappealing room. Predictably, Marjorie started on her spiel.

"I'll bring out some cookies. I buy them in bulk but they are just as good as anything you can get at Trader Joe's," she began. But, Jack, with his deep voice and thick Israeli accent, interrupted her.

"Marjorie, my dear, this is not a social occasion."

I'd never heard Jack talk before. I'd seen him a few times and I suppose I knew that he *could* talk, but I was pretty sure this was the first time I heard his voice. More astoundingly, I'd never seen anyone successfully shut Marjorie up before, ever.

Jack waited until he was sure he had everyone's full attention.

"Boys, we are here to talk to you about something serious," Jack began. "Am I correct that you disabled the filters on the school computers?"

"Yes, Dad," Ben said, his head hunched between his shoulders.

"Yes, Mr. Greenberg," Sam echoed, also looking down.

"Well, that is pretty impressive computer knowledge." Both boys looked up at him in surprise. "No one taught you how to do it?"

"No," said Sam with real enthusiasm, "Ben and I figured it out from books and some sites on the internet. We learned a lot about how the computer system works and we were even able to enter as administrators. That's how we disabled the filters."

"Well that shows a lot of ingenuity and talent, and I'm proud of you for that." Jack paused and let his compliment sink in before he continued. "But you obviously did not realize that the school could figure out who did it."

"I guess we didn't cover our tracks," Ben admitted.

"No, and more importantly, you really did not think through the consequences." Jack spoke slowly and calmly. He continued: "As a direct result of your actions, some children were directed to inappropriate websites."

"We didn't think about that either," Ben said, sounding truly sorry. "We were just trying to see if we could do it. We were going to put back the filters. We just ran out of time."

Jack looked to me for permission to address Sam. When I nodded, Jack asked, "Well, Sam, what do you have to say?"

Sam stared at the carpet and mumbled something about seeing if they could do it. He added that he was sorry.

"Now boys, there is something else I want to discuss with you, and I am going to ask your mothers to stay, even though this might be a bit embarrassing."

I didn't think it was possible, but Sam and Ben seemed to shrink even smaller, melting with shame into the couch. The phone rang and Marjorie leapt for it but was thwarted mid-air by a look from Jack. Instead, she retreated and everyone just sat and listened to it ring. I'll hand it to Jack, I thought, the man knows something about dramatic timing.

I couldn't imagine a scene such as this one at my house. Sam would never have sat still to listen to me; he would have just yelled at me to shut up, or insisted that I pick up the phone. Jeremy couldn't be bothered to talk to his son about such matters and, besides, had set a crummy example by being a total workaholic and then, years later, marrying Kim-ber-ly, a woman sixteen years his junior. Jack, however, seemed to wield the quiet authority necessary for the job. I expected him to address the big busty blondes issue in the manner of a World War II sergeant providing VD warnings to his new recruits, but again I was surprised.

"I understand that you boys visited some pornographic websites." Ben reddened. Sam just kept his eyes firmly planted on the plush beige carpet. "I just want you to know that I understand your interest." Sam looked up momentarily, curious. Ben's color faded slightly and he looked less lobster-like. "We men are visual creatures and we are attracted to the female form. That is how nature intended us to be. Your curiosity is normal and even healthy." Jack let the point settle in.

OK, I thought, here's where Sam will begin presenting a thoroughly obnoxious defense, arguing that he shouldn't be held accountable for his normal, healthy behavior. But I was happy to see that I was mistaken. Sam seemed to be really listening, rather than mounting a counterattack.

"Interest in women is normal for kids your age, but you went about it the wrong way, damaging school property, and going after some mean-spirited pornography. Real men desire women, but we also respect them." Jack paused and looked directly at the two boys, even though neither one could return his gaze.

Jack resumed: "The sites you were on were not respectful." Again, Jack let his words hang in the air. "It is not manly to treat a woman like an object. Do you understand?"

Two nods from the boys prompted him to continue. "You like playing TIE Fighter, correct?"

Incredibly grateful for the change of subject, both boys piped up in agreement. "Ben is actually better at it," Sam acknowledged with a grace I'd no idea he possessed.

"Well, it is fun to play TIE Fighter, but I'm sure you understand that a computer-simulated game is not like a real war."

"Your father was a helicopter pilot in the Lebanon War," Marjorie chimed in. "He knows what he's talking about."

"Thanks, my dear," Jack said. He threw Marjorie a warm glance and then resumed. "Pornography is like computer games—merely a simulation. Do not ever confuse it with reality. Those women are nothing like real women." The two boys listened attentively, curious, despite themselves.

"It would be unhealthy for you to imagine that real women think, or act, or even look that way. Those women are fakes—paid actresses. Real women are much better." Here, I swear to God, Jack winked at Marjorie.

Jack concluded his remarks to the boys by stating, without equivocation, that there was to be no pornography in his home and that Ben was forbidden from accessing it anywhere.

"I just will not stand for it," Jack said rising to his full height and towering over the two little boys who seemed frozen on the couch.

"Yes, Dad," Ben said sheepishly.

"Yes, Mr. Greenberg," Sam added, to my surprise.

Jack's face betrayed no emotion. His voice was stern, but not unkind. He continued, "I know that you boys meant no harm, but you did something really wrong. There has to be a consequence, and there will be no arguing."

No arguing? Was that possible? I had a lot to learn from Jack.

"Ben," Jack continued, "in addition to any punishment imposed by your school, you are barred from all computer use for a month. That includes the internet at the library and the computer at Sam's house. You will have to write all your homework out by hand. Sam, your mother will have to decide the nature of your punishment. I hope you will show her the same good manners you have demonstrated here. As you can imagine, this is very tough on your moms, and you boys should be especially respectful." With that, Jack excused himself and left the four of us speechless.

Eventually, Marjorie regained her composure and offered me some coffee. She also offered to have Sam spend the three-day suspension at her house, where I felt confident the restrictions would be observed and he wouldn't get into further trouble. I offered to provide pizza for both boys, but Marjorie brushed it off saying it would be no trouble to make them grilled cheese sandwiches. I smiled to myself, thinking that Marjorie's soggy sandwiches would serve as another punishment for Sam. Marjorie did accept my offer to pay for the supplies for a work project Ben and Sam would do as part of their suspension.

Under the circumstances, I felt I had to accept Marjorie's insistent coffee invitation. Around the kitchen table, Ben and Sam ate cookies and sulked. Marjorie explained to me that it was undoubtedly Ben's computer skills that got the kids into temptation's way in the first place. She would have to have a serious talk with Ben's computer tutor. Great, I thought, Ben contributed the computer genius; Sam contributed a desire for busty blondes who like it up the ass. Ben, to his credit, looked as if he wanted to die, though, to his further credit, he remained polite to Marjorie as she chattered on.

On the silent ride home, I replayed the scene in my head. I doubted Jack's admonition to show me some respect would have any tangible effect, but I was very grateful for his effort. I was also thankful for the silence in the car. Mostly, I couldn't wait to see Rob and talk to him.

20

Day one of Sam's suspension from school started out well, with Sam ready to go at 7:00. He hadn't apologized to me, but his being ready to go to Marjorie's and serving himself a bowl of cereal was a delightful change—and just maybe an indication of some contrition.

Conversing with Rob was everything I'd hoped for, and slightly more than I'd bargained for. He was so empathetic about the crime ("how awful for you"), even though I didn't give him full details about the various adult sites. Rob was also very complimentary about Jack's handling of the sensitive issues involved. "It's good that he didn't try to shame the boys. Interest in women is natural at that age. I used to swipe a *Playboy* from the corner drugstore occasionally." Rob cast an eye to see if I was scandalized, and I told him that he'd have to do a whole lot better than that to impress me.

As I told him more about my adventure, I noticed that Rob was uncomfortable when I was mimicking Marjorie.

"Is something wrong?" I asked.

"I sort of know Marjorie and Jack from work," Rob explained.

"Sorry," I cringed, remembering that Jack was the CFO of the local hospital.

"Your imitation is dead on," Rob smiled conspiratorially, "but I really can't listen to it. I know she can be a challenge sometimes, but she does a tremendous amount of good for the community."

I recalled last Breast Cancer Awareness Week, when Marjorie accosted me, plied me with various flyers, and tried to recruit me for the hospital's breast cancer fun-run. She reminded me that even if I wasn't in good enough shape to run, I probably could still stroll the five kilometers, if I took it slowly.

"You're right," I conceded, "she does work hard and doesn't get a lot of credit."

I was pretty sure that I'd milked all the possible humor and pathos out of the events of yesterday when Rob threw me a curve ball. "So what did your ex say about all this?"

"I haven't told him. I'm sure he's too busy with his own porn queen to do anything about it, anyway."

"Are you sure that's right? It's not as if you've given him the chance. A lot of fathers would want the chance to respond the way Jack did. Maybe you should broach it with him."

"Not all fathers are like Jack, believe me," I said with vehemence. "Some people don't deserve to have the privilege of acting like a father," I added with intense feeling, my eyes suddenly spilling tears.

Rob hopped off his treadmill and motioned for me to go sit with him at the juice bar. He patted my hand while big, fat, hot tears plopped down my face.

"Exactly how long has it been since your divorce?"

"About four years," I muttered.

"It's still so raw for you, I'm sorry." Rob continued to squeeze my hand. "Don't punish Sam. He needs his dad, not just a friend's dad, no matter how wonderful Jack is. Clearly your ex has some serious problems—who could ever leave such a beautiful, kind, funny woman? But that isn't Sam's fault. Besides, let him be a dad and take some of the pressure off you, for God's sake. You've been suffering alone with all the challenges Sam presents. You need some help. You deserve some help. And Sam needs his father."

I was dubious that Jeremy could do anything, but realized that Rob was right. I'd been hiding how bad the situation with Sam had become. Who besides Rob knew the hell that child was putting me through? Sam's cursing and verbal abuse had gone virtually unchecked, and I often dreaded going home to him. Even Joanie and Lydia had no idea how bad things were. I joked about the "little felon" and, unsurprisingly, no one except Rob—wonderful, insightful, non-judgmental Rob—had listened carefully enough to take me seriously. I portrayed Sam as a typical teen, not the monster he sometimes was. But if he was a monster, what was I?

21

In the locker room, I donned my normal work garb: blue suit, silk blouse, pearls, hose, and low pumps. My dress size hadn't changed, but everything hung on me in a much more flattering way. Though no one could mistake me for hot, I was looking a whole lot better.

When I arrived at work, I entered my inner office and was immediately presented with a glazed doughnut and a cup of tea. Molly had printed out my schedule of appointments and laid them on the far right-hand corner of the desk, next to the pink message slips I'd yet to return from the day before. My email was already fired up, and I had a document to review for Corey before noon. My first priority, however, was to arrange to meet with the often-absent, ever-tardy Teresa Williams. The woman had missed six of the past ten Mondays. When I reviewed it outside Dr. Braunstein's office, I'd come to the realization that Teresa's file had "gone on a bender" written all over it. I felt I had to confront her. There was an employee assistance program and even a regular AA meeting on the corporate campus; she just had to be willing to accept the help. Teresa had risen to a serious position of responsibility in the operations and administration division and her absences occasionally held up other departments when her signature was needed for major purchases. Teresa wasn't highly educated—she had a two-year associate's degree—but she had worked her way up from secretary to an assistant vice president in charge of purchasing and supplies. She was trustworthy and efficient, at least when she was there.

As I was waiting for Teresa to arrive, I reluctantly phoned Marjorie to see how the boys were doing. She was cooking Hungarian goulash, another one of Jack's favorites, and announced each ingredient as she added it to the pot. As for the boys, Marjorie assured me that she was vigorously enforcing the no electronics policy and had them assembling a bookcase that she had purchased from IKEA. Marjorie launched into a discussion about the megastore, its prices (excellent), the crowds (huge), and the difficulty of transporting the shelves home (unspeakable, but for the fact that she could speak about it for five full minutes). Marjorie informed me that when the boys were done with the shelves, they were going to go through a bunch of donated toys that she had collected for the hospital, making sure all the pieces were included and that each game was clean and complete. Rob was right; Marjorie really did do a lot for the hospital. I didn't give her enough credit, but she sure didn't make it easy.

My mind must have been wandering because I was startled when Marjorie asked me with some impatience, perhaps for the second time, whether Sam could stay the night so that the boys could go to the Youth Group at the synagogue. It was the rabbi's night to lead the group. Hmm, I thought, there's a respite for me and a punishment for Sam. Win-lose, just as that rotten kid deserved. I quickly agreed and tuned out again as Marjorie extolled the virtues of the rabbi, though I vaguely registered that she wasn't complaining for a change. I couldn't be less interested in Rabbi Reuven or his ability to relate to kids. Big deal, I thought, as she talked. I bet that rabbi has never had to deal with the likes of Sam. Besides, I was going to go to Joanie's synagogue book group, and that was more than enough Judaism for me.

I toyed with trying to get off the phone—my other line was blinking indicating that Teresa was waiting in the outer office—but I did feel I owed it to Marjorie to listen politely after all she and Jack had done. Besides, I had a perverse interest in seeing how long she would go on if not interrupted. About four minutes later, with a few "uh-huh's" and "really's?" thrown in by me to indicate that I was still alive on the other end, Marjorie's call waiting put an end to my little experiment. "I'm sorry, Claire, but I just have to take this." I began to say that I understood, but Marjorie had already ditched me for the next caller.

This was my cue to usher in Teresa, who seemed appropriately nervous. As always, she was stylishly dressed and in full makeup. She must have been wearing three coats of foundation. I wondered if she smoked as well as drank and maybe the makeup was to cover the ravages of her lifestyle on her skin.

Before I could even begin, Teresa looked at me unflinchingly and informed me that she knew her absenteeism had become a serious problem. She appreciated the warning, and said she would address the issue. All of this was stated in a clipped tone as she held my gaze. Teresa immediately looked away and it was clear that as far as she was concerned, this meeting should be over. Understandable, I suppose. But I couldn't let this faux-confession stand without some serious discussion.

"Look," I said, "maybe it's worth exploring the underlying causes of your absences from work."

My words just hung in the air. Clearly, she wasn't going to make it easy, and I was going to have to initiate the touchy subject. Well, that's why I'm paid the big bucks, I reminded myself.

"I think I know what's going on," I said in my most sympathetic, non-judgmental tone.

A look of panic crossed Teresa's face, but I continued anyway. She just had to confront the truth if she was ever going to deal successfully with her problem.

"I think you have a substance abuse problem. It explains the missing Mondays, your lateness, and the accidents."

Immediately, her expression, which had looked truly terrified, turned into something else, something I couldn't quite identify. Well, her secret was out and the worst was over. She would go from fear to anger, but that was all part of the process.

"I see you have this all figured out," she said tightly.

I tried to be understanding about how shameful this was for her and how much denial was a part of her problem. She was obviously not ready to face her demons, but at least I wanted to try.

"I don't mean to invade your privacy, but this is affecting your work. We have some programs that could be helpful to you." I was met with stony silence. This was irritating but not, in my experience, unusual. Her absenteeism was enough to initiate a performance review with an eye towards termination, yet she insisted on making this difficult. I continued, "You have a long history with our company and we want to help you. Addiction to alcohol or drugs can affect not only work but also your personal life."

I wasn't sure, but I think she squelched a cry. Maybe I was getting through.

"I understand your concerns and I'll work my hardest to fix the problem," Teresa said with what I assume she thought of as great dignity. As I saw it, her full-faced war paint was now accompanied by a suit of armor. And I wasn't convinced that I'd even made a dent.

22

With Sam under rabbinic supervision, I decided to go over to Joanie's house to prepare for the upcoming book group. Eventually, Joanie would be getting out of bed and confronting the fact that what I considered clean might not meet her more exacting standards. I planned to help Aaron with dinner and then get scrubbing.

Imagine my surprise when I entered the kitchen and the place smelled of pine, bleach, and whatever the smell of no-smell is. This was a big improvement over the not-so-vague whiff of diaper pail that had been hanging over the place. The laundry was ironed and neatly folded. The countertops sparkled, and I, for one, would have been perfectly happy dining off the gleaming kitchen floor. Did Aaron hire a service? If so, it was time to bury Joanie's dead body, because only over that particular impediment could a cleaning crew have entered Joanie's home.

The kids were all sitting at the kitchen table coloring in new coloring books with washable markers. Even Jake was assiduously scribbling over Superman's outline. The kids were chatting and exchanging colors.

"I want boo," Jakie demanded, and Sarah brought it over to his high chair. I noticed that Aaron and the kids were eating some kind of homemade cookies. Where were the yodels? What was going on? I looked around and saw the source of the various welcome, if unsettling, changes. I hadn't noticed her at first because her head was buried in the freezer.

"Hi, Claire. Uh, let me introduce you to Beverly," Aaron said.

"Beverly, this is Claire Mandelbaum. She lives next door." Beverly removed her right latex glove and shook my hand.

"Beverly Fineberg," she announced, and then proceeded to the sink to wash her hands.

I was struck by how tall and thin Beverly was. OK, thinness is something I always noticed, but Beverly's was truly striking in an Audrey Hepburn sort of way. She was wearing a simple belted navy dress under an apron with a map of Israel on it. She had large diamond studs in her ears. Despite the hot September weather, Beverly wore pantyhose and some fancy designer flats. Beverly's hair was short, blonde, and spiky—certainly the most edgy part of her appearance, which otherwise looked as if she had stepped out of a 1960s sitcom.

"Joan is resting. I'm just helping out a bit, getting ready for the book group tomorrow night," she explained as she continued washing her hands. "The place was filthy," Beverly whispered conspiratorially, "but you know how men are, and besides, Aaron has his hands full."

Now, I would be the first to acknowledge that my cleaning abilities aren't the greatest and certainly not the locus of my core self-esteem, but filthy? She found the place filthy? If so, the woman would obviously need a hazmat suit to enter my kitchen. A quick look around the house confirmed that Beverly had brightened up the whole house. I wouldn't say that I'd drink from the toilets exactly, but they probably would be less germ-infested than some of the glassware sitting by Sam's computer.

"Bev, is there anything I can do to help?"

"Beverly," she corrected, "I prefer Beverly. The only one who calls me Bev is my husband and it's only because after sixteen years I've given up on trying to get him to stop. I can't get him to get a decent shave either, but that's another story," Beverly continued as she stood on a ladder to dust above the fridge.

I was surprised she didn't just shave him herself. Beverly struck me as the ultra-competent do-it-yourselfer—the kind of person who builds her own furniture, sews her own clothes, and cuts her own hair. It sounded as if she'd have no problem slapping her husband's face with a few hot towels and giving him a shave.

"Is there anything I can do to help you out?" I asked again, and then added, "Joanie's right; you're amazing." That's what's great about words like amazing and incredible. They allow one to be truthful without giving offense.

"Oh, I enjoy cleaning up," Beverly said, clearly pleased with the perceived compliment. "It gives me a sense of real accomplishment to roll up my sleeves and tackle a place like this. I'll be back tomorrow to bring dinner and set up for the book group."

She surveyed the kitchen with evident satisfaction and suggested to me that Aaron could probably use help with getting the kids to bed. This seemed to be the one job she wasn't champing at the bit to perform. I noticed that throughout dessert Beverly kept on wiping the kids' faces while they were still eating, a pointless task that irritated them immensely. She just couldn't help herself.

I herded the kids out of the kitchen and Aaron and I tackled the various bath and bed preparations. When that was finally done, I returned to the kitchen where Beverly had just finished scouring the oven. Joanie would be very pleased with how everything looked. Beverly really had done a mitzvah. She announced that she was headed for the grocery store and then home to bake for the book group.

"Reuven is running the Youth Group *again*," Beverly stated with a pronounced rolling of her eyes. "The synagogue has a youth director, but Reuven insists on spending time with the kids. He'd be better off meeting with some of the *machers* who might actually donate something to the *shul*, but he loves hanging out with the teens. At least I can look forward to a quiet evening without his messing up the kitchen."

Of course! It suddenly struck me. How could I have failed to put two and two together? Beverly was married to the rabbi who was leading Sam and Ben's Youth Group. Ha! Her husband would be in for a shock when he met my misanthropic pornographer. But maybe I was being too hasty in dismissing the good rabbi. After all, he managed to avoid a close shave with Beverly, and that seemed impressive.

23

The next morning I went to the gym even though I knew there would be no chance of seeing Rob there. Mondays and Thursdays he always had early rounds. Still, the effort was worth it. The belles of the locker room no longer intimidated me. I saw how hard these beauties worked at it—scrubbing away at pores, curling their eyelashes with scary looking implements, and styling their hair with humongous blow dryers. I also saw how dissatisfied they were with their appearance, despite all that fuss. What a no-win game the whole beauty thing was. By contrast, the actual exercise had an immensely salutary effect.

I found the mindless stepping soothing as I contemplated my to-do list. I reminded myself that I had to call Jeremy, if only to prove that I was right and he'd be way too busy to concern himself with the felon's antics.

At work, the highlight of my day was the meeting I set up between Corey and the guy who made the racist comment in the cafeteria fight. We met in a small but comfortable conference room. Corey's suite would have been too intimidating. Corey offered the guy a soda or coffee, which the guy, biting his lips, declined.

"Thanks for coming in," Corey said. It wasn't like the guy had much choice.

"I want to talk to you about what happened during the fight in the cafeteria," Corey began. "When I hear the word 'nigger,' I think of my hard-working grandfather who never received the respect he deserved. White people called him 'nigger' and 'boy' though he was a deacon in our church and a successful businessman. That term brings me great pain. It's not something you can just say because you're mad at a black man. When you use that word, you insult every African American."

"I'm sorry. I wasn't thinking . . . I was just so mad."

"I understand that you were angry—and maybe you had a right to be. But that kind of talk affects everyone."

"I know, I know. I didn't mean it. I just wanted to say the most vicious thing I could think of. It sort of popped out."

"Stick to asshole—that's an equal-opportunity insult," Corey advised.

The guy smiled. "You got that right. There are assholes of every color."

"Do you think you can apologize to Harris?"

"He's an asshole all right, but I guess I do owe him an apology. Will you talk to him and get him not to keep switching the station on the radio at the dock?"

"We'll work something out. If the guys at the loading dock can't agree on music, then we'll have to turn off the sound system altogether and that won't be good for anyone. We can work it out if we all come from a place of respect."

"I swear, I meant no disrespect, especially to you."

"I know, man. Just learn from the experience," Corey replied. "That's all we can ask of ourselves."

After the employee left, Corey and I repaired to his office suite, which was twice the size of mine and possessed real, as opposed to kiddy, art.

"You're amazing," I said.

"Aren't I though?"

"Seriously, you have the perfect touch in these situations. You make a human connection."

"Yep, I'm the Racist Whisperer."

"Come on, Corey, you made a difference, and this corporation is a better place to work because of conversations like that."

"I suppose," he grudgingly conceded.

I switched to his favorite subject, his daughter Keisha, who was in her first year of law school at my alma mater.

"The kid works nonstop," Corey said. "I worry about her health. Did you kill yourself at Cornell?"

"No. I worked hard but I didn't kill myself. Jeremy, on the other hand, he used to pride himself on never needing more than five hours of sleep, and most of the rest of his time was spent studying or in class. A hot date was sitting next to him, holding hands in the library."

"Sounds like fun," Corey deadpanned.

"There was one occasion in the stacks. . . ."

Corey's eyes widened. "Boundaries, Claire, boundaries," he said with a look of panic on his face.

"Are you sure? It's a hot story."

"Absolutely, before I have to forbid Keisha from ever setting foot in the library."

"OK, I'll spare you. You should tell Keisha to feel free to call me if she has any questions or wants some moral support."

"I'm keeping my daughter as far away from you as possible. Moral support," Corey snorted. "How about immoral support?"

We chatted some more about Corey's son, who was an engineering student, and then Corey asked me about Sam.

"Total monster," I said with energy but without a trace of the sadness I really felt. I couldn't bring myself to tell him about Sam's porn escapade. I was embarrassed by how Sam was so out of control, and I didn't want Corey to see what a weak, ineffectual mother I was.

"See this head?" Corey said, pointing to his shiny dome. "I used to have a lot of hair on here. Pulled it all out. Know why?" Corey paused to achieve the full dramatic effect. "Teenagers! Keisha and Patrick made me tear it all out. If I'd known they'd turn out so well, I wouldn't have done it. Have faith, Claire, it gets better."

"When?" I asked plaintively.

"About the time they turn nineteen or so."

"I'll be bald by then for sure," I said.

Back in my office, I tried Jeremy on his private line at the firm, but he wasn't in. It occurred to me that maybe he was working on a brief from home so I called there. I was horrified when Kimberly picked up on the third ring. Oh well, she and I had to talk sometime.

"Hi, this is Claire Mandelbaum, Sam's mom."

"Hi, Claire, it's Kim," Kimberly said, sounding nervous. Good. Let her be uncomfortable. Although my marriage had broken up long before Kimberly came on the scene (Jeremy abandoned me in favor of spending time with clients, not tootsies), I still resented the woman.

"I'm calling to talk to Jeremy about Sam," I said.

"Is Sam OK?" Kimberly sounded genuinely concerned. Didn't she have a pedicure appointment or a gardener she should be fucking?

"Well, he's gotten into some trouble at school."

"I'm so sorry to hear that. I hope it isn't anything serious. Is there something we can do?"

"I just need Jeremy to call me as soon as possible."

"He's traveling right now, doing some depositions in Indianapolis."

Wow, that sounded familiar. I guess the honeymoon was officially over.

"I'll be sure to let him know," Kimberly said. "Sam's coming over this weekend, right?" she added with what sounded like eagerness. Had she met the boy?

"That's the plan." This was the first time Sam would be at their new place.

"Well, please let us know if there is anything you want us to do, or if there are any restrictions on his activities. We want to be supportive of whatever consequences you impose for his behavior at school."

"Thanks, that would be a help," I said. And a first. Since when did Jeremy know or care what happened with Sam at school? But this tootsie could talk the talk of "consequences" and "appropriate behavior." Maybe she would get Jeremy to call.

I sat at my desk and stared into space. Molly walked in to inform me that Teresa had called in sick today. I just rolled my eyes and made a note to talk to her the next day—that is, if she made it in to work.

24

I arrived home on the early side. Sam was heating up some leftover pizza in the microwave. The kitchen was in its usual state of chaos; soda cans and wrappers from Sam's fast-food delights littered the sticky counter surfaces. I was saved from a sink full of dirty dishes by the fact that we almost always ate on paper plates. We treated the planet as shabbily as we treated the kitchen. Sam was reading *The New Yorker*. I guess that's what the desperation of no-electronics leads to. It helped that I'd taken the precaution of disconnecting the TV cable and hiding the remote.

"Hi," I said, testing the waters.

"Oh, hi, Mom," Sam answered more civilly than I can recall having heard him in a while. I decided to go for broke. "How was the time at Ben's?"

"Pretty cool," Sam said noncommittally as he chomped on some pizza. "Jack taught us how to use the power drill and we put the bookshelf together."

Wow, a full sentence and none of it an indictment of me or my many personality flaws. I was on a roll, so I continued. "How was the Youth Group?"

"Good," he said without looking up. A short response, but not, I noted, a negative one.

I started to head for my room to change clothes but Sam continued.

"Mom, can I go to Youth Group this Sunday night? They're playing broom ball. It's like hockey, but you play indoors with a rubber ball and brooms. Rabbi Reuven challenged each kid over thirteen to a man-on-man faceoff. I'll need a broom."

Our broom will finally see some action, I thought. "Sure," I began but then realized that Sam would be at Jeremy's and maybe they'd made plans. "Let's call your dad and Kimberly to see what the plans are for this weekend."

I tried but there was no answer at Jeremy's house.

"I really want to go," Sam said. "It's not fair that just because you and Dad got divorced, I can't go to Youth Group."

"Look, Sam, I'll talk to your dad, that's all I can do."

He glared at me. I wondered, was this child abuse or merely an infringement of Sam's right to free religious expression? How did this Rabbi Reuven have such an instant hold on my son? For all I knew the guy was running a cult or a drug ring. But if he was good enough for Marjorie, he must have been carefully vetted.

"There's nothing to do," Sam complained.

"And why would that be?" I asked sharply. He just glared at me again and took his magazine to the couch. Sam plopped his filthy sneakers on the couch pillows. At least my couch isn't white, I reassured myself, though no one would ever mistake the ambience of this place for homey.

I turned to the condolence cards and was surprised to spot Jeremy's handwriting on one of the envelopes. I made myself a cup of tea and set to reading the note written on thick, cream-colored, monogrammed paper. Jeremy's square block letters read:

> Dear Claire,
>
> I was saddened to hear of Alvin's death. He was a courtly gentleman who treated me with immense kindness. I recall with fondness our visits when he and I played golf. I still have the watch he gave me for my thirtieth birthday, and will give it to Sam someday. Even though Alvin and I hadn't talked much in the past few years, I kept tabs on him through Sam and understand that he was in good health until the very end.
>
> I imagine this is a tough time for you, Claire, and I hope you will let me know if there's anything I can do for you to ease the burden. Please accept my condolences for your loss. He really was a great guy.
>
> Jeremy

A lovely gesture. I hated it when Jeremy subverted my image of him by acting like a mensch. It made things so confusing. Focus, I urged myself. Remember the time when Jeremy went back to California to review documents four days after Sam was born, leaving me to cope with a screaming baby, sore nipples, postpartum depression, and hemorrhoids. As I was reliving this affront, my phone rang. It was Kimberly. Again she sounded nervous, and I was especially glad. Kimberly informed me that Jeremy would be back in town on Friday evening and that we could talk when I brought Sam over for the weekend. She assured me that it would be no problem taking Sam to Youth Group.

"I love Rabbi Reuven!" Kimberly chirped.

Well, he *is* good with the teenagers, I thought.

"That's wonderful. See you Friday," I said in a cold, clipped voice and hung up the telephone.

Immediately it rang again. It was Aaron, sounding panicked, asking me to come over right away. Joanie needed to go to the hospital. I hung up the phone, screamed something incoherent to Sam—he wouldn't have listened even if I'd been comprehensible—and tore across the yard to where Aaron was leading Joanie to their minivan. Aaron had hired a sitter for the evening's book group, so he just needed me to hold down the fort until the sitter arrived and to do something about the Sisterhood ladies, who would be coming over in an hour and a half.

I felt tears spilling from my eyes, but I tried to pull myself together, knowing that the last thing Joan needed was any added drama or worry. She was a ghastly sight, pale and clutching her stomach.

"I'm bleeding," Joanie said as Aaron carefully helped her into their minivan.

"I wanted to call an ambulance, but Joanie was afraid it would upset the kids," Aaron said.

"The hospital is only fifteen minutes away," I reassured him. "Drive safely and she'll be fine."

"It's going to be OK," I told my best friend. "I'll come to the hospital as soon as I can," I added, squeezing her hand. I gave Joanie a kiss on her forehead, and they were off.

I returned to the house where Jake was crying in his crib, the twins were fighting, and Sarah was watching TV. I separated the twins and noticed that Jake needed a diaper change, bad. I held my breath as I changed him and dumped—a term I use advisedly—the contents of his cloth diaper into the toilet. At least Sam is toilet trained, I thought to myself; that's one thing the kid has going for him. Why couldn't Joanie use disposable diapers like a normal person? Irritated and still not-so-faintly smelling of shit, I deposited Jake back into the crib and ran to get the ringing doorbell.

At the door stood Beverly, wearing a sleeveless beige silk pantsuit, sapphire earrings, some serious eye liner and peachy lip gloss. Instead of flats she sported white high-heeled sandals, which must have put her height up to five-ten or so. She looked tall and vaguely intimidating, but then again I was always intimidated by the ultra-thin, well-put-together look. Beverly's biceps were clearly defined as she hoisted a large, lined wicker picnic basket. I was guessing that *rebbetzins* had closets full of baskets just for such occasions. Propped on top of the basket was an apron and a copy of the book *The Far Euphrates*, with little post-it notes jutting from the margins. There was no question about it—Beverly was hard core.

"Hello, Claire," Beverly shifted her burden entirely to her left hand so that we could shake hands.

"Hi," I said, feeling slightly queasy about the handshake mid diaper-change. I invited Beverly in and realized with relief that I'd no cause to worry. Beverly raced for the sink and began to scrub her hands then donned an apron with a recipe for matzo ball soup on it. I washed up myself, retrieved Jake, and gave the kids a five-minute warning for dinner. Beverly had brought a full-fledged meal—lentil soup, chicken, broccoli, mashed potatoes, and homemade cookies for dessert.

"Any allergies I should know about? I made some of the cookies without nuts just to be safe."

"No, they can eat everything. But Beverly, I should tell you, Joan is in the hospital."

"Oh, no," Beverly exclaimed. "That's too bad. Is she OK?" Before I could respond, Beverly continued, "What are we going to do about the Sisterhood book group?" She sounded anxious. "Do you think we have enough time to call everyone and change the location? We could do it at my house, I suppose. Does Joan have a Sisterhood list?"

"I don't know," I told Beverly, not even caring to hide my annoyance. "Right now, I can't think about anything except Joan."

"Of course, of course. This is her fifth? My goodness. Four healthy children and she's having a fifth. She's how old . . . almost forty, right?"

I was too stunned to say anything. Beverly continued, "Let me get the food ready. These are the meat dishes, right? I'm going to call my husband on his cell phone. He'll answer right away. Knowing him, he'll want to rush right over to see Joan. I can't get him to wear a mask or gloves at the hospital, but I make sure he has lots of sanitizer and that he removes his shoes before he comes back into the house. All I need is Reuven bringing home some antibiotic-resistant, flesh-eating bacteria."

In my opinion a flesh-eating bacteria was just about what was called for. I wished some bug would eat away Beverly's tongue, and maybe her peach-colored lips for good measure. Poor Rabbi Reuven. Given a choice between hanging out with Beverly and playing broom ball, it was no contest.

The kids were disconcerted by the sudden departure of both parents. Sarah wanted to know when her mom was coming back. I was evasive but Sarah kept on asking. Beverly interjected, letting us know, in a sing-song voice, that dinner was ready. The kids took their places at the table. Zack announced that he was hungry only for cookies, which he had spotted on the counter. Rachel was crying because Zack had taken her favorite Snow White drinking glass. Jake, whom I'd placed in his high chair, was banging his sippy cup, making a huge racket. Beverly, for all her take-charge attitude, occupied herself wiping invisible spots off the kitchen counter. I made the executive decision to skip the soup and filled each of the kids' plates, serving them quickly. Once the food was on the table, things calmed down a bit. The poor kids were just hungry and thrown by the deviation from their regular routine.

"Very nice, *yiladim*," Beverly commented with faux enthusiasm. "No dessert until you finish every bite."

"Actually, that's not Joan and Aaron's policy. The kids just have to give everything a try."

Beverly didn't say anything, but raised her ultra-thin eyebrows, which were my next target for the flesh-eating bacteria even though her slender arches would hardly make much of a meal.

"*Yiladim*, what would you like to drink? I have 7UP and apple juice," Beverly announced.

The kids started to yell simultaneously.

Sarah said in a panicked voice, "We're not allowed to have soda, ever."

Meanwhile, Zack started chanting: "7UP! 7UP!" And Rachel soon joined in.

I served juice all around, but Zack kept up his rather loud lobbying.

"These children certainly don't have proper table manners," Beverly whispered to me.

I didn't say a word. I just grabbed one of Beverly's cookies and bit into it. I was starving and if I kept on chewing I would be less likely to say something I would later regret. Delicious, I had to admit. I'd have to get the recipe. Undoubtedly, it begins with, "Take a blow torch to your oven. . . ."

Then, as if things couldn't get worse, Marjorie appeared at the door. I hadn't thought about it, but of course she would be in the Sisterhood book club and, naturally, she and Beverly would be the best of pals.

Beverly greeted Marjorie with an air kiss and began to consult with her about what to do regarding the evening's book club meeting. It took Marjorie a minute to understand the situation, but as soon as she did, Marjorie sprang into action. Once she ascertained that Joan had gone to White Plains Hospital, where Jack worked, she called to let him know. She explained, as soon as she got off the phone, that Jack would call the emergency room and make sure Joan was seen quickly and not left in the waiting area.

"Has Dr. Lewis been called?" Marjorie asked. I wasn't sure, so Marjorie left a message with his service, just to be on the safe side.

"Poor Joan, she must be worried sick," Marjorie said to me, careful to make sure the kids didn't overhear. Marjorie put her arm on my shoulder. I was bracing for a discussion about AP Science, but instead Marjorie asked me how she could help.

"So is the Sisterhood going to meet here? It's getting too late to reach people to cancel," Beverly said.

"So be it," Marjorie replied. How apt, I thought.

Marjorie and I bathed the kids and put them in pajamas. She helped Sarah sound out some words in her bedtime story, which to my amazement, Sarah seemed to really enjoy. The twins were in bed listening to a music tape. As I was rocking Jake, Marjorie came in.

"Maybe you should talk to Sarah. I think she's a bit anxious about her mom," Marjorie said. "Meanwhile, I'll help Beverly set up. I think she's right that the meeting will have to be here. Don't worry, I'll make sure the place is cleaned up."

"With Beverly here, I doubt that's a problem," I observed.

"Right," Marjorie said and flashed a wide, beautiful smile, something I'd never seen her do before.

"I can stay after the sitter leaves until either you or Joan and Aaron get back," she offered.

"That might be really late," I cautioned.

"So be it," Marjorie said and headed back to the kitchen.

In Sarah's room a dim night-light glowed, illuminating Sarah, who was sitting upright in bed, crying.

"Lie down, sweetheart," I said as I stroked her hair and tried to reassure her that her mom would be home soon.

"I can't go to sleep until Mommy gets back."

"Sweetheart, that's going to be very late. You need your rest."

"But I can't go to sleep without the *shmah*," she protested.

"Auntie Claire will say it with you."

"You know the *shmah*?" she asked. "The whole thing?"

"Yes, I do, and I would be really happy to say it with you."

"You don't say it, you chant it. A chant is kind of like a song."

"OK, I'll chant it with you."

Together we chanted the central tenant of the Jewish faith, proclaiming the oneness of God. We got to the place where Jews are commanded to love God with all our heart, soul, and might. Can you command love? I couldn't even command Sam to put his glasses in the sink. According to the prayer, we were to teach these things (love of God, not bussing one's dirty dishes) to our children, speaking of them when we lie down, and when we rise up. I realized that I was fulfilling the mitzvah exactly, saying the *shmah* with Sarah right before bed. The tradition realizes that children are taught not just in formal classrooms but also in the everyday experiences of walking around, doing errands, going to sleep, and getting up. Maybe loving God and cleaning up after yourself aren't that different. How badly had I mangled that part of Sam's education? He excelled at all the formal learning but hadn't managed to learn the daily obligations and kindnesses that living in a family should entail. Our times in the morning and the evening were points of conflict, not teachable moments. How could I have failed so miserably?

As Sarah drifted off to sleep, the babysitter, Laura, arrived. Beverly fed Laura cookies and inquired about Laura's parents and Laura's older sister at Brandeis. As I prepared to go, Beverly handed me a care package. "For Joan and Aaron. It might be a long night."

"Thanks," I said, peering around the spotless kitchen. "Thanks for everything."

25

My Bubbe spent her last weeks in White Plains Hospital, so I was plenty familiar with the place, having snuck in after visiting hours on many occasions. The trick is to wear comfortable shoes and look like you know where you're going. The ER, however, was relatively unfamiliar to me. I'd only been there once, when Sam was five and needed stitches when he split his lip after a playground tumble. Needless to say Jeremy was supervising Sam at the time, reviewing a trial transcript while he was supposed to be watching the kid.

Upon entering the ER's wide automatic doors, I was immediately confronted with a receptionist. I introduced myself as Joan Cohen's sister and was directed down a long hallway painted a bright baby blue. I was assaulted with "that smell," the special odor hospitals manage to exude, a heady disinfectant bouquet with floral undertones and a splash of urine. Joan was in "room" nine; her space was enclosed by a wrap-around curtain in fabulously ugly pastels. She lay in the bed looking very pale. I bent over to kiss her and held her hand. Joan didn't speak or crack a smile. Her eyes were wide with fear.

Aaron filled me in. The ER doctor had checked on Joan, as had the rabbi. Dr. Lewis was on his way. There was really no news yet. Everyone would have to wait and see. The ER doctor had told them that second-trimester miscarriages were rare, and in all likelihood, Joan and the baby would be fine. They were waiting for Dr. Lewis to come before they would order any tests. I gave the food to Aaron, who was evidently starving, and offered to stay with Joan while he went to the cafeteria. He declined but asked me to get him a Coke.

I took the cavernous elevator to the basement cafeteria, where I purchased a Coke loaded with ice, just the way Aaron liked it. As I was paying, I heard someone call my name. I looked up and saw Rob, dressed in surgical greens, heading toward me.

Was this some sort of mirage? I wondered. Was it possible that the person I most wanted to see at that moment was right there in front of me in his green surgical scrubs? I felt a rush of gratitude and relief.

"Rob!" I exclaimed, "Thank God you're here."

"What is it? Is everything OK?" Rob asked with concern.

"My friend Joanie is in the ER. She's pregnant and having some trouble."

"Of course," Rob said with sympathy, "Joan Cohen. I was up to see her a while ago. How's she doing? How are her spirits?"

"Not good right now. She's feeling awful and I think she's really scared. I'm glad you were there to take care of her until Dr. Lewis arrives."

"Dr. Lewis is the best. She'll be in good hands. Meanwhile, don't hesitate to call me over if there's anything I can do. I'll be in the hospital for at least another half an hour. I have two more people to see."

"Thanks," I said and gave him a hug. "Thanks a lot."

So my man of mystery was an ER specialist, I thought as I headed back to the ER. That explained the constant proximity of his cell phone, the regular early morning hours every Monday and Thursday, and the fact that he worked almost every weekend. It also explained his compassion and his ability to connect with lots of different people. Maybe his schlumpiness came from his being so busy saving lives that he didn't have time for a decent haircut. I wished I could stay and talk to Rob. I wanted to tell him about Sam's youth group and to let him know how Marjorie had really come through. It would have to wait for another time. Meanwhile, I was grateful that he was on the scene. Joan would be tickled to know that her ER doctor was my big crush.

26

I returned to sit next to Joan and hold her hand. Aaron went outside to call to let Marjorie know we wouldn't be back for a few hours at least. I glanced around the awful cubicle, taking in the coldness of the place—the stainless steel, the tiled floor, and the chairs with surfaces that made human excretions an easy clean-up job. Joanie was silent. I thought of telling her about meeting Rob but decided against it. It wasn't the time for anything light-hearted. Instead, I squeezed her hand, happy just to sit there in silence if she wished. On the other side of the curtain, the nurse was interviewing a patient. She wasn't being overly loud, but Joan and I couldn't help but hear everything.

"Ms. Peters, how did you get those bruises on your arms?"

Joan and I exchanged glances but didn't speak.

"I don't know. I bruise pretty easily. I actually came in because I bumped my head on a door. The bruises aren't hurting me," the woman on the other side of the curtain answered.

"We'll attend to your head, but the bruises are a concern. I also note in your medical chart that you split your lip six months ago."

"Yes, I tripped and busted my lip."

"And dislocated your shoulder."

"If you say so."

"We checked over with Yonkers Hospital. According to their ER files you've come in with injuries three times in the past two years."

"I guess I'm just accident prone."

"Ms. Peters, it's obvious that someone is hurting you. I need to make a police report."

"Please, please don't do that," Ms. Peters begged, sounding scared. "It will only make things worse."

"By law, I have to report suspected abuse," the nurse stated.

"I'm leaving if you call the cops."

"You need some stitches and we have to monitor you for a concussion."

"I'm begging you. Please don't get involved."

"You can't just keep covering up the bruises with makeup. You could be seriously injured."

"I know how to take care of myself. He doesn't mean anything by it." Ms. Peters sounded like she was crying. Joanie and I locked eyes again. Neither of us said a word.

"Assault is a crime," the nurse continued, keeping her voice low and remaining remarkably calm.

"I don't care. I'm out of here. Don't bother sending the cops. I'll tell them what I told you. I hit my head on a door. Christ, you people are busybodies. Thanks for nothing. Don't you dare send me a bill," the woman shouted as she flung away the curtain and quickly ran down the hall.

"What was that about?" Aaron inquired as he slipped back in. Neither of us answered him. Aaron shrugged and reported that the kids were all asleep and that Sam had walked Laura, the sitter, home. According to Marjorie, Sam had gotten hungry, had no idea where I was, and wandered over. Beverly gave him some dinner and then suggested that he walk Laura home. Apparently, Sam was quite the gentleman. Even Joan couldn't suppress a wan smile at this revelation. Aaron turned to Joan, kissed her forehead, and ran his fingers through her hair. "So, how's my girl?" he inquired.

"I don't feel right," Joanie said, panic creeping into her voice. "I think the bleeding is getting heavier. When will Dr. Lewis be here?"

Dr. Lewis was delivering a baby upstairs and sent word that he would come down from the maternity floor as soon as possible. But I didn't like the way Joanie was looking or sounding and decided to find one of the ER doctors on call. As I turned the corner, I ran into Rob.

"Rob, thank goodness, Joanie needs you." Rob looked deeply concerned, and he quickly followed me into Joanie's area.

Aaron's face brightened when he saw Rob. In fact, Aaron came over and shook Rob's hand, telling him how glad he was to see him again. It was good that I'd fetched a doctor, my doctor.

Rob approached the bed and held Joanie's hand. "Joan, I'm so sorry you're having a rough time," he said.

"I'm just waiting for Dr. Lewis. I'm afraid something's really wrong. I'm scared for the baby," Joan replied.

Aaron turned to me, "Claire, have you met our—"

"Sure, we know each other," I said, thinking this was no time for introductions.

"Of course you're scared," Rob said to Joanie. "Anyone would be in your situation. You're in a good hospital, Joan, where everything possible will be done for you and your baby."

Rob was just as wonderful a doctor as I thought he would be—kind, reassuring. I was getting ready to leave the room so that he could examine Joanie.

"Would you like me to recite some psalms?" Rob asked. "It sometimes makes waiting a little easier."

"Yes, please. I think that might help."

What was going on? Why was Rob reciting psalms? Shouldn't he be taking her vitals or something? Enough with the bedside manner, for which I had to give the guy an A-plus. Couldn't he do something for her?

Vaguely I could hear Rob intone, "I turn my eyes to the mountain, from where will my help come? My help comes from God, maker of heaven and earth. He will not let your foot give way; your guardian will not slumber. . . ."

I was about to give way myself. What the hell was going on?

The next minute, Dr. Lewis entered the already crowded space.

"Rabbi Reuven, so nice to see you," I heard Dr. Lewis say as he shook Rob's hand. Rabbi? Rabbi? I felt that I could barely breathe, but I had to hold it together for Joanie's sake. The three of us, Rob, Aaron, and I exited the area so that Dr. Lewis could examine Joanie. We stood at a discreet distance from Joanie's curtain. The smell of the place made me feel nauseated. The light from the fluorescent ceiling fixtures bounced off the linoleum floors and the pattern on the pastel curtain began to dance. I realized that I hadn't had anything to eat since the cookie at Joanie's house, and before that, I wasn't sure. My eyes were open, but all of a sudden I couldn't see. The next thing I knew I was lying on a bed and Rob was holding my hand.

27

"Please tell me I didn't faint," I implored Rob.

"It would be a lie, but I'll tell you that if it will make you happy. Apparently, some people just have to be the center of attention," Rob teased.

"Does Joanie know that I passed out?"

"No, she's still with Dr. Lewis. He is going to run some tests. What happened? Were you just stressed out? Hospitals have that effect on some people."

"No, Rabbi," I said, pointedly. "I was just caught off-guard."

"Since when do you call me Rabbi, Claireleh?" Rob asked, not letting go of my hand.

"Since I found out you were the famous Rabbi Reuven," I answered.

"But you know who I am," Rob said, incredulously. "You knew that I'd been called. You even tracked me down in the hospital. Who did you think I was?"

"You were dressed like a doctor," I accused.

"I was just wearing this get-up because I had to visit someone who is very susceptible to infection. I also wore a mask and those little shower caps over my feet."

"Beverly will be thrilled," I snapped.

Rob blanched and dropped my hand. I hadn't meant to sound shrewish. And I certainly hadn't meant to mention Beverly. I was just so confused. Rob brought me some apple juice, though he didn't meet my gaze. Slowly, I started to put things together. He didn't come to the gym on Monday and Thursdays because those are the days when they read Torah and the morning *minyan* started early. Of course Rob worked weekends—ironically, Saturday, the Jewish day of rest, is a prime working day if you're a rabbi. And if Rob was actually the infamous, saintly Rabbi Reuven, then he spent last evening with Sam.

"So, *Rabbi*. . . ."

"Cut it out," he ordered. I'd never seen Rob angry before. I realized that I was being a jerk, but it was hard to control my emotions. I felt like such an idiot.

"You've met Sam, I take it."

"Nice kid," Rob said, his voice still a little strained. "He came to Youth Group last night. I figured you sent him with Ben so that I could meet him."

"No, it was Marjorie's idea." Marjorie, whom he knew from work—from the synagogue, not the hospital. My God, how could I have been so deluded?

"He behaved OK?" I asked.

"He was great. We baked challahs for some of our shut-ins and made cards."

"No way," I exclaimed. This night was too much for me.

"Way," Rob countered in his best imitation of a teen. "It helped that Sam was sitting next to a lovely red-headed young lady," Rob added. "They had a very animated conversation."

This couldn't be happening. I felt like I was in an episode of *The Twilight Zone*. Rob, a rabbi? Sam, a pleasant teenager capable of polite conversation?

Rob, who didn't seem to get the magnitude of my disorientation, continued to chatter. I tried to force myself to pay attention, though I wasn't quite all there. I tuned back in as Rob was reminding me that teens are often at their worst at home. Any opportunity for them to demonstrate their good side was to be encouraged.

"I guess people are always on good behavior with you," I commented.

"Everyone but you, apparently," Rob said with a smile. "It's very refreshing," he deadpanned.

I didn't respond. I just sat on the bed looking vacant.

"I was sure you'd known for months—ever since our breakfast at the Sage Diner." I saw the justice in his remark. I'm sure from his perspective it couldn't have been clearer. Still, I couldn't bring myself to say anything.

"There are only two people in the world who call me Rob anymore—you and my mother. I love my Hebrew name, but there is something so special, so genuine to me about being plain old Rob." He was tearing up. "I'm just so grateful that I have one friend who calls me Rob and doesn't treat me like some separate species. Someone who doesn't watch her language imagining that I couldn't hear the word 'shit' without being scandalized or tattling to the big man upstairs."

"Oh, shit, I'm so fucking sorry," I said with feeling, getting a smile out of him. "I'm . . . just a little overwhelmed right now, but everything will be OK."

Rob hugged me and dabbed his eyes. "It's been a hard night for all of us," he said offering me some peanut butter crackers and some more apple juice. Soon I was steady on my feet, so we went out to check up on Joanie, the rabbi and I.

28

Aaron intercepted us on our way to see Joan. One look at his face and I knew something was terribly wrong.

"Dr. Lewis is going to schedule an ultrasound, but he couldn't hear the baby's heartbeat. I think there's a good chance we've already lost the baby," Aaron whispered as he paced in front of Joan's room.

"Has Dr. Lewis spoken to Joan yet?" Rob asked.

"Not yet; he doesn't want to say anything until he's sure. My God, this will kill Joanie."

"Let's take it one step at a time," Rob said. "We don't know anything for certain yet. Let's try to keep her spirits up."

Joan looked worn out and anxious as the three of us re-entered her room. In response to her urgent questioning, Aaron told her that Dr. Lewis said he needed to run some tests. Rob sat with Joanie, holding her hands. He began to pray in deeply moving tones. "Oh merciful God who watches over his people Israel, we pray for the health of *Rut Yocheved bat Miriam* and her child. Please keep them and protect them. We place our trust in You, our Rock and our Redeemer."

Joan, though still looking extremely frail, appeared comforted by Rob's words. I was just reeling from all the events of the night, keenly aware that I had no rock on which to lean, no source of comfort in times of trouble. Although I couldn't share their faith, I did envy it.

It looked like even under the best of outcomes, Joan would be in for a long night. Fortunately, Jack Greenberg had arranged for Joan to be transferred to a regular room with actual walls and doors. Someone with good sense made sure it wasn't in the maternity wing.

Joan insisted that Aaron go home so that he could be there for breakfast and getting the kids off to school. I offered to stay over in the hospital, but Joanie instructed me to go home too, announcing in a weary voice I'd never heard from her before that she just wanted to rest. Who could blame her? I arranged to meet Rob again Friday morning; not, obviously, at the gym, but at the hospital cafeteria at eight.

By the time I arrived home, it was past midnight. I stopped by Joan's house to see if there was anything I could do before going to sleep. I noticed the kids' lunches were made and that there was Shabbes dinner in the fridge—challah, matzo ball soup, brisket, carrots, apple cake, all neatly packaged in plastic containers, labeled with precise instructions on how to warm each item. Beverly also left a note in neat, almost calligraphic handwriting, detailing the various child-care arrangements. Beverly let Aaron and Joan know that they were in her "thoughts and prayers."

I had a brief conversation with Marjorie, who looked tired. She told me that things had gone well with the book group. Everyone was worried about Joan and sent their love. Apparently, everyone professed to enjoy the cookies Marjorie brought. Given that these were a cheap off-brand purchased on clearance, Marjorie was bursting with pride and a sense of personal vindication. Normally, the whole cookie thing would have driven me around the bend, but I figured that after a night of yeoman's service, Marjorie was entitled to her idiosyncrasies. Also, Marjorie endeared herself to me by observing that Beverly was a bit high-strung.

"I don't think Aaron really needs instructions on how to heat up a pot of soup," she commented. "So be it," Marjorie sighed as she left. So be it indeed.

The next day started well enough with Sam's on-time departure for school. The little felon was re-entering law-abiding society, and with any luck, he had been rehabilitated. I headed for my breakfast rendezvous with Rob. We met and filled our trays with hearty breakfast fare and Rob poured himself oily-looking coffee that looked to soon burn a hole in its styrofoam cup.

"I notice that you aren't offering me your bacon this time," Rob remarked as we ate breakfasts so high in fat I suspected that the cafeteria was drumming up business for the cardiology unit.

"You're welcome to it. I believe that if you find yourself in a hospital cafeteria, God owes you some bacon," I explained.

"Interesting theology," he mused. "That's not what they teach you in rabbinical school, though some of my classmates believed that there should be a deliciousness exception to the *kashrut* laws."

"I doubt this bacon would qualify. I'm only eating it to be transgressive," I said smugly.

"Just like Eve, you want the one thing you can't have," Rob observed.

My eyes widened and my pulse raced. Did Rob realize what he had just said? Was I that transparent? Did he also want something that he couldn't have? Was I the one who would tempt him with forbidden, if slightly low-hanging, fruit?

For a moment, neither of us spoke. Our awkward silence was broken when we spotted Aaron, who joined us and told us that Dr. Lewis had completed reviewing the tests and was on his way down to meet him before talking to Joan. Rob and I exchanged worried glances.

Two minutes later, Dr. Lewis arrived and ushered us into a private conference room. As Aaron sat down, Dr. Lewis placed a huge hand on his shoulder. "Well, the good news is that Joan will make a full recovery," he began, and then turned to face Aaron directly. "But I'm sorry to tell you that the ultrasound confirms that the baby died in utero." A long moment passed and Dr. Lewis resumed. "We'll analyze a tissue sample, but the truth is we rarely know why this happens. Sometimes it's a chromosomal mutation, sometimes a problem with the cord, and sometimes there's an anomaly in the placenta. The fact that Joanie has had four healthy, live births indicates that this was probably a one-time thing, though miscarriages do become more prevalent with the increased age of the mother. I'm truly sorry about the baby."

My heart sank. Aaron looked just awful. I'd never seen him so haggard. Almost in a whisper, Aaron thanked Dr. Lewis and agreed to meet in Joan's room after Dr. Lewis finished making his maternity rounds.

As soon as Dr. Lewis left, Aaron buried his head in his hands. "Poor Joanie," he said without looking up. "This is going to devastate her."

"We'll all be here to help her," Rob reassured him.

Aaron lifted his head. "Rabbi, how could this happen? How could God do this to Joan? She is such a good woman, such a good mother."

"You're asking a profound question. I can't explain why good people suffer. Nobody can. Suffering and loss are part of life. But God put us here on earth to comfort each other." Rob put his hand on Aaron's sturdy forearm as he spoke.

I imagined that Rob gave this explanation a lot in hospitals and *shiva* homes, but it didn't come across as canned. Rob clearly believed what he was saying and cared deeply about Aaron. He was right that the best thing we could do, in fact, the only thing, would be to offer Joan comfort and support.

29

I don't quite know what I expected from Joan—hysterical crying? Angry thrashing? What she displayed was infinitely more disquieting. Joan simply retreated into an unapproachable silence. She barely met anyone's gaze, and when she did, her eyes looked dead.

Joanie needed to stay in the hospital for what everyone was euphemistically calling a "procedure." Her miscarriage hadn't fully expelled the fetus and the extra tissue, so Dr. Lewis would have to vacuum it out. He assured Joanie that she was going to be fine and after a few menstrual cycles she could get pregnant again, but Joanie didn't even seem interested. She also refused Rob's offer to say a prayer, which, I noticed, didn't seem to ruffle him at all.

Physically, the room was a big improvement over the ER cubicle. The hospital smell was fainter and there was some natural light. Without the blinking equipment, one could perhaps have been persuaded that we were in a two-star hotel with incredibly bland food and cheerful room service. The one big problem—and I mean big—was Joanie's hospital roommate, Imogene Walters, who must have weighed at least 300 pounds, 50 of which came from atop her head where a mound of teased "blonde" hair was perched in a do that might have been all the rage circa 1960. Imogene immediately introduced herself to us and wouldn't shut up. Despite the noise from her television, which she played at top volume, Imogene kept on trying to engage all of us in conversation. Joan didn't speak at all but Aaron, out of an awkward sense of politeness, answered Imogene's questions about why Joan was in the hospital, where the Cohens lived, what their family was like, etc. His replies were clipped but old Imogene didn't seem to get the hint. When she ran out of questions she observed, "At least you have the other kids." When this statement went unanswered, she added, even more loudly, "When you think about it, it's a blessing that you never got to know the baby. That would have made it much harder." Joanie didn't respond; she didn't even seem to notice. Aaron, however, was clearly pained by Imogene's comments.

"If this woman tries to look on the bright side one more time, I'll hit her with a metal bedpan, right in the head, and then point out how lucky she is that the bedpan was empty," I muttered hotly to Rob.

"She's just a lonely old woman, one sandwich short of a picnic," Rob whispered, apparently using another phrase learned from the Youth Group set.

Rob immediately went over and started to chat up Imogene. He drew the curtain around the two of them to shield poor Joan and Aaron. Rob asked Imogene about her family, her church, her health. He insisted on seeing pictures of all the grandbabies. Rob then asked Imogene if it would be OK if he came back to visit her sometime soon. She was tickled pink. She actually flirted with him, telling him in a voice that was as coquettish as it was loud that a handsome gentleman such as himself was always welcome. That guy can schmooze up anyone, I marveled.

At the end of their conversation, Rob, almost conspiratorially, asked Imogene for a special favor. Could she turn down the TV a bit and let Joan rest? The doctor really needed Joan not to talk just now and to sleep if she could. Imogene assented gladly. The woman was putty in Rob's hands. It wasn't at all clear that Imogene understood what Rob's being a rabbi (which she pronounced "rib eye") meant. Join the club, I thought. Did Rob consider me just another Imogene—a fat, annoying (if well-meaning) woman who needed to be humored and managed?

Rob had other congregants to visit in the hospital—I was still not on board with the whole rabbi thing—and had to prepare his Friday night sermon. I wondered what his sermons were like. Had I been getting mini-sermons at the gym and not realizing it? No, I concluded, during our talks Rob wasn't preaching. Our relationship was special because we interacted normally, without all the formality, deference, and weirdness that came with his position. I was determined to try to maintain that sort of relationship, though I realized that I didn't want to let on to Joanie that Rob and I knew each other from the gym.

I had to at least put in an appearance at work. There was a meeting about various employee assistance programs, and I had Teresa Williams to deal with. She either had to get some help or be given the boot. I just hated to leave Joanie, especially when she was in such a bad way. I kissed her and promised that I'd come by her house tomorrow, but she didn't even look my way. At least, I thought, thanks to Beverly, the food was all ready. Words sometimes fail, but everyone has to eat.

30

After work I returned home to get Sam ready for his weekend at Jeremy and Kimberly's. Normally, I was pretty laissez-faire about what the kid wore, but my pride intervened when it came to sending Sam to hang with his new, young step-mama. Imagine my shock when I saw Sam stuffing his navy blue suit into his overnight bag.

"Do I have a clean fancy shirt?" he asked.

"Going to another funeral?" I responded.

"If you must know, me and Kim are going to services tomorrow. Ben is reading Torah and Rabbi Reuven invited me to go."

I was stupefied into silence. Or at least temporary silence, until I opted for stupidity instead. "You're going to *shul*?" I asked incredulously.

"It's no big deal," Sam said, rolling his eyes.

Since we did have a big deal coming up—while facing the honeymooners, I had to explain what the miscreant had been doing at school—I really couldn't afford a freak out just then. Had my demonic son finally found the perfect way to rebel? I had to hand it to the kid, he did have a sense of irony. I would just have to confront on another occasion the fact that my son was clearly on his way to joining some crazy Jewish cult led by the married man upon whom I had an insane and pointless crush. So I found him another shirt—still in the package—and let the issue go. In fact, I let Sam choose the radio station, some horrid misogynist rap, for our ride across town to greet the happy couple. "Fuck that bitch" indeed.

Kimberly greeted us at the door. My heart sank when I saw that she was even more beautiful than I'd feared. Kimberly looked positively Twiggy-like in a cobalt blue knit dress with crocheted neckline and sleeves. Her hair, short, shiny, and dark, was cut at a sharp angle to frame her face. Her bright blue eyes shone through wire-framed glasses that were just on the right side of artsy-fartsy. I looked down dejectedly at my crumpled blue suit and the obligatory tea stains on the chest of my pale pink silk blouse and felt ungainly—let's face it, elephantine—by comparison.

I suppose I expected to see a garish McMansion monstrosity replete with grand entryways, spiral staircases, vaulted ceilings, media rooms, imported Italian tile, etc. Jeremy could certainly have afforded it. So I was shocked to discover that he and Kimberly lived in a cozy, tastefully furnished, center-hall colonial, walking distance from the Hudsonville train station. The kitchen was clearly updated, but someone had taken pains to make sure the look complemented the old feel of the house. Kimberly apparently adored gadgets, but the kitchen, with its deep, rich wood floors and matching cabinets, didn't feel sterile or overly modern.

"Jeremy should be home any minute," Kimberly said.

How I remembered those long evenings with a cranky toddler and dinner turned cold, waiting for Jeremy to come home. He kept on promising that he'd catch the very next train, but could never quite pull himself away from his desk. I wondered how many evenings Kimberly ended up watching television until she fell asleep, the way I used to. Kimberly made me a cappuccino while we waited for Jeremy to arrive.

"Would you like to see the rest of the house?" Kimberly offered, desperate as our silence became uncomfortable. I'd no inclination to do anything to make her feel better but agreed to a tour. Curiosity about the house trumped my desire to watch Kimberly squirm. Reluctantly, Sam led the way upstairs and we viewed his room. There were two twin beds with striped bedspreads in bright primary colors, a large closet, a chest of drawers, and a computer that was newly out of its box.

"Sam, your dad and I were hoping you knew how to set up the computer. We put a high speed cable in your room."

"Sure," Sam said with real enthusiasm, and immediately got to work unraveling wires.

I spotted clothes hanging in the closet, and Kimberly explained that she and Jeremy wanted to make things as convenient as possible for Sam with clothes and other items at their house so that Sam could easily go back and forth. I even saw a pair of Sam's favorite running shoes in there. I bet step-mama was more diligent about doing the laundry too. The room also contained a writing desk and a book shelf that held a thesaurus, a dictionary, and some science fiction. Although Jeremy and Kimberly had been in the house less than two weeks, Sam's room had evidently been a priority and was fully set up for his lordship.

"Here's the guest room," Kimberly said, pointing to a gorgeous space with a broad-paneled wood floor graced by small rag rugs. There was a brass bed covered in a striped maroon and pink bedspread. A matching cushion covered the built-in window seat. On the back wall stood a huge mahogany dresser with brass pulls and a tilting built-in mirror. The room was lush and inviting without being frilly or overdone. Knowing that Jeremy's talent for decor was limited to artistic placement of socks and underwear on the bedroom floor, I figured that all of this had to come from Kimberly. She was, after all, an art teacher at the fancy local prep school.

"We're not quite finished decorating," Kimberly informed me. "I still have to sew the curtains."

Sew? I thought. Was Kimberly also churning her own butter to pass the time while Jeremy slaved away at the law firm?

"This is my favorite place in the house," Kimberly announced as she ushered me around a corner. If it's her bedroom with a heart-shaped, king-sized bed, I'll puke, I told myself. It wasn't. Instead, Kimberly invited me into a bright room with a large loom, a sewing machine, a spinning wheel, and shelves full of yarns and fabrics. She pointed to a yellow and white cloth suspended from the loom. "I'm weaving a *challah* cover for Rabbi Reuven as a thank-you gift. He taught me for my conversion and did the wedding. Do you know Rabbi Reuven?"

"Not really," I said.

I checked out the hall bathroom, which had a huge claw-foot tub, the underside of which was painted blue and matched the sink made out of a large Delft Blue ceramic bowl. Note to self: the smell of potpourri beats the smell of shit. As I dried my hands on the plush, tasseled guest towels, I swore to myself that this woman would never see the inside of my house. Ever.

Just then I heard Jeremy arrive home and I steeled myself for our talk. We engaged in a brief, awkward hello. We never touched anymore, so he and I just stood there, looking ridiculous. We moved to the kitchen table where we sat without Sam, just the three of us—Jeremy, me, and the interloper with the eye for design.

With Kimberly present I was determined to be on good behavior. No need to let her realize too soon how every rotten thing Jeremy undoubtedly said about me was true. So, without embellishment or reserve, I told them about the sins of the son that had been visited upon the mother and upon Hudsonville Middle School.

"Gosh," Jeremy said with no expression.

"This must have been just awful for you," Kimberly said.

"It was pretty bad," I admitted. "But Sam has been so tough lately. This isn't even the worst of it. He screams at me and calls me a 'psycho' and a 'fucking bitch' all the time. I just can't take it. I don't know what to do." To my utter horror, I felt my eyes welling up. It was too late to pretend. Too late to preserve any dignity at all. I just lay my forehead over my hands on the table and wept.

"I had no idea," Jeremy said softly.

"How would you? You're never around for Sam."

I wondered, had I actually said that? It was the type of thing I often thought, and sometimes said, but I wasn't aware that I'd been talking. I'm losing it, I thought.

"Of course, you're right," Jeremy replied. "I haven't been around enough for Sam. I've been too wrapped up in my work. It cost me my marriage to Claire, and I won't let it cost me my relationship with Sam, or with you."

Huh? Dripping snot or not, I had to lift up my head to get a look at what the hell was going on with the pretty-boy lawyer I'd been married to for almost twelve years. He redirected his attention to me and said, "Claire, I'm sorry you're going through all this, especially right after Pop died. Kim is right: I haven't been there enough for Sam. Kim wouldn't marry me until I promised to quit the firm and spend more time with family. I'm going to be chief in-house counsel at an insurance company in White Plains. The hours should be much better, and there will hardly be any traveling. I promise you I'll be more involved with Sam's schooling and I'll try to help with his behavior. It's time to take some of the burden off you. I have all of December off between jobs and I'll take

Sam for his entire winter recess—more if you'd like. You really do deserve a break."

Two weeks without Sam? I couldn't believe it. And Jeremy was quitting the firm to spend more time with family? Amazing. In addition to my disorientation, I felt a sudden pang. Why was he willing to do this for Kimberly, when he hadn't been willing to do it for me?

"Your taking him for winter recess would really help," I said quietly. Kimberly had placed a box of tissues next to me and had set out another cappuccino for me to drink.

"Tell us what you'd like us to do regarding Sam this weekend," Kimberly said gently.

"I already plan to talk to him about how he's treating you," Jeremy said. "But is there anything else you'd like us to do?"

"Well, could you monitor what he's accessing on the internet and maybe find out what kind of progress he's making on reading *A Tale of Two Cities*? Also, he wanted to go to Youth Group Sunday night."

"We're going to *shul* tomorrow and Youth Group sounds like a great idea," Jeremy said. "Rabbi Reuven really has a way with the kids. In fact, he was the one who first suggested that we take Sam for the winter break."

"When did he suggest that?" I asked, wondering how long Rob had known that Jeremy was my ex.

"He mentioned it to me after I picked up Sam and Ben from Youth Group Wednesday night," Jeremy said.

"*You* picked up the kids?" I was incredulous. Jeremy never drove Sam anywhere. He was always busy at the office or on the road. His apartment in the city had been a cramped one-bedroom that was totally inappropriate for hosting Sam. For one thing, the fridge was always empty. Since our divorce, Jeremy often ate all three meals and a midnight snack at the office. Jeremy's car was garaged and rarely driven at all, let alone to chauffeur a kid. Time with Sam was a Knicks game or a restaurant meal, never something as prosaic or as helpful as a ride to an activity.

"I've been telling Jeremy that car rides are great for talking to kids. You have a captive audience," Kimberly said.

"Now that I'm living in Hudsonville again, I'm going to make a real effort to do my fair share with Sam," Jeremy said. "We can take him to *shul* even on weekends that he isn't with us, and if you need any last-minute help, Kim gets done at school by 4:00."

I didn't know what to say. Now that Jeremy had traded up, he was interested in Sam. Was he angling to take Sam away from me? Would I mind?

Sam was summoned to join us and Jeremy explained that he was very disappointed with Sam's lapse of judgment and his treatment of me.

"Mom is mad at me 24/7," Sam said. "According to her, I never do anything right." Sam didn't look me in the eye.

"I know your mom can get pretty angry sometimes, but that's no excuse for being disrespectful or cursing at her," Jeremy said firmly.

Hello, I thought, I'm here. I was literally as well as figuratively the elephant in the room. The angry elephant on a non-stop rampage. Isn't that what drove Jeremy away? Hadn't he hated coming home because I was angry all the time? Was Jeremy going to empathize with Sam about what a bitch I am to live with?

"It's time for me to go," I said stiffly. "See you Sunday night, Sam."

Sam ignored me.

"Say goodbye to your mother, Sam," Jeremy said sternly.

"Bye," Sam said sullenly.

Kimberly walked me to the door. "Have a restful Shabbat," she wished me. "You deserve it."

31

My Shabbat was anything but restful. I went over to help Aaron with the kids. Marjorie was just dropping off Jake, who looked happy and cozy in his pajamas.

"Don't you just love kids in these footy pajamas?" Marjorie asked.

"I have bad associations," I replied. "When Sam was small, that was the first sound we'd hear on winter mornings—the shuffle of those no-skid feet announcing that, like it or not, a new day had begun."

"Jake and I had a great time," Marjorie announced with enthusiasm. "Who likes grilled cheese?" she quizzed.

"I do!" volunteered Jake.

"And what did we have in the bath?"

"Duckies!" shouted Jake.

"How many duckies were in the water?"

"Five!" Jake proclaimed.

"That's right," said Marjorie, beaming at Jake. "Two in front of you and three behind you makes five."

I wondered how long it would take Joanie to deprogram the poor kid. Still, I had to take my hat off to Marjorie: Jake looked like he had a great day, which was more than I could say for Sarah. Sarah knew something was up. She was whiney and tearful all evening, rejecting the pizza we ordered and unwilling to listen to any bedtime stories, arguing that only Mommy knew how to read them.

"Mommy's in the hospital. She is a little sick, but she'll come home tomorrow," Aaron explained.

"Is the baby born yet?" Sarah asked.

"No, sweetheart, we lost the baby," Aaron said softly.

"Then find it," Sarah demanded.

"Sarah, honey, the baby died," Aaron explained patiently. As far as I knew, Sarah's only acquaintance with death was her goldfish, over which she had cried bitter tears.

"Will the baby come back?"

"No, Sarah, the baby won't come back. Someday maybe we will have a different baby, but this baby, baby Mimi, is gone."

"Did you flush the baby down the toilet like you did with Goldy?"

Aaron looked horrified.

"No honey," he answered. "It's different with babies. I promise you that Mommy is coming back and we'll see her tomorrow," he reassured her.

Eventually we got Sarah to bed. I arranged to return the next morning so that Aaron could pick up Joanie from the hospital.

As I walked through Joanie's garden in the still, starry night, more than anything else, I just wished I could talk to Rob. Turns out those two cappuccinos left me plenty of time for reflection as I stared, wide-eyed, at my bedroom ceiling, heart and thoughts racing. Jeremy had been an awful husband and an absent father. I wasn't wrong about that. But nothing I had to offer him was sufficiently alluring to make him want to change. Kimberly succeeded where I'd been a big, fat failure. I'd been angry and aggrieved all the time, and, according to Sam, I still was. Who wants to come home to that? Really, why was I so angry all the time?

32

Joanie returned from the hospital Saturday morning and went straight to bed. Her face was drawn and her auburn curls were matted. I don't think she'd showered or shampooed for days. For the entire weekend, she didn't emerge from her room. She barely ate and hardly spoke. Aaron and I tried to let her rest undisturbed, but despite our best efforts, the children kept on sneaking into her room, asking for stories and wanting to give Mommy hugs. Though normally energized by the presence of her happy, boisterous children, Joanie seemed barely to notice them. Even when Zack entered her room with a lollipop in his mouth—a violation of every nutritional edict and restriction on mess-making Joanie had ever issued—she said nothing and just gazed vacantly into the distance. Joanie, who regularly rose at five to exercise before the kids woke up, now just slept all day. Joanie, who baked her own bread, grew her own vegetables, and ground her own peanut butter, raised no objection to our ordering take-out two nights in a row. Joanie, who was vigilant about neatness and order, didn't even bother to mop up a drink that spilled on her bedroom carpet. Where had my friend gone?

Even scarier than her prolonged silences were her obsessive comments about the baby, delivered in a flat, quiet voice. "I knew there was something wrong," she repeated over and over. "I didn't feel a kick," she said. And most heart-wrenching, "I let my Mimi die."

I felt totally out of my depth. Never had words seemed so pointless. Aaron arranged with a nursing service to send someone Monday morning. I would take the twins to school and Marjorie offered to take Jake again. Four adults could somehow muddle through and perform (badly) all the tasks that Joanie accomplished in a day. Scheduling and logistics we could handle, but none of us knew what to do for Joanie, who showed no sign of recovering from this crushing blow.

When I arrived at home on Sunday after my exhausting and depressing weekend, I saw that Sam was already back. *Shul* was "fine" and Youth Group was "good." The kid wasn't particularly loquacious, but he was civil and that was plenty.

Monday morning, Sam left home without a fuss—did his eggs not suck for once or was he becoming more reasonable? I went over to Joanie's to help with the morning craziness. Marjorie stopped by Joanie's room to say a quick hello, something I heretofore didn't realize she was capable of. I was amazed to hear her tell Joanie that she, too, had suffered a late term miscarriage.

"I lost a little girl. She would have been eleven years old last week," Marjorie said softly. "You never forget, but it does get easier."

I never thought of Marjorie having any tragedy larger than Jack's dinner being cold or Hudsonville High School cutting back on its advanced-placement offerings. I suppose I never really thought about Marjorie's interior life or even imagined that she had one, given that most of my energies were directed at avoiding conversations like the one that followed in the kitchen.

"I don't know why Joan buys real Cheerios. The store brand is just as good. I defy you to tell the difference," Marjorie declaimed as she packed up diapers, wipes, and toys for Jake.

How could Marjorie switch gears so quickly from tragedy to kvetchy farce? She seemed unaware of any incongruity.

"We're going shopping, right, Jake?" Marjorie asked in a friendly voice with a beaming smile on her face. "And you're going to be my helper. Would you help me find the bananas and the bagels?"

"Bagels!" Jake shouted.

My God, children are easily bought, I thought. His mother could be curled up in a ball of depression, but hand a kid a carbohydrate with some cream cheese on it and he's happy. Marjorie informed me that she'd bring Jake back after dinner in his pajamas, but she had a meeting on Tuesday and couldn't take him that day.

"Besides," Marjorie lowered her voice, "Joan has to start interacting with her kids."

I knew Marjorie was right. Joanie's behavior was taking a terrible toll on the older kids. Jake happily announced "baby goned," but the twins and Sarah were confused and worried by Joanie's lack of interaction and the withdrawal of her warmth. It was like a fire had gone out. I was at a loss.

"Maybe Aaron should call Rabbi Reuven," Marjorie suggested. Great, I thought as I packed the twins up for school. Life was getting a little too uncomplicated.

33

The work day whizzed by in an unending flow of phone calls, meetings, tea, and doughnuts. I made an appointment to see my boss, Corey, later in the week. The problem with Teresa Williams wasn't resolved, and I needed his input. She was such a valuable employee and one of our few women who had worked her way up the employment ladder from secretary to manager, so I hated to lose her, but her absences couldn't continue. I called Joan's house a few times, but someone must have taken the phone off the hook and her cell phone went straight to voicemail. I decided to go there early and see if the Cohen family would enjoy my specialty—mac 'n' cheese with a side of broccoli. It used to be one of Sam's favorites when he still had anything pleasant to say about me or my cooking.

I let myself in the back door. Jake was in the kids' playroom glued to a DVD of some performers in animal suits singing inane songs. Sarah was in the family room watching cartoons. None of this would be happening if Joanie were on the job. I peeked into Joanie's room. Joanie was sleeping and the nurse was knitting. Joan was having trouble sleeping at night and had begun sleeping through the day. The nurse joined me in the kitchen and told me that physically, Joan was fine, but her spirits were still very low. As we were talking, Aaron arrived and paid the nurse. Aaron looked like hell. His face was haggard, his shirt rumpled, and he looked lost. Without Joanie's picking out his clothes Aaron resembled one of those eccentric bachelors who never goes out without a bow tie but occasionally forgets to wear pants.

"I don't know what to do for her. I called. . . ."

Aaron was interrupted by the doorbell. I hurried to the door and opened it, expecting the twins and their babysitter. I called out in the friendliest, most cheerful tone I could muster, "Hello there!"

"Hello there to you, too," Rob said, smirking. He was dressed in a blue pin-striped suit with a gorgeous blue and yellow tie.

"Ro . . . Rabbi!" I caught myself just in time; Aaron was right behind me. "How nice to see you," I said as steadily as I could manage.

"I was hoping there was something I could do to help Joan."

The three of us repaired to the kitchen. I made tea and distributed Marjorie's cookies, which I grudgingly had to admit weren't too bad. Rob listened sympathetically, nodding and interjecting supportive comments as Aaron and I described Joanie's lack of affect and recounted what little she'd said. Rob explained that there was no traditional *shiva* for a lost baby. Even infants under a month old didn't receive the full mourning ritual when they died. However, modern rituals had evolved and he would talk to Joanie about them to see whether some formal acknowledgement of the loss might bring her some comfort. Rob had also brought some books for the kids about miscarriage and loss. He told Aaron that kids sometimes worry that they caused the miscarriage by having negative thoughts about the baby or were afraid that they might die as suddenly or inexplicably as baby Mimi. The books looked sad, but beautiful, with great illustrations.

Just then the twins did burst in.

"God is here," Zack announced to Rachel as soon as he saw Rob.

Despite our sorrow, the three of us burst out laughing.

"So can God stay for dinner?" I asked.

"I'd love to, but Bev is expecting me. I'm already half an hour late."

"Rabbi, you can use our phone to call home if you'd like," Aaron offered.

"No that's fine, Bev's used to my being late."

"Must be hard for Beverly to be married to God," I observed. "During sex, does she start yelling, 'Oh God, Oh God'?" I asked.

Rob looked stricken. Aaron looked shocked. "Claire, this is our *rabbi*," Aaron said incredulously.

"I'm sorry, Rabbi," I said, mortified. "I'm sorry, Aaron, I was just joking and got carried away."

"No problem," Rob assured Aaron. "No problem," Rob said softly as he placed his hand on my forearm. "I really wish I could stay." I wished his touch would linger. I believed him when he said he wished he could stay.

Switching from his quiet tone to his camp counselor bellow, Rob announced, "Rabbi Reuven is going to read to you while Daddy and Aunt Claire make dinner." Rob took me aside and said, "As soon as the kids start eating, I'm going to talk to Joan. You've been doing a great mitzvah helping out Aaron and the kids while Joan recovers. I hope you're taking care of yourself, too."

"I'm going to the gym tomorrow morning," I said looking straight into his green eyes.

"I'm glad to hear it," Rob replied.

34

What a pathetic life. Only someone of my lameness and girth could transform a visit to the gym into an illicit assignation. Big deal. I was planning to walk the treadmill next to Rob. Rabbi Rob. Rabbi Reuven. Yet, my joy in seeing him, my excitement at my stupid secret was undeniable. Rabbi Reuven is my friend! I know him better than all of you!

Rob was already there when I arrived at the gym, and in violation of the club rules he saved the treadmill next to him by draping his towel over it. I happily started walking next to my fellow transgressive.

"Shalom, Rabbi," I said with a grin.

"Shalom, yourself, bad girl," Rob said. "Have anything else wildly inappropriate to say to me?"

"Yes, but I'm waiting to say it in front of Marjorie," I said.

"So you're going?" Rob asked.

I must have looked confused because Rob explained that Marjorie had invited him to Friday night dinner and said something about including me and Sam. I hadn't heard about it.

"So be it," I said in my best imitation of Marjorie.

"Claire!" Rob scolded, but he couldn't hide his smile.

We fell into a good rhythm. Walking and talking, we caught up. I let Rob know that things had been somewhat better with Sam.

"I gather you spoke to Jeremy. How long have you known that Jeremy was my ex?" I asked him pointedly.

Rob swore that it was only when Jeremy picked up Sam from Youth Group that he made the connection. Once Rob realized that Jeremy was Sam's dad, he tried to do some good by suggesting to Jeremy that he take Sam over break. It was hard enough to get Rob to acknowledge the slightest flaw in Marjorie, so I knew he wasn't going to dish any dirt on

Kimberly, who apparently had become the model Jew and whose main sin, as far as I could tell, was to win Jeremy's love and attention, where I'd failed to do so.

Mostly, we talked about Joanie.

"I think she blames herself," I told Rob. "Joanie feels that she somehow failed as a mother. That's why she's having trouble connecting with her kids right now," I ventured.

"Her grief and confusion are understandable," Rob said. "Her body let her down. God let her down. The *Mishnah* says that a one-day-old infant who dies is like a full bridegroom to his parents. The same is true if you lose a fetus at six months."

Suddenly it dawned on me how hard this must be for Rob, who desperately wanted children but couldn't have any. Could he really console Joanie, who was upset about losing her fifth, when he had no children at all?

"Is this hard for you personally?" I asked gingerly.

"You mean because I can't have kids?" he asked in a low voice.

I nodded.

"A little. But I'd like to hope that my personal disappointment allows me to be more compassionate toward Joan. It helps to think that my own heartbreak can help me reach out to others."

"You do, you do comfort others," I assured him. "I can tell already that your visit helped Joanie. She got out of bed for the first time after you spoke to her."

We agreed that it would be a slow process. Joanie might get pregnant again, but there would only be one Mimi for Joan, and Mimi was lost forever. How painful it was for Joanie to lose her heart's desire. But wasn't this true for each of us in our own way?

Later that day I did receive an invitation for Friday night dinner from Marjorie, which I accepted with alacrity. Afterwards it occurred to me that not only Rob, but Beverly, would be in attendance. Like Rob, I was to be confronted with denial of my one true wish, thrust into the presence of one who possessed it, but hardly seemed to value it.

35

Another morning without a blow up! No screaming, no cursing, no throwing things, and I'm not just talking about myself. Sam was actually civil. I even got a "Hi Mom" when he entered the kitchen. Spared the morning scream-fest, I had enough extra time and psychic energy to conduct a massive sweep and managed to corral the cups and glassware abandoned throughout the house. Remarkably, only a small portion of the retrieved items was actually growing hair, though the three-day-old chocolate milk had its own pungent howdy-do.

I loaded the dishwasher as Sam ate his eggs and bagel. One couldn't call our morning interactions animated or even convivial, but I happily settled for peaceful.

"Why aren't you eating breakfast?" Sam asked.

"I'll grab a couple of doughnuts at work after the gym," I replied, stunned by his interest.

"Isn't that kind of counter-productive? I mean, you work so hard to exercise and then you just ruin it all with doughnuts."

"Turns out I like both exercising and doughnuts," I replied waiting for his usual observations that I'm a stupid, weird bitch who never acts normal.

"That's cool," Sam said and returned to the comic book he was reading.

Interested to see how far I could push the boy, I ventured into territory I hadn't touched in months.

"Is your homework all done?"

"That's what the bus ride is for," Sam said without looking up but without any notable hostility. Enough for one day. I was permitted the question, no need to quibble over the answer. The kid was still bringing home good grades, so he must be meeting his obligations.

"More juice?" I offered.

"Thanks," he replied without looking up, holding out his glass with one hand while he turned the page of the comic with the other.

Amazing, I thought. Amazing.

My success with Sam buoyed me for the tough morning ahead. The time had come for a final showdown with Teresa. She'd missed the previous Monday. That woman had to get with the five-day workweek or find another job. I knew the conversation would be extremely difficult, and that Teresa's defenses would be up. I could just imagine how disdainful she was of me, my schlumpiness, and my attempts to be helpful. Teresa put a lot of care into her appearance and she undoubtedly thought of me as a frumpy, know-nothing, Ivy-League tee-totaler, which, let's face it, I sort of am. Nevertheless, I was determined to try to gain her trust and see if I could help her conquer whatever addiction was plaguing her work life.

At the office, I ate two jelly doughnuts. I was ravenous and they were gone in a trice as I reviewed Teresa's file. I could see that she no longer had kids at home so I couldn't appeal to her on that score.

I asked Molly, the repository of all company gossip, about Teresa's husband. The guy couldn't enjoy living with a drunk, so maybe that was an effective angle to explore. Molly informed me that Duane Williams used to work on the loading dock. In fact the two met at the company twenty-five years ago.

"Why'd he leave?" I asked. "Did he get a better job?"

"Don't know," Molly said furrowing her brow. "It was before my time."

"So what's he doing now?"

"I think he's on some kind of disability," Molly replied. "Teresa has to take him to the doctor sometimes. He's got some chronic something-or-other."

Poor man, I thought—in chronic pain and relying on a drunk to bring home the bacon.

Just then Teresa arrived and Molly ushered her in. Even though it was a hot October day, Teresa was dressed fashionably, if primly, with long sleeves and a scarf around her neck. If ever there was a person in the world who could use a little bit of the unbuttoned look, it was Teresa. She looked armed for battle with her ramrod straight back and her multiple layers of makeup. The only incongruities were her obviously bloodshot eyes and her slightly swollen lip, though she had minimized the effect of the injury with clever use of lip-liner.

"Ms. Mandelbaum," Teresa began stiffly. Everything about this woman was stiff.

"Please, call me Claire," I urged with more friendliness than I felt.

"Claire," Teresa continued, allowing a brief, forced smile, "I know I promised no more absences. The reason I missed work on Monday was because of a fall. I tripped and banged my lip on a cabinet.

"Do you have a doctor's note?" I asked. The time for phony excuses was officially over. The agreement we reached last time was that all medical absences would have to be documented.

"Well, I'm actually between family doctors right now. . . ."

"But I assume you went to the hospital? That's a nasty bump," I observed, all the while imagining Teresa falling-down drunk too embarrassed and incapacitated to go anywhere.

"Well, I've had some bad experiences at White Plains and I didn't feel up to driving to Yonkers," Teresa continued.

"Couldn't your husband have driven you over?"

At the mention of her husband, Teresa flinched. "Please, keep him out of this," she said unsteadily. For goodness sake, I thought, he lives with you; he's got to know what's going on.

I pondered how I could bring up her addiction in a way that Teresa could actually hear it. Her job was in jeopardy and yet she still wasn't willing to face the truth. The addiction had taken over her life. Perhaps she relied on the booze or whatever substance it was to give her strength to face the pressures of her job and the demands of caring for a disabled husband.

As I was trying to strategize what to say next, Teresa interrupted my thoughts and said in a flat voice, "I'm truly sorry I've inconvenienced the company so much. I guess I'm just accident prone."

Slowly, pathetically slowly, and late in this game, a light began to dawn.

"I think I know what's going on," I said quietly.

"Yes," she said dryly. She had regained her composure entirely. "I have an attendance and a tardiness problem."

"Yes, but that's not the real issue," I said. "And you don't have a substance abuse problem."

She suddenly looked less sour and less in control.

"I apologize for being an idiot," I continued. "Someone is hurting you."

My statement hung in the air. She didn't even bother to deny it. The poor woman dressed that way and painted her face to cover the bruises. She was being hurt at home and the pressures from work only made it worse.

"You can't continue this way," I said gently.

"I know I've missed a lot of work. . ." Teresa began.

"I couldn't care less about work right now. Teresa, are you safe?"

"I don't know," she said softly as her eyes welled with tears. We sat for a moment in silence. "Two months ago I would have laughed off the question," Teresa continued, "but now I'm scared." Slowly she unwound the scarf around her neck and I saw dark red marks on her throat. "He tried to choke me. My eyes were so bloodshot and the bruises were so ugly I just couldn't come in on Monday." Tears leaked from her eyes, streaking her foundation.

I wanted to ask why the hell she stayed another minute with her husband. I was tempted to wonder aloud how such an intelligent, tough, well-put-together woman could allow someone to mistreat her that way. Luckily, I asked the right question instead.

"What can I do to help?"

"I don't know. I think I need to leave him, but I'm frightened. If I leave, Duane would have nothing to lose. He's threatened to kill me in the past, but I just thought it was the beer talking. He's always been a little aggressive when he drinks, but since he can't work anymore, he's been depressed and angry and has been taking it all out on me. He hangs around at home all day, watching TV, drinking beer, getting mad. When I get home he finds fault with everything I do. He says I'm a stuck-up bitch, that I think I'm better than him. It's not true! I don't think that. Honest to God. I just want to live in peace. . . ." She trailed off. I passed her the tissues.

"Teresa, you have to be safe," I said. "I can help keep your job safe—don't worry about that," I assured her, "but we have to make sure that you're physically safe."

"I can't leave. He's home all the time. I can't pack my stuff up. He wouldn't let me go."

"Do you have a cell phone?"

"He smashed it. And when he's mad, he pulls the landline out of the wall."

"Are you really ready to get out?"

"After what happened last Sunday," she said, adjusting her scarf, "I think I am. I passed out. I could have died. I'm not giving up on seeing my grandbabies."

"You have grandchildren?"

"Not yet. But I figure that if I can live long enough, my kids might settle down and give me some." She actually smiled. The brittleness was gone. It was as if I was seeing her for the first time.

"Where are your kids?"

"One's in California and the other is in Oregon."

"Do they know what's going on?" I asked.

"They know their dad is having trouble," Teresa replied, "but they have no idea how bad it's been. He's always been a mean drunk, but now he's getting drunk all the time, and he's much more violent than he used to be."

"Does anyone else know?" I asked.

"I think my secretary might suspect, but I haven't talked to anyone. You're the first person I've told."

We needed a plan. As Teresa sat on the couch in my office, I contacted my friend Toby at the domestic violence shelter. We needed to get Duane out of the house long enough to pack Teresa up and get her to a safe house. Teresa also needed to secure an order of protection and to let her kids know what was going on. There would be tons of details—canceling credit cards, removing items from the safety deposit box, taking half the money out of their joint checking account—Toby gave us a whole checklist. But for now, physical safety was the top priority. Teresa adamantly refused to go to the police but reluctantly accepted my insistent suggestion that we photograph her neck and lip. Turns out she also had huge purple bruises on her arms from where

Duane had grabbed her. My private bathroom came in handy. Oh, the perks of being upper management! Teresa washed off layers of makeup to reveal a rainbow of bruised and mottled skin. I took photos with my cell phone and emailed them to my account. Modern technology documented a problem as old as humankind.

"I could pretend to send you to a conference. That would allow you to pack up," I suggested as Teresa reapplied her makeup.

"Duane might not let me go," Teresa said, uncertainly. "And besides, what I really want, I couldn't possibly pack up in front of him. I want the kids' albums, my gardening books, my letters, and my Dawn doll collection." She'd obviously given this some serious thought.

"What are Dawn dolls?" I couldn't help asking.

"Sort of like Barbies, only cooler," Teresa explained with a smile. "They were really popular in the seventies. They sold at half the price of Barbies, and were all the rage with the girls in my neighborhood. I've been collecting them since I was a little girl."

"I could see where packing up photographs and dolls for a conference might appear suspicious," I agreed. "How about if we send Duane someplace?"

"He almost never leaves the house anymore."

"Not even for a Rangers game?" I asked, and our plan began to fall into place.

36

The only person I knew who could get me good tickets to any sports event in New York on short notice was Jeremy. We had to talk about stuff with Sam anyway, and I had to admit that our last few encounters were friendly, so I decided to give it a try. I called Jeremy and we agreed that he would take Sam for the last two weeks in December. Amazing. Then, I broached the question.

"Are you up for doing a mitzvah?"

"Absolutely," he responded. "What's up?"

Without naming names or giving the details, I explained Teresa's situation. "The only way I can get this woman to safety is if we get her husband out of the house. As soon as she's safely at the shelter, I'll file for an order of protection."

"How can I help?" Jeremy asked.

"Well, your fancy-pants firm always has good seats to sporting events, right? How about a fabulous ticket to a Rangers game?"

"Happy to oblige. In fact, I can get him a rinkside ticket. Why don't I take Sam to the same game? We'll sit a few seats back and if he leaves early, I could give you a call."

"Jeremy, this guy is dangerous. I don't want you or Sam to go near him."

"Understood."

"But if you could keep an eye on him from a distance, that would be fabulous."

The next few days were nerve-wracking. I was still spending part of every evening and morning at Joanie's house. Slowly, she was re-engaging with her kids and her life. A lot of my mental energy was spent fretting about Teresa. We got her a special 911 phone that would immediately notify police of her location. She didn't have to talk into it or anything, just press "1" and it would send an alert to the local cops. We made advance arrangements with the police, notifying them that if they received a 911 call from Teresa's phone, it could involve a dangerous domestic dispute. I prepared the paperwork for the order of protection, delineating the latest incidents and Teresa's well-founded fear for her safety. Eventually we'd want Duane out, but for now, she had to make it out of the house and out of the marriage without harm.

Although she didn't change any of her other finances or touch Duane's disability check, Teresa rerouted the direct deposit of her not insubstantial salary to a new account. For the first time in her entire life, she would have her own money. Until this point, everything she earned had gone to either her father or her husband. Teresa operated on allowances from the men in her life, who doled out cash for groceries and questioned each item on her credit card. It was liberating, but clearly also disconcerting, for her to imagine having her own money to spend as she pleased.

Teresa managed to make it to Thursday, the night of the game, without getting hurt or giving herself away. She'd convinced Duane that she'd won the ticket in an office raffle. She would drop him off at the train station, where he would catch a train to the city, and then take a subway to Madison Square Garden. She counted on having at least four hours to pack up her car and get out of there. Teresa told me that she'd been careful to make absolutely no advanced preparations.

As soon as she dropped him off, Teresa called me. "He's been drinking, but I think he's OK."

"Just get everything done as quickly as possible," I told her. "No matter what, put your safety first. I'll call if there are any problems on my end. Be sure to pick up the phone. If you don't, I'm going to assume there's trouble and call the police."

"OK, I'm on it."

Teresa was going to pack entirely on her own. She didn't want to risk involving anyone else, and she certainly didn't want anyone else's car in front of the house.

I was a nervous wreck. I couldn't even watch TV. At 7:07 the game would start. Duane would be engrossed and Teresa would be on her way to safety.

At 7:20 Jeremy called. “Hey, Claire, I don’t see the guy. There’s no one sitting in his assigned seat.”

“Could he be out getting a hot dog or something?”

“I don’t know. He missed the faceoff.”

“Maybe he’s just running late,” I suggested.

“I guess, but why would the guy come late? Look, I’ll call you in another half hour.”

I called Jeremy again fifteen minutes later. Still no Duane. I decided I’d better call Teresa.

“Hi there,” I said, trying not to sound as alarmed as I felt. “Duane hasn’t shown up yet at the Garden. Teresa, I think you need to get out of there.”

“But hardly anything’s packed,” she cried. “I thought I’d have more time.”

“I’m sorry, but I think you need to go. Teresa, nothing’s irreplaceable but you.”

“I just need a little more time. Even if he turned right around, he couldn’t be back from the city for another forty minutes or so.”

“Teresa, please,” I begged. “Look, let’s not waste precious time arguing. I’ll call you again in fifteen minutes. Make sure you pick up the phone.”

My heart raced and I could actually feel my blood pressure rising. If anything happened to Teresa I would never forgive myself.

I called Jeremy again. He confirmed that Duane was still a no-show.

“Do you need us to come home?” Jeremy offered.

“No, that’s very kind of you but there’s nothing you can do. Enjoy the game with Sam and call me immediately if you see a tall guy with a crew cut and a beer belly.”

“You’ve just described fifty percent of the guys here. But I’ll keep a look out, and if anyone takes that seat I promise I’ll call.”

There were ten minutes left before I could call Teresa again. There was no point in interrupting her packing again and slowing her down. The second hand on the kitchen wall clock was mocking me, making an ungodly racket. I’d never felt so helpless. I paced. I actually wrung my hands, a gesture that seemed natural though I can’t recall ever having done it before. Oh, how I wished I could talk to Rob. Oh, how I wished I could pray.

My cell phone rang and I lunged for it. It was Marjorie on the line.

"Sorry, Marjorie. I have an emergency, I have to keep the phone free."

"Claire, are you O—" Marjorie didn't even get in the "K" before I hung up on her.

Finally it was time. My hands were shaking as I punched in the numbers. Teresa picked up on the second ring.

"All clear. You'd be proud of me I'm just stuffing things into suitcases, not bothering to fold a. . . ." There was a pause. "Oh, hi, Duane," I heard Teresa say. I was able to hear only some of what transpired next. Teresa was explaining that she'd gotten the phone from work. She asked Duane, "How was the game?" and the phone went dead.

Immediately I called 911 and requested Officer Arnold, the cop we had consulted. We'd arranged things with him ahead of time and he promised he'd go to Teresa's if there was any trouble. When we were connected, Officer Arnold told me that he was on another call but would be there soon. Meanwhile, he dispatched a black-and-white to Teresa's house. He assured me that they would be there in less than five minutes.

God, I thought. A lot could happen in five minutes. I couldn't stand it another second. I jumped in the car and raced like a madwoman to Teresa's house, which was less than a quarter of a mile away. With any luck I'd lead a patrol car right to her house. Unfortunately, no one stopped me and there were no cop cars in front when I got there.

I ran to the door and leaned on the bell. Duane came to the door. I could smell the beer on his breath.

"Mr. Williams?" I asked as sweetly as I could, trying not to hyperventilate. "I'm so sorry to bother you at home, but there's an emergency at work and I must talk to Teresa."

"She's not home," he growled, shutting the door in my face.

I rang again, leaving my thumb on the doorbell, which kept on ringing, ding-dong, ding-dong, keeping pace with my racing heartbeat.

"For fuck's sake," he screamed as he jerked open the door. "Teresa isn't home. Leave me alone."

I had to keep him talking. If he was talking to me, he couldn't be pummeling Teresa.

"Can I leave her a message? I wouldn't bother you if it weren't really urgent."

There was a crash from behind the door. He turned to look and I could see Teresa running out the back door.

"Help!" she screamed. "Help!" she repeated. "Call the police."

"Now look what you've done, you stupid bitch," Duane said. His face took on an ugly expression as he lunged forward to slap me. Luckily, he was pretty drunk and unsteady on his feet, and I was able to dodge the blow. Duane stumbled. I ran to my car and locked myself inside. Duane was right behind me. He was banging on the hood with his fists and the whole car shook. I saw the neighbors across the street let Teresa in. I leaned on my horn and called 911. I hung up as I heard the sirens and saw the cruiser approach.

The uniforms came to my car as Duane was kicking the driver's door. Duane was so wasted or angry or both that he didn't have the sense not to hit the cop who approached him. They had Duane on the ground, handcuffed, after he took a few wild swings.

Moments later, Officer Arnold arrived on the scene. He was over six feet tall, bald, with a muscular chest and biceps bulging through his button-down shirt. Though I was desperate to see Teresa, Officer Arnold insisted on interviewing me first. I told him as best I could what had transpired that evening and asked again after Teresa.

"She's OK, ma'am. A little shaken, but OK."

"Where is she now?" I asked.

"A medic is checking her out and then we'll take her statement."

"And Duane?" I asked.

"He's in custody, ma'am."

"Is there any chance he'll be out tonight?"

"No, ma'am. He assaulted an officer. We don't take too kindly to that. He's not going anywhere but jail tonight."

"You're sure she's all right?" I asked again, sobbing with relief.

"Yes, ma'am. But I'll bet she could use a friend right now." I took that as my cue to pull myself together.

I hurried over to Teresa, who was just emerging from the neighbor's home.

We hugged and I squeezed her tight.

"Thank God, thank God," I murmured.

She was very pale and I saw from Teresa's face that she'd been less successful in dodging Duane's blows than I had.

"Are you OK?" I asked, determined to keep it together.

"I'll be fine."

Teresa had to give her statement to Officer Arnold. I got to stay once I explained that I was her lawyer, which I kind of was. I was licensed to practice in New York and Teresa was now officially my pro bono client.

Officer Arnold raised his eyebrows, and I thought I could detect a bit of a smirk on his face. I was dressed in sweats and I doubt that I looked very lawyer-like.

"You're one full-service lawyer, ma'am," he said, looking me up and down.

"If the client dies, you don't get paid," I explained.

He gave me a wide smile as he nodded his head in apparent approval of my business model.

Teresa walked Officer Arnold through the events of the night. Apparently, Duane never got on the train to New York. He drank a few extra beers at the station and managed to get so drunk that they wouldn't let him board. He fueled his frustration with a few more drinks at the station and then took a cab back home, surprising Teresa in the middle of her phone conversation with me. Although he was drunk, Duane eventually noticed the open suitcases and realized that Teresa was packing up to leave him. He smashed the phone and then told Teresa that they were both going to die that night.

"He meant it," Teresa told us quietly. "His voice had this eerie calm. He brought in a huge knife from the kitchen and made me watch as he lopped off the heads of all of my Dawn dolls."

"Oh my God, that's awful," I exclaimed. Officer Arnold shot me a look. I resolved to keep quiet for the rest of the interview.

"He said he was practicing," Teresa said flatly, "and when he was done with the dolls, it would be my turn, then his."

"We'll make sure to monitor him in jail, ma'am; he'll be on suicide watch," Officer Arnold told her, intuiting that even after all that happened, Teresa didn't want any harm to come to Duane.

After the police were done talking to Teresa, she and I went back to the house to clean up. We collected the mangled, decapitated bodies of the dolls Teresa had lovingly collected since she was a little girl. I noticed that the rest of the house was spotless.

"You were right. I should have just left without my stuff. These Dawn dolls are no good to anyone now," Teresa said, and for the first time since this ordeal began, she started to cry. "But at least you have your clothes, and your books, and your albums. And most important, you're safe," I said, squeezing her hand.

Teresa stood in the middle of the room looking around helplessly. Now that she was no longer in danger, she didn't seem to know what to do or where to turn.

"Come to my house tonight," I insisted. "You've been through hell; you shouldn't be alone right now. Though I should warn you, my place is a bit of a mess."

Teresa agreed to come with me. After I called Jeremy and told him everything was OK, we packed an overnight bag and drove to my house. I took a detour along the way and bought five different flavors of ice cream—the good, artery-clogging stuff.

"I don't know about you," I said, "but I feel like we've been through a war. At the end of a war there should at least be a little ice cream."

37

I woke up at 6:00 a.m. to a scratchy rhythmic sound. Teresa was scrubbing my kitchen counters. I tried to protest, but Teresa was unmovable.

"You saved my life; I'm cleaning your kitchen. It's an old Italian tradition. You weren't kidding when you said the place was a mess."

I didn't even bother to pretend to be offended. The place was pretty gross.

"Do you always get up this early?" I asked as I made us some coffee.

"That's when I get my housework done. Duane would be sleeping off his beer and the house would be peaceful. I'd get the place really clean, do laundry, and do as much advance prep for dinner as I could. The only challenge was the bedroom. With Duane home all the time, there never seemed to be a good time to get in there to do a deep cleaning."

"Oh, so that's what the hour from six to seven is for," I said as I passed her the cream and sugar. "As you can see, I've been sleeping right through cleaning time."

"Seriously, why are you living like this? I'm not saying that you have to clean it yourself, but you can afford to hire someone to come in."

"Well, I guess I'm a natural slob who inherited my Bubbe's disdain for any woman who didn't do all the cleaning work herself. I realize it's sexist and stupid."

"Not to mention a health code violation," Teresa added. "I'm going to put up some red sauce in your slow cooker. . . ."

"I have a slow cooker?" I asked in astonishment.

"Yep, bottom right cabinet, towards the back. This kitchen could be great, Claire. You have everything you need."

"Except the will to clean it at six in the morning."

"Get somebody else to do it. Meanwhile, I'll have some sauce ready for you for tonight."

"Sam and I are going out to a friend's for dinner tonight. There's no need to bother," I told her.

"OK, I'll make it for you and you'll have it another night. I'm Italian on my mom's side and I learned the recipe from my Nonna. It has to cook for at least five hours."

"Wow, you're hardcore," I observed.

Teresa smiled. She looked relaxed with no makeup and her hair in a bandana. I doubt she got a lot of sleep the previous night and she was still puffy under her left eye where Duane had slapped her, but clearly she had a huge weight lifted off her shoulders.

"Whatever else happens," Teresa said, "I'll be at my desk at 9:00. I can't thank you enough."

"I'm just grateful that it all worked out and you're safe. I'm going to file the motion for a protective order and get the ball rolling on some of the legal stuff. Officer Arnold promised me that they wouldn't release Duane without giving us advance notice, but just in case, I'll amend the protective order to bar Duane from going to the house, the company campus, or getting closer than 100 yards to you."

"Is there any way we can get Duane into treatment? He's not a bad guy when he's not drinking."

"Now that he's in trouble with the law, he may be a whole lot more motivated to seek help for his drinking problem. What he probably needs is a residential program, which your insurance will probably pay for. I can talk to the prosecutor. But for now, I want the bail set high and I want him in jail drying out."

Sam had slept at Jeremy's house, so it was a particularly quiet and calm morning. Teresa insisted that I eat something before I went to the gym. I don't think I'd realized before how bossy she was, though honestly, I didn't mind. It helped that her French toast and poached eggs were delicious. I was tempted to invite her to come live with me permanently. She could be my wife any day.

"You're welcome to stay on for few days. And I'm not just inviting you so you can reform my dissolute habits. I'm going to take your advice and hire a cleaning service."

"Thanks, but I want to go home. I want to thank the Kenneys, my neighbors from across the street, and I just want to be in my own bed."

"That makes sense. I think I'd want the same in your position," I said, not that I could really fathom what Teresa had been through. My two minutes with Duane were scary enough and I had the size-ten shoe imprint on my car door to prove it.

"I really don't even know what to say to you," Teresa said her eyes filling with tears. "How can I thank you? I could never have left him without your help, and, literally, you saved. . . ."

"Please, you don't have to say anything. We both have a lot to be grateful for. I'm just so relieved everything turned out OK." We hugged and agreed we'd talk later in the day, after she called her kids.

I decided to look in on Joanie before heading for the gym. Things were certainly better, but Joanie still wasn't back to her old self. The kids were still getting cold cereal for breakfast—something they loved—but it was a clear indicator that Joanie wasn't fully back in the saddle.

As the kids ate, I had a second cup of tea with Joanie and Aaron, and whispered to them about the events of the night before.

"How awful. Can you imagine feeling unsafe in your own home?" Joanie asked, grabbing Aaron's hand and squeezing it tightly. Their eyes locked. The kids looked up from their cereal. We could all sense the deep feeling in the room.

38

Sam and I arrived at Marjorie's house just as Rob and Beverly were walking in.

"Rabbi Reuven," Sam called and rushed up to meet Rob.

"*Gut Shabbes*," Rob said, sticking out his hand. "Great to see you, Sam."

"Nice to see you, too," Sam replied, returning the handshake.

Who the hell taught him to do that? I wondered.

Rob introduced Sam to Beverly, who looked stunning in a pink and white checked suit with a black silk camisole underneath. Pink teardrop pearls hung from her ears and she wore two-inch black heels that made her slightly taller than Rob. Man, that woman knew how to dress.

"How is Joan doing?" Beverly asked me as we handed our coats to Marjorie.

"Better," I said. "But she still has a long way to go."

"She certainly has her hands full with those four little ones. Please give her my very best and let her know that she's in my thoughts and prayers," Beverly said.

I apologized to Marjorie for my abrupt hang-up the night before. It felt like a week had gone by, but it was less than twenty-four hours earlier that I'd been frantic about Teresa.

Next, Jack introduced me to Seth Feldman, a short, slim, and dapper man with a thin mustache. Within the first few minutes of our meeting, Seth let me know that he was head of cardiology at White Plains Hospital, on the New York Philharmonic Society board of directors, and, most ominous of all, recently single. I immediately regretted my decision to wear lipstick and something a bit low-cut. I was trying to look nice that evening, something I rarely attempted and even more rarely pulled off.

Dr. Feldman was obviously my ambush blind date. It was unclear whether he knew about this set-up in advance.

We gathered awkwardly around the dining room table, which was set with china, crystal, real silverware, and cloth napkins. Beverly was seated on my left, Dr. Feldman on my right. Jack sat at the head of the table and Rob sat opposite me between Sam and Ben. Rob and the boys seemed to be reliving, with great animation, the highlights of the broom ball playoffs. Marjorie sat at the foot of the dining table near the kitchen. Next to her was Ben's older brother Stuart, who apparently was going to help serve the meal.

We began with *Shalom Aleichem*, the song for greeting the Sabbath, and I was startled by Rob's voice, which was rich and soulful with a subtle vibrato. Rob made the blessing over the wine and Ben and Stuart said *motzei* over the *challah*. We sat down to Marjorie's homemade matzo ball soup. It was delicious, if a bit sweet for my taste. Chunks of carrot and translucent wedges of onion bobbed against the obscenely large and fluffy matzo ball. Marjorie shared her chicken stock recipe with Beverly, not that Beverly had asked. I caught the fact that the secret ingredient was sweet potato while half-listening to Dr. Feldman proclaim his love of chamber music. Words like "transcendent" and "intimate," and then, more disturbing, "deeply penetrates." Was this guy still talking about music or did he just ask me to have sex with him? I was pretty sure that he was still talking about Brahms' chamber and not mine, but I had to admit my mind had been wandering during his long and passionate declamation.

"I once had the distinct pleasure of seeing André Previn direct Smetana's *The Moldau*," Dr. Feldman announced in a booming voice to the entire table. "I have placed four violins on long-term loan for some very gifted Julliard students. The school kindly invited me to a master class taught by the Maestro. Did you know that Mr. Previn's first love is chamber music? In any case, you, Rabbi, certainly you would be intrigued by the Smetana."

Rob, so abruptly torn from his broom ball play-by-play, looked like a deer caught in the headlights. Beverly couldn't hide her concern, rightfully recognizing Dr. Feldman's foray as a test that Rob hadn't studied for and couldn't pass.

Jack, however, stepped in. In his thick Israeli accent Jack began, "Of course, all Jews recognize the melody for *Hatikvah* when we listen to that piece. Are you aware, Seth," (which Jack pronounced as "Set") "that the Czechs deeply object to the title you used? Moldau is the name the German occupiers gave to the river. Czechs prefer the name Vltava for the river and for Smetana's symphonic poem. Last time I heard Smetana's *The Vltava* was with my mother in Israel. The entire auditorium stood up for the theme that we Israelis have co-opted for our national anthem."

Wow, I thought. I love Jack. Dr. Feldman clearly hadn't known that tidbit about the piece and now apparently had to choose between being musically ignorant or appearing to be a Nazi sympathizer.

Beverly, however, wasn't pleased with the direction the conversation had taken. She obviously saw no percentage in taking Dr. Feldman down a peg or two. She leaned across me and asked the deflated doc for suggestions about an adult education program at the synagogue. "We would so appreciate your input and were hoping that you might be able to prevail upon some of the music students you sponsor to play."

This cheered up Dr. Feldman enough to mention his last meeting with the late Isaac Stern, whom he pronounced "a magnetic personality." Stuart and Marjorie cleared the soup bowls, and I noticed that Sam and Rob continued their animated conversation. At least someone is having a good time, I thought.

As Stuart passed the salad around, Dr. Feldman chose a new topic, closer to his professional interests. "Go easy on that dressing, Rabbi," he advised.

Rob looked up from his plate.

"Don't forget, Rabbi, I know your cholesterol levels. I see too many men your age with premature heart attacks. They know nothing about proper nutrition. They think they're still nineteen and can eat whatever they want. For instance, some of the men who come to see me claim that they've switched from high fat lunches to salads, but when I inquire further, it seems that they also throw in a few hard-boiled eggs, pile on the cheese, and slather buttermilk dressing all over it."

"There's no dairy in this meal," Marjorie interjected, horrified. "Our kitchen is strictly kosher."

"Of course," said Dr. Feldman. "But that means you use margarine, which is full of dangerous trans-fats."

"So you find that even with adequate exercise, diet is an important factor for lowering cholesterol?" Beverly asked pointedly, looking right at Rob, who smiled sheepishly.

"Absolutely," Dr. Feldman agreed. This initiated an animated conversation between Beverly and Dr. Feldman about proper diet for the middle-aged set. They had a particularly rousing discussion about omega-3 eggs and whether free-range added to nutrition. I felt like the fatty yellow yoke surrounded by lean, virtuous egg whites.

"I can tell that you're very knowledgeable, *Rebbetzin*, do you have any nutritional training?" Dr. Feldman asked.

Beverly flushed with pleasure. "No, but I do think people have a duty to take care of themselves and learn the facts about health and nutrition. God gives you only one body, right? You have to take care of it."

So being fat wasn't just unhealthy, it was also ungrateful? According to Beverly, I was pissing off God. Did Rob concur with this view? God sits idly by during the Holocaust but intervenes to punish those of us fatties who have second helpings or cover our salads with creamy dressings? Surely, I thought, Rob would be offended by her sanctimonious tone.

"Bev, tell Seth where you work," Rob encouraged, sounding not at all irritated by Beverly's obvious dig at his eating habits.

"I work at the Hadassah Thrift Shop," Beverly said. "We raise money for the hospital in Jerusalem and we're able to help local young women who are looking for affordable, quality work clothes."

"Bev is being modest," Rob interjected. "She runs the place and stocks it with gorgeous, used professional clothes, which she solicits from houses of worship all over Westchester. Recently, Bev received a New York State grant to help women coming off welfare re-enter the job market," Rob continued with obvious pride. "Bev assists these women in getting the right interview outfit. She also runs resume workshops, and conducts mock interviews. It's a real mitzvah and a perfect fit with her entrepreneurial skills. If she wasn't a *rebbetzin*, she'd have been a CEO." I was struck by the realization that Rob spoke with genuine affection.

"Reuven, please," Beverly said, embarrassed but also clearly gratified.

"I should tell my ex about this place," Dr. Feldman said bitterly. "Shopping for clothes with my credit card was her favorite hobby. Now, of course, she's too fat for most of the clothing she bought. If she donated them, at least all those expensive designer items could go to some use."

"We'd be grateful to get the donations, I'm sure," said Beverly.

"Can anyone shop there?" I asked, more out of politeness than interest.

"Yes, we encourage everyone to shop. The women going from public assistance to work use vouchers, so for us to have any cash flow, we need other folks to buy as well."

"There are beautiful clothes and really good bargains," Marjorie added.

"I try to make sure everything is in good condition and arrange the shop by size and color," Beverly explained. Leaning over, Beverly smiled sweetly and told me in a conspiratorial whisper, "We have some lovely things in your size, I'm sure."

Delicious as it was, the rest of the meal—chicken, carrots, potato kugel, and chocolate cake with trans-fat frosting—was hard to choke down. Did Beverly really believe that I was worried about finding my size? Did she think I was afraid that the shop carried nothing above a size 8? Had she meant to insult me or did she just assume that any woman my size would need such reassurance?

As I accepted a second slice of cake, Beverly and Marjorie started chatting about books. I was surprised to hear how much recent fiction Marjorie had read. It turned out she was an English major at Tel Aviv University; that was where she met Jack. Artfully, Beverly tried to switch the conversation over to the synagogue library. She was clearly hoping that sometime soon it would be called the Feldman library, bankrolled by the music-lover and fatty-hater on my right.

I was desperate to go home, but it was rare to see Sam so happy and so full of life. Besides, my date, who apparently wasn't a big reader, had turned his attention back to me. In response to his questions I explained what I do.

"So you're a lawyer?" he asked archly.

"Yes. A Cornell '01 grad," I replied.

"Hmm, I'm a Cornell grad myself," he said meaningfully. "Although, I don't know, can a lawyer and doctor find true love?"

OK, this was definitely a date and he was trying to be charming despite my girth, which was big of him.

"As long as we avoid the subject of caps on med-mal recovery, I'll bet we could manage to get along," I was irritated to hear myself say. Apparently everyone else heard it too. Although not exactly a declaration of love, this was way more encouraging than I'd meant to sound.

"We'll have to test that hypothesis, sometime," Dr. Feldman said with a smile. "Maybe you could come with me to the Philharmonic."

"That would be lovely," I lied. Note to self: I'm always busy. Or if we do go out, order Fettuccine Alfredo and cheesecake. That would give him a heart attack.

"I just need to clear off. Why doesn't everyone go into the living room?" Marjorie invited.

"Rabbi, would you care to play some chess?" Jack asked.

"I'd love to. Boys, do you want to play?" Rob replied.

"I fancy myself quite a chess aficionado; may I join you?" Dr. Feldman asked.

"Sure, that would be great," Rob said warmly, and then turned to Jack. "How many boards do you have?"

"We can set up three," Stuart said with enthusiasm, and then looked at his mom.

The boys were told that if they cleared the table they could join the chess mania in the living room.

"Let me help you in the kitchen," Beverly insisted as she went to her bag and retrieved a pair of yellow rubber gloves.

Marjorie was flabbergasted. "You actually carry those around?"

"Well, I want to protect my hands and it isn't sanitary to share gloves," Beverly said.

In a replay of what I remembered from my Bubbe's house, the women headed off to the kitchen to clean up while the men went to the living room to play chess. We chatted as we washed dishes and Beverly scrubbed the kitchen into a high gleam. At the risk of being hit with every recipe, I complimented Marjorie on the fantastic Shabbes dinner.

"I'm glad you liked it," she said. "What did you think of Seth?"

"He seems to love classical music," I said noncommittally.

"I hope you don't mind my inviting him. He's been going through a rough time since his wife left. Jack says that he's really been thrown by it."

"What happened?" I asked.

"Well, we probably shouldn't talk about it. . . ." I could tell that Marjorie was dying to tell me and only the presence of the rebbetzin was inhibiting her.

"Was it another man?" I prompted.

"Not exactly," Marjorie said slyly.

"Another woman?" I asked, intrigued.

"At least she won't have to pick up dirty socks and underwear," Beverly said.

Marjorie gave me a meaningful look and redirected our conversation—or at least I hoped that's what she was doing. "Claire, you look great. Have you lost weight?" she asked me.

"A little," I said, very pleased. "Mostly, I've toned up a bit. I've been going to the gym."

"Oy, the gym!" Beverly exclaimed. "Reuven eats a dozen blintzes with gallons of sour cream but then insists on going to the gym whenever he can. He's obsessed with the place. God forbid he should miss a morning."

I was thrilled to hear what Beverly was saying. Those mornings at the gym were just as important to Rob as they were to me. And, whereas I was fleeing the angry one who was thrilled to have me leave the house, Rob had to get by Beverly.

"Rabbi Reuven is great with the kids," Marjorie observed.

"That's because he's just a big kid himself," Beverly said with a sigh but without any bitterness. "I wish he would spend more time cultivating potential donors like Seth Feldman," she said wistfully.

"He's playing chess with Seth right now," I said.

"Knowing Reuven, he won't let Seth win," Beverly said.

"Maybe Seth will beat the rabbi," I suggested.

"Not likely. Reuven's a chess master," Beverly said.

"Oh yes, Rabbi Reuven challenges the kids to a chess competition every year where he plays over twenty simultaneous games," Marjorie gushed. "He's very talented."

"He hustled games in Washington Square Park when he was at the Seminary. I used to wander around the vintage clothing shops while Reuven would earn enough for us to have dinner at the Second Avenue Deli," Beverly said with what could be mistaken for nostalgia.

39

It had been thirty days since baby Mimi was lost. Joanie was unquestionably doing better. She was re-engaged with the kids and back to many of her old routines. She was cooking, gardening, and doing yoga, but she didn't quite have her old sparkle. Aaron told me that she still cried in the shower when she thought no one could hear her.

Although traditionally there was no *Shloshim* service for a miscarriage, Rob had told me that new rituals had been created for mourning the loss of a baby in utero. We all agreed that some sort of ceremony was called for and the thirtieth day after Mimi died seemed right.

We gathered in Joanie's house. Jake and the twins were with a babysitter down the street, but Sarah was there sitting next to Joanie and holding her hand. Marjorie and Jack had arrived. I was touched to see Dr. Lewis. Joanie's pediatrician and her husband had come, as had a bunch of Sisterhood ladies I didn't know and a friend from Joanie's yoga group. Aaron's mother was on a three-month freighter cruise, which was just as well. She was a difficult, highly critical woman even in the best of circumstances. She believed herself too young to be a grandmother and every time Joanie spit out another kid, it was another wound to her mother-in-law's vanity. The woman was none too welcoming about Jake, and God knows what ridiculous things she would have said about Mimi's loss being "for the best."

We gathered in the living room, and just as we were about to begin, I was startled to see Sam slip in the back and waive awkwardly to Rob. It never occurred to me to invite Sam to this, but either Rob or Joan must have done so. Rob began by encouraging everyone to sit in a circle. Then he quoted from the Book of Job, "*Adonai Natan, V'Adonai*

Lakach, Yehi Shem Adonai Mivorach. God gave to us, and God took from us. Blessed be the name of God."

God was something Rob and I didn't talk about. Did Rob really believe that a loving God took Mimi away from Joanie and Aaron? If such a personal God made the choice to whisk away this innocent, unborn child, should He be getting top billing in the ceremony? How about a little anger instead?

"We gather here today to mourn the untimely passing of Mimi, a child we never got to know but a soul already much loved." Rob's voice remained steady and comforting. "Even though Mimi never made it to our world, she affected it profoundly. Mimi's conception was evidence of the deep love between Joan and Aaron. Mimi embodied a connection to the Jewish people that is reflected in the daily lives of the Cohen family. She became a repository for our collective hopes for the future. We had visions of Mimi's birth, her naming ceremony, her bat mitzvah, her graduation from college, her wedding."

Tears were rolling down Aaron's cheeks. Marjorie looked stricken. A bunch of the Sisterhood ladies were weeping openly. Joanie looked pale but composed, holding Sarah's hand.

Suddenly, I flashed on a scene at the cemetery over thirty-five years ago. My father was sobbing. Grandpa Sam was propping up Bubbe, who was barely able to walk, and Lydia was holding my hand. She must have been about thirteen at the time. Lydia walked with me hand-in-hand to the hole in the earth where people took turns shoveling dirt onto the pine box below. Pop recoiled after the reverberating thump that followed his shovelful as if he'd suffered a physical blow. I remember feeling deeply grateful for Lydia's hand in mine. All the adults were so mired in their grief that I think they forgot I was even there. Lydia had been at my side ever since we were both called into the principal's office and told that my mother had died. I was nervous when it was my turn to shovel the dirt, but Lydia helped me and never let go of my hand. I could still remember the support her hands gave me as our fingers intermeshed. Perhaps Sarah and Joanie would provide that sort of comfort for each other.

Rob continued, "Instead of gathering for these happy occasions, we are here with you, Joan, Aaron, and Sarah, to express our grief at your terrible loss. We acknowledge your pain and we share it with you. You have lost a precious part of your family. We have all missed out on the *nachas* of watching Mimi grow into a daughter of Israel."

Rob's words evoked raw emotion and the grief felt almost physical, like a heavy blanket that weighed on everyone's shoulders. But there was, undeniably, another force in Joanie's living room as well. The sorrow that wrapped us together wasn't warm or cozy, but it connected us together in a powerful, honest way. However smothering the sadness was, none of us had to experience it alone. We were in it together with Joanie and Aaron.

Rob asked Aaron and Joanie if they would like to say a few words. Aaron began, reading haltingly from a crumpled page he extracted from his shirt pocket: "We will never fully recover from losing Mimi, but I already see that Mimi brought our family many gifts. She reminded us that life is unpredictable and that we have to cherish every day. She reminded us that birth is a miracle that we sometimes take for granted. She reminded us that we have been blessed with four healthy children, and that their health and growth is our reason for living. In memory of Mimi, we are making a contribution to our synagogue's youth group and to The Gateway, an organization that offers help to New York City youth. Our hope for her was that her life would include service to the people of Israel and to the wider world. She will never get that chance, so Joan and I decided that we will do the mitzvah in her name. Had Mimi lived, we would have been able, thank God, to give her everything she needed, materially, intellectually, and, I hope spiritually. Many kids are not so lucky. These two organizations fill a crucial need for children, and the money we set aside for Mimi's schooling will go to these causes."

Joanie spoke with more composure than I could have possibly mustered. She had no notes. "Mimi," she began, "you were named after my mother. I thought her life was too short, and she lived for sixty-three years. I wish you could have met all the wonderful people who were prepared to welcome you. Dr. Lewis would have helped bring you into this world. Dr. Rao would have kept you healthy. Your big sisters, Sarah and Rachel, would have taught you how to make friends and be a cool girl. Rabbi Reuven would have you leading the *Adon Olam* by the time you were three. When I wasn't looking, Auntie Claire would have fed you cookies from a box, which, if you were anything like your siblings, would have been your favorite kind. I can't help feeling that I let you down, my girl. I wish things could have been different. I promise to remember you always. I'll try to be more caring and compassionate because of you."

"*El Maleh Rachamim*, God full of compassion," Rob resumed, "please watch over the spirit of *Miriam bat Aharon v' Rut Yocheved*, Miriam, daughter of Aaron and Joan, *sh'yetzah l-olama*, who is now gone to her own world."

The group—even Sam—answered with a somber "Amen."

"May God who blessed our ancestors, Abraham and Sarah, Isaac and Rivkah, Jacob, Leah and Rachel, grant peace to this bereaved family. Shelter this family in the wings of your love and grant them peace. *Adonai*, source of all healing, help Joan and Aaron to find comfort among those who are here to mourn, and among all the mourners of Jerusalem. Joan, Aaron, Sarah, please allow us to comfort you and to offer our condolences."

Rob then led the group in the mourner's *Kaddish*, a special prayer in praise of God. The last time I'd heard it was at Pop's *shiva*. What God did to deserve all this praise, I'll never know. But I could see that it made Joanie feel better, and that was enough for me.

I suddenly realized the one person who was missing—Beverly. I asked one of the Sisterhood ladies who had set up coffee where the *rebbetzin* was and she told me that Beverly had sent the rum pound cake, but had been feeling unwell at the last moment and had been unable to attend herself.

All I wanted to do was throw my arms around Rob and weep on his shoulder. Instead, I had to content myself with a formal greeting.

"Nice to see you again, Rabbi," I said.

"Nice to see you, too, though I hope in future we'll meet at happier occasions," Rob said looking deeply into my eyes.

"It was a lovely service."

"I'm glad you thought so. I hope it was meaningful for Joan and Aaron."

"I think it meant a lot to everyone."

"I see Sam is here. I'm going to go say hi to him and compliment him for doing the important mitzvah of comforting the mourners," Rob said and departed, leaving me to talk with Bertha, Dr. Lewis' wife, who looked like a squat version of Eleanor Roosevelt.

"Did you taste the *rebbetzin*'s cake?" she boomed. "It's to die for. The *rebbetzin* is a talented baker." Apparently, Bertha, like me, could choke down some dessert even when she was very sad.

"Enjoy it in good health," Rob called to Bertha. Rob was having an earnest discussion with Sam about what happens to people when they die. I was trying to listen to his conversation, but Bertha was a commanding presence.

"In my day, when you had a miscarriage, the doctors just told you to get over it," Bertha continued. "Even my husband was trained that way, though now he knows better. He adores Joan and feels just terrible for her loss."

"Dr. Lewis was wonderful at the hospital," I said.

"People don't know it," Bertha leaned over to tell me, "but it kills him inside whenever he loses a baby, even when there is nothing he could have done. He has to act strong for the families, but it's hard on him too."

"We're always so keenly aware of our own hurts, but we rarely think about how tough it is for others, professional people especially," I observed.

"Well just look at the rabbi," Bertha said, nodding in agreement.

"What do you mean?" I asked.

"He looks out for everyone, but who looks out for him?"

"Well, he has Beverly," I said, suddenly riveted by this conversation.

I didn't know Bertha well, but the look she gave me couldn't be mistaken for anything but skepticism, tinged with contempt for my weak powers of observation.

"She's not here now," Bertha observed. "Cake—I don't care how good it is—is no substitute for moral support." Bertha lowered her voice, which still carried considerably. "Dr. Lewis, like any husband, has his faults. But you'd never hear me trumpeting them at the Hospital Auxiliary League fundraiser," Bertha said in a pointed whisper.

"So, Beverly's very critical?" I asked in as innocent a tone as I could muster.

"That woman has an opinion on everything," Bertha exclaimed without a hint of self-irony. "When I was doing the ordering for the gift shop, something I've done for twenty years without any complaints from anyone, she started interfering, making suggestions about new items I could order from these fancy catalogs of hers. All those yarmulkes she wanted me to order. Seriously, I don't care what old person in Jerusalem was making the merchandise she wanted me to sell. It just wasn't right for the gift shop."

I had this delicious image of a mud-wrestle between Bertha and Beverly. Sorry, Bertha, you might be heavier and louder, but Beverly would play dirtier if it meant getting her way.

It was time to go, so I rounded up Sam.

"It was really great that you came to this," I said to Sam as we cut across Joanie's garden.

"It's not like you invited me."

"No, I didn't. That was a mistake on my part. I underestimated you."

"I'm not as bad as you think I am."

"Sam," I said, tears flowing down my face as I was overcome with the emotion of the evening, "I don't think you're bad. I know you've got a good heart, and I know it's been hard for you this year."

"I'm really trying to do *kibood av v'aim*, the way Rabbi Reuven talked about, but I don't think you even notice."

"Rabbi Reuven talks about honoring your parents?" I asked, astonished.

"He talked about it at the Youth Group *dvar torah* and told us that even if our parents are unreasonable, they still deserve respect."

"Well, I am unreasonable," I said as I blew my nose.

"See, Mom, I'm trying to tell you something and you're making a joke out of it. That's why it's so hard to talk to you."

"You're right. I'm sorry. And I have noticed that you've been more respectful lately."

"I'm trying. To Dad and Kim too."

"Well, I've noticed it and I appreciate it," I said.

"Rabbi Reuven is starting a chess club on Saturday afternoons. It's in the youth lounge. Can I go? I can bike there myself."

"Sure, of course you can go." I went for broke and put my arm around the kid. He didn't flinch.

40

It was Thanksgiving Day, and I was spending it blissfully alone. Sam was with Jeremy and Kimberly, and for the first time in years, I didn't have to fly to Florida the Wednesday before Thanksgiving, the busiest, most horrendous travel day of the year. Joanie had invited me over for a festive meal, as had my boss, Corey, but I declined both offers, thrilled to be in the house by myself with nothing to do except read. I'd purchased the whole *Little House on the Prairie* series and was enjoying immensely my regression into girlhood.

At around 11:00, the phone rang.

"Hey Claire, it's Lyd," said the voice on the other end of the line.

"Lyd, how great to hear from you!" I exclaimed, genuinely thrilled to hear from my cousin.

"You're one crappy correspondent," she said.

"Same back at you, or did your fingers get frostbitten in the Italian Alps?"

"Nah, I've just been having too much fun. How about you?"

"Can't honestly say that's the reason I haven't been in touch. I'm so glad you called."

"Well, I wanted to wish you a Happy Thanksgiving," she said.

"You too. Are you doing anything over there to celebrate?"

"Yeah, a bunch of American academics got together. This law professor gave a talk entitled 'A Short History of Every Broken Promise to the Indians.' It was a blast. Turns out there isn't a treaty we've honored. Those Indians should have just let the Pilgrims starve. Anyway, after the talk, we had polenta and quail, our Italian version of turkey with stuffing. What are you planning? You gonna have turkey?"

"Not unless they make turkey-flavored ice cream. I had coffee ice cream for breakfast and, as a nod to the holiday, I'm having pumpkin ice cream for lunch."

"What about dinner?"

"Butter Pecan. I need my protein," I said.

"Sounds good. So, what's new with you?" Lydia asked.

I couldn't bring myself to tell Lydia about Sam's computer-porn escapades, but I recounted my experience with Teresa, and Lydia was really interested and supportive.

"Do you think Bubbe and Grandpa Sam ever knew that your dad hit Aunt Ida?" I asked Lydia.

"Hard to know," Lydia replied. "No one ever talked about it. My mom was embarrassed more than anything. She always made excuses for him. Besides, Bubbe had to save all of her disdain for your dad."

"They really hated Pop, didn't they?"

"You don't know the half of it. Your mom was the baby and the favorite. Alvin was most definitely not who they had in mind for their darling daughter. Bubbe used to scoff at Alvin's career. 'Grown men chasing around a ball, these are the people you work for?' And your mom, she wasn't just pretty. She was smart. You know, she was pursuing her masters in math before she got sick. Bubbe and Grandpa Sam didn't think anyone was good enough for her, but certainly not your short, foppish, smooth-talking dad. They hated him from the first date, when he brought her home late and, if my mom's version can be trusted, with her shirt on inside-out."

"Well, I didn't inherit the math ability, but it's nice to know I got the floozy gene from my mom."

"What do you remember of her?"

"I remember sitting in the living room watching her twirl around in an evening gown, all made up and ready for a night on the town with my dad."

"She was elegant. Very Jackie O."

"I also remember one time I peed in my pants and she was really nice about it. She just helped me clean up and told me not to worry about it. 'It happens to everyone,' she said, and I was so relieved that she wasn't mad."

"That's a sweet memory. Hold onto that thought, you'll get old and be peeing yourself again before you know it," Lydia said.

"Something to look forward to. You know, I don't really remember much from when she was well. I was only four when she was diagnosed."

"That's when I started hanging out with you big time. My job was to keep you busy and happy."

"Was it torture for you?"

"Nah, you were a good kid and you did sort of idolize me."

"You let me give all your Barbies haircuts," I said with nostalgia.

"I hated those Barbies anyway. My father really gave it to me for letting you ruin the dolls," Lydia said.

"He hit you?" I asked.

"Yeah, with a belt. The guy had an anger problem and the littlest thing could set him off."

"I was terrified of your father."

"Join the club. Though yours was tough in his own way. Remember your twelfth birthday?"

"Not really."

"Well, Bubbe and Grandpa Sam made a party. They were too Orthodox to have a bat mitzvah for you, but twelve was considered a special birthday. Forty-five minutes into the party, Bubbe is on the phone demanding that your dad come for birthday cake. She was *shreiying* at him."

"Did he end up coming?"

"An hour later, once whatever game he was watching was over, he came by with an unwrapped plush football. It was obvious, even to you, that he had just regifted something from his closet."

"Wow."

"Alvin just wasn't into the whole kid scene. Losing your mom really seemed to shatter him. Did he connect with anyone after her?"

"Certainly not the various women who pursued him. Anyone who got too close or demanded too much attention was out. He focused on his own comfortable, predictable world. He was good to Sam. And Pop was unbelievably supportive of his clients—intensely involved in their careers and willing to drop everything to help them. He stood by guys through injuries, drug use, and collapsed marriages. I wish he'd cared half as much about me."

"It's hard to lose a parent when you have a lot of unresolved negative feelings, believe me, I know," Lydia said.

"I sometimes think every screwed-up relationship I have is just another pathetic replay of my attempts to attract Pop's attention. How ironic that the guy who spent so little time with me shaped who I am today."

We were silent for a moment.

"Another thing that's happened since we last spoke," I resumed, "my friend Joanie lost her baby." I told Lydia about Mimi and described the gathering to observe *Shloshim*.

"It was so sad, but the rabbi was amazing," I heard myself saying. "He really offered comfort to Joanie and Aaron. All of us. . . . Well, anyway, it was a beautiful service. What's new with you?"

"I've met this woman, Cinzia, and we're having the usual relationship issues," Lydia said. "She's wildly possessive. I don't know why I thought I'd be able to escape the dyke drama by going abroad. Still, she's gorgeous and sexy and I'm having a lot of fun when we aren't arguing. What's up with you in that department? Did that date ever pan out?"

"Nah," I said, barely able to recall the movie date that fell through. "Lyd, can I tell you something in confidence?" I asked, my heart suddenly pounding.

"Sure," she said.

"You know that rabbi I mentioned?"

"The one who helped after Joanie lost her baby?"

"Yes. Well his name is Rob. I'm the only one who knows that."

"Well, your secret is safe with me," Lydia said dryly.

"Can you be serious for a minute? This is important."

"Sorry, Claire, go on."

"Well, Rob and I have a special friendship."

"Is that code for you're fucking him? If so, I'm very impressed. It's right behind defrocking a priest in the bad-girl department."

"No, it's platonic."

"Then what's the big secret?" Lydia asked.

"Well, it's just that we have this really close friendship. It's hard to describe. I'm the only one who calls him by his English name, the only one who knows the real him. And, we have great talks. We really get each other."

"But nothing's happened physically?"

"No, he's married. Well, maybe we do flirt a bit. But to be fair, when we first met, I didn't know he was a rabbi."

"OK, let me see if I have this right. You've been flirting with your married rabbi and only you know his true name is Rumpelstiltskin."

"He's not *my* rabbi. He's Joanie's rabbi . . . and I guess now he's Sam's rabbi too. We're not really flirting. We have these deep talks. I think we really love each other. At least, I feel that I love him."

"You have all these deep talks, but you don't know how he feels?" Lydia asked.

"I know it sounds stupid, but we talk about everything in the world except our relationship."

"How can this possibly go anywhere?" Lydia asked. "I'd kinda understand if you were just fucking him late at night on the *bimah* under the flicker of the eternal light. That would be hot. But this just seems weird."

"We go to the same gym and we talk at least three times a week."

"Do you ever see him outside the gym?"

"Well, I ran into him a lot when we were all helping Joanie after Mimi's death."

"But you don't go out for coffee or lunch?"

"We went out for breakfast once, but generally no," I said.

"And let me guess," Lydia continued, "you've never called him at home."

"I don't even have his number," I admitted.

"Claire, this guy sounds like bad news. If he were really your friend, it would be above board. He sounds squirrelly and emotionally unavailable. Just like you know who."

"No," I said with vehemence. "You're wrong about that. He's emotionally really present. He's just physically unavailable—at least I think so."

"Sounds like he's using his ministering skills to get into your head, maybe also your pants."

"He's not calculating that way," I protested. "Rob is the kindest, most loving person I know."

"Well, can you just be Rob's friend and get yourself a real boyfriend?"

"I suppose I could try but I want him. The truth is, I really want Rob. My heart leaps whenever I see him. I don't think I've ever felt this way about anyone."

"Your heart leaps?" Lydia echoed, not even trying to mask her sarcasm, which crossed the Atlantic loud and clear. "Claire, take care of your leaping heart. This sounds like a set-up for getting hurt. Just be careful. Be a little self-protective."

"He's nothing like Jeremy," I told her.

"That's a point in his favor. But he seems equally unlikely to fuck you," Lydia observed, "and you could use a little action."

"Can't argue with that," I conceded. "But can we drop the subject?"

"OK, OK. How's the boy?" Lydia asked.

"Slightly less monstrous," I said.

"Well that's good news. Is he home? Can I say hello?"

"No, he's at Jeremy's."

"So you're all alone on Thanksgiving?"

"And very grateful for it," I said. "My new friend Teresa's coming over and we're painting the kitchen tomorrow afternoon. She's helping me rehab and redecorate the house. The kitchen is going to be a color called Resolute Blue."

"Well, as long as you're sure," Lydia quipped.

"It's about the only thing I'm sure about," I said honestly, and we said our goodbyes.

41

We were sitting in Earth, the loveliest restaurant in Hudsonville, which boasted local, organic cuisine in a decidedly non-hippie setting. Real tablecloths for lunch. The prix fixe included appetizers and dessert, but the cappuccino I ordered would probably be an extra seven bucks. I couldn't tell exactly because Joanie was the only one who received a menu with prices. Around the small, round table, elegantly appointed with silver, crystal, and red roses, sat Joanie, Marjorie, Rob, and me.

Joanie had invited us for a special thank-you lunch for helping her when she was so depressed. The best bread in the world was whisked to our table with some herb-infused butter. I noticed that Rob didn't stint on the butter when Beverly wasn't on patrol.

"Rabbi, if I order champagne, will you have some?" Joan asked.

"So long as I don't need to make *kiddush* over it, I'm fine."

Joanie ordered some of the good stuff (I could tell it was the good stuff because it was dry rather than sweet the way I like it). After everyone's glass was filled, Joanie made a toast. "To three wonderful friends who helped me in a dark time. Thank you for your friendship, your loving-kindness, and all your help. I couldn't have made it through without you."

"*L'chaim*," Rob said as we all clinked glasses.

I inadvertently placed my champagne glass on my dessert spoon and the contents tumbled onto Rob's place setting. A little even got on his pants. The waiters rushed in to replace the plate and cutlery. I felt absolutely mortified, flashing back to a similar fancy dinner with Pop. I must have been about nine. Pop castigated me for spilling my water, curtly informing me that he wouldn't take me out if I was going to behave like a slob. I wanted to sink under the table. I was surprised when Pop's date leapt to my defense, reminding him that it was just an accident and that I was just a young girl up way past her bedtime. She patted me on the hand and told me not to worry about it, everyone spills sometimes. That night was the last I ever saw of her.

Focusing on the present, I realized that the only way I could make my gaffe worse would be by applying my napkin to his wet pants. I let Rob handle it and apologized repeatedly, offering to pay for the dry cleaning.

"Seriously, these pants were headed for the cleaners anyway. No harm done," Rob said, waving off my apologies.

Joanie was truly back to her old self and in fine form, regaling us with stories from Jake, whose language ability was growing exponentially every day.

"Nowadays, the kid will only answer if you address him as Spider-Man. I asked Jake if he was pretending, and he answered, 'No, Mama, I'm real-ing.'"

Marjorie pronounced Jake precocious and creative and had the good sense not to declare that the fabulous meal we were eating could have been purchased for less at some cheaper joint. Instead, we all enjoyed the delicious fare. I was the only one of the three of us who didn't keep kosher, but I saw no reason to scandalize anyone during this celebratory meal. I ordered fish like the rest of them.

"Did Seth ever call you?" Marjorie asked.

"Seth?" Joanie asked with animation, "How come I never heard about Seth?"

"Seth Feldman," Marjorie explained. "Claire and he were both over for Friday night dinner a couple of weeks ago. The rabbi was there too."

"He's all wrong for Claire," Joanie said without equivocation.

I could tell Rob was paying close attention.

"Well, it was worth a try. Seth's probably not ready to date yet." Marjorie conceded.

"Maybe I could date his ex-wife," I offered.

Marjorie narrowed her eyes, trying to see if I might be serious.

"Claire, behave yourself," Joanie scolded in mock irritation. "The rabbi's here. Sorry Rabbi, I can't take Claire anywhere."

"Rabbi, did I offend you?" I asked sweetly.

"Not at all," Rob answered gallantly. "I wish all my congregants would take a cue from you and behave a little less well around me. It makes for far more interesting conversations."

"Well, as long as the subject is Claire's love life," Joan said, smiling at me, "whatever happened to that guy at the gym you had such a crush on?"

"I don't know what you're talking about," I said quickly, hoping I didn't look as panicked as I felt.

"Of course you do," Joanie tried to jog my memory, "the chubby guy with the great smile."

Rob's eyes positively danced at the word "chubby."

"I never said he was chubby, I just said we both needed to get into shape."

"Okay, but I'm talking about the one who quoted children's books all the time. Last time we spoke about it, you were wild about him."

I could just feel how intrigued Rob was by this turn in the conversation.

"Oh, I think I know who you mean," I said, trying to sound nonchalant. "He turned out to be different from who I thought he was."

"I'll bet he was married," Marjorie piped up. "Those creepy types are always married. At least Seth is available."

"He wasn't creepy at all. He was . . . is . . . great, in fact. Really great," I said, venturing a glance at Rob. "But things just didn't work out for a romantic relationship."

Joanie wasn't going to give this conversation up easily, but I was saved by the appearance of a tanned elderly couple at our table.

"Rabbi, I thought that was you," said the bejeweled woman in a mink coat, "but I couldn't be sure because you aren't wearing your *yarmulke*." The woman's hair was so tightly coiffed and so full of hairspray that a Category 5 hurricane couldn't have blown a strand out of place.

"Hello, Elaine," Rob said, rising to greet her. "Hello, Harry," Rob said, turning to shake the hand of a red-faced, white-haired gentleman in white pants, white shoes, and a pink short-sleeved shirt. Even fashion-impaired moi realized that this couple just couldn't agree on a season.

"Rabbi, what are *you* doing here? Are we paying you so much that you can afford to eat at such a fancy place?" Harry asked. Without waiting for an answer, he added, "You haven't ordered any *treif*, have you?"

"No, Harry, the rabbi's eating the salmon," Elaine announced, inspecting Rob's plate.

"The lobster is delicious here . . . or so I'm told," Harry said with what he probably believed was sly charm.

"How is Davida doing?" Rob asked them.

"She's expecting again," Elaine said. "It's her third. God willing, by you and Beverly too."

"That's right, Rabbi, when are we going to hear the pitter-patter of little feet at your house?" Harry asked.

"I went to high school with a Davida Goldenberg," I interjected. "Could that be your daughter?"

"Why yes," said Elaine, first noticing that anyone else was sitting at the table. "Hudsonville, Class of '92. Then she went to Berkeley, where she met her husband, who works in Silicon Valley. She has two beautiful daughters and now is expecting a son."

"That's lovely," I gushed, before Mrs. Goldenberg could reach for her pictures of the Silicon Valley princesses. "I'm sorry," I continued, "I shouldn't detain you any further, I see you folks are on your way out. But please give Davida regards from Claire Mandelbaum."

"Is that your maiden name?"

"Yes."

"So you never married?"

"Married and divorced," I answered. "Not everyone is as lucky as Davida. She'll know me as Claire Mandelbaum. Please give her my warmest regards. So nice to meet you."

As soon as they were out of earshot, I informed my luncheon companions that Davida Goldenberg was the biggest pothead at Hudsonville High.

"I wonder if Elaine and Harry are aware that she used to give blow jobs to a not-so-select-few football players under the bleachers."

"Claire!" Joanie admonished, "The rabbi is here."

Although I'd anticipated that Rob would enjoy the well-deserved hostility directed towards the Goldenbergs, he seemed truly uncomfortable, twisting his napkin in his lap. Instead of replying, Rob changed the subject, making an inelegant segue.

"Speaking of the youth of America," he said, and then proceeded to tell Joanie about his plans for the new youth lounge dedicated in Mimi's memory. Rob described the new ping-pong and pool tables, the electronic gaming areas, the computers, the tables for chess and other board games, the comfortable chairs and couches, and the popcorn maker for the "classroom" where Rob delivered his *dvar torahs*. "I want them to integrate their Jewish learning and Jewish identities into their daily lives and not see them as separate," Rob explained. "This will be a place for them to hang out and to connect with being Jewish."

"Rabbi," I said once we had all expressed enthusiasm for the planned improvements, "I want to thank you for talking to the kids about honoring their parents. I think Sam took it to heart."

"He's a great kid. We have someone in the group on crutches and he is always so helpful to her."

"Her?" I asked meaningfully.

"Sam's mom can't be the only one looking for love," Rob said with a sly smile.

Marjorie began a long discussion of the behavior of her son Ben, Sam's partner in crime. She made a special point of letting Rob know that Ben didn't need any help in honoring his parents, but Ben could use some encouragement in applying himself more to the Science Olympiad.

"To get into a good college, you need more than just good grades and high SAT scores nowadays," she pontificated. We all listened politely. She had been heroic in taking care of Jake and in helping Joanie in so many other ways. Marjorie deserved some time to discuss what was on her mind.

She continued at length, criticizing Ben, whose only failings seemed to be not being Stuart, her oldest son (though she never quite came out and said it), and hanging out with ne'er-do-wells like my kid. While she spoke, I focused on her kindness to Joanie's kids and had no trouble enjoying my sole, which was swimming in a frothy foam of deliciousness, nestled on a bed of tender asparagus and topped with crisp potatoes—easily the best thing I ever ate, although the zucchini fritter appetizer with crème fraiche was a close second. The waiter brought the desserts—apple tart for Joanie and Marjorie, homemade mango ice cream for Rob, and cheesecake for me, surrounded by strawberries.

Without thinking, Rob reached over and scooped up the strawberries that garnished my plate. "You can't have these, Claireleh, but I can," he said flashing me a smile.

I don't know if Marjorie had noticed, but Joanie's eyes widened and her eyebrows shot up. She was clearly stunned by the intimacy of Rob's gesture and the way he spoke to me. Even Rob, with his easy-going manner and informality, didn't just help himself to food off strangers' plates. And he'd disclosed that he must know me in another context, aware as he was of my strawberry allergy. But my comfortable, loving, confused, and altogether screwed-up relationship with Rob was something I couldn't discuss with Joanie. Tellingly, she never asked me about it.

42

With Joanie pretty much back to her old self and Sam behaving like a semi-reasonable teenager (which is to say surly but not unspeakable), I found myself falling into a pleasant routine at work and the gym. Rob and I had gotten to the point where if one of us was going to miss, we'd send an email. The emails were always very short, and written so that even if Beverly saw them, she would have no cause for concern, other, of course, than the fact that I was encouraging Rob to go to the gym at all. I always addressed the emails to "R," so that Rob and I could keep my use of his English name our little secret in case Beverly or his secretary snooped. "R—Skipping gym on Friday, meeting at work. *Gut Shabbes*—C." That was the extent of it.

On a Tuesday in early December I received such an email from Rob. "Have to miss, see you tomorrow." He didn't show up on Wednesday either. I was disappointed but it sometimes happened that last-minute things would interfere with his attendance at the gym so I didn't give it much thought.

The following night, Jeremy dropped Sam off and, for the first time since our divorce, actually came in for a cup of tea. Ever since Jeremy helped me out with Teresa, we had been getting along famously. He often ferried Sam around for Youth Group and after-school activities, and we would sometimes chat briefly in my front hallway after he dropped Sam off. It was an oh-so-civilized display of post-nuclear-family parenting. We were apparently again capable of pleasant, light conversation. Jeremy and I hardly seemed to be the same two people who only five years before had engaged in painful and pointless screaming matches about why we never had sex anymore.

That night, Jeremy was euphoric. He had finally finished at the firm.

"If I never take another deposition it will be too soon," Jeremy said as he sipped his decaf Earl Grey, something he drinks all the time and got me hooked on when we were married.

"I thought you loved litigation," I said with surprise.

"Turns out I'm good at it but I don't really love it. There's a difference. Kim taught me that. Kim's taught me a lot of things. Truth is, I wouldn't have cared if Kim had converted or not. She was the one who was interested—insistent really—that we explore Judaism. I learned a lot while Kim was studying for conversion. I'm actually planning to take a class at the seminary this spring," Jeremy said.

"Wow." That's all I could say.

This whole Jewish observance thing was even more mind-bending than the fact that Jeremy had quit the firm. I suppose this type of midlife crisis was better than getting hair plugs, driving a fast red convertible, and acting like an ass. But, to be fair, Jeremy did have the hot young wife, so he hadn't evaded the cliché entirely.

"How's your work going?" Jeremy asked, interrupting my thoughts. I was surprised; he rarely inquired about anything in my life outside of Sam, even when we were getting along. Apparently, Kimberly had totally rehabilitated the guy. And, annoyingly, he was looking more handsome now than ever with grey at his temples and a weathered look achieved by the network of fine wrinkles framing his eyes. He'd clearly been working out some, and his shoulders were broader.

"I guess I'm lucky; I really like my job," I replied. "Sometimes I wake up after a hard weekend with you-know-who and just say TGIM—thank God it's Monday."

"Sam can be a handful. But I admire you, Claire. You spend time with him. You've made the investment. I can't believe how much time I've let slip by."

"Look," I reassured Jeremy, who appeared to be genuinely remorseful, "you're giving him your time and attention now. That's what matters. I think your spending time with him has really made him happier and he's certainly been better behaved."

"Thanks. That's really nice of you, especially under the circumstances. You've really borne the brunt of caring for Sam. You know," Jeremy continued tentatively, "I'm taking a pretty big pay cut going in-house. And I've had some serious expenses lately. . . ."

Aha, I thought. This is why Jeremy is being so nice. He's about to cut off child support. I should have seen this coming.

"I'm a little behind in saving for Sam's college," Jeremy said. "I can't believe how much money I wasted on restaurant meals over the years. But Kim and I have a strict budget and we're planning to be more aggressive in putting money aside for Sam's future."

I was instantly mollified. "It's OK, Jer," I said. I hadn't called him "Jer" in years. "Sam's rolling in it. Pop left the kid a small fortune. We just have to make sure he makes it all the way through high school without me killing him."

"That's fantastic!" Jeremy said, clearly relieved. "I still want to contribute, but this takes some of the pressure off. I'm glad Pop was able to leave something substantial for Sam's education. And you, Claire, you're heroic."

Heroic, I thought, admirable too, but obviously not fuckable. Oh well. I couldn't complain. Jeremy had lost interest in me way before Kimberly came along, and things were so much better with Sam now that Jeremy was actively involved in Sam's day-to-day life. It wasn't just that Jeremy drove or offered an extra pair of hands. Sam clearly craved attention from Jeremy, and it meant a lot to Sam that Jeremy had moved back to Hudsonville and left the firm, at least in part to be more available as a dad.

"Keep on spending time with Sam. That's what he needs."

"Well, Kim and I are really excited to be taking him for the rest of the month. We'll be home and I, for the first time in twenty years, will be without a job to go to."

"Don't you two want to travel or something?" I asked. "Don't get me wrong, I'm grateful for your taking him. I've got to close out Pop's condo and there's a hassle with selling it. Apparently, the buyer also has to purchase a membership in the golf course—and that's an extra seventy thousand dollars. . . ."

I stopped talking. There was something more. I could just sense that there was something else Jeremy had to say. There was a reason he'd stopped in for tea. It wasn't just to commiserate about Sam, or praise my efforts, or even to talk about college expenses. Something was up.

"We're not going anywhere for a while," Jeremy said. There was a long pause. "Kim's pregnant. She's due in May. I wanted to tell you in person."

We sat silently for a minute.

"I know you wanted to have more kids," he said, averting his gaze from me. "I hope this isn't hard for you."

Was it hard for me? Was I supposed to want pretty-boy's latest spawn as my own? Did I resent the reminder of how much younger Kimberly was than me? Or the fact that he obviously had sex with her? Joanie's kids served as constant examples of how much physical work little ones entail. And Sam reminded me daily of how uncute they can become. I felt oddly unemotional about the whole thing. Why not take the high road?

"Come on," I said, "This is great news. Mazel tov."

"Thanks." Another long pause ensued and Jeremy resumed. "I know that I made some stupid, immature choices when we were together. I was so damned focused on being a powerhouse lawyer that I never stopped to ask myself what I valued or what made me happy. Kim showed me what I'd been missing."

Enough already about Kimberly, I thought, though it brought me some satisfaction to see that Jeremy was still a bit of a clueless oaf. But, to be fair, he was trying to be a better father to Sam and a better person. That had to count for something.

"It takes two to tango," I said to Jeremy. "I didn't exactly make it fun to come home at night. There are many things I wish I'd done differently too."

This had the benefit of being not just nice, but true. As the hurt from my failed marriage diminished, I increasingly realized that Jeremy's lack of attraction to me was mostly about him—his preoccupations, insecurities, and needs. I could have been a supermodel and he would still have worked late and pled fatigue when I wanted some sexual attention. He found stability in work and couldn't handle my volatility and my intense need for closeness. Recasting Jeremy from villain to anxious, lost soul made me feel better about both of us, and more open to facing how I contributed to the problems of our marriage. Our law school romance should never have gone further than our wild spring-break romp in Mexico. But I wanted kids, and Jeremy was Jewish and clearly going to be able to provide for a family. My cousin Lydia had tried to warn me not to marry him, but I didn't listen.

"Does Sam know he's going to be a big brother?" I asked.

"I was going to tell him tonight, but he was so out of sorts because Rabbi Reuven wasn't there, so, I decided to wait."

"The rabbi canceled Youth Group?" I asked.

"No, he just didn't show up," Jeremy said. "They planned on playing a game called 'Stump the Rabbi,' and Sam actually prepared some questions on Jewish history and Jewish ritual. He did a lot of research on the internet and he and Ben had some fabulous questions. Man, was Sam irritated when, after the kids waited around for a half an hour, the youth director announced that they were all going to watch the movie *Yentl* instead."

"Didn't anyone call the rabbi?" I asked.

"I guess so, but no one managed to reach him. I'm sure he just had an emergency or something. Sam tends to overreact when he's disappointed."

"No shit," I said.

So Sam was disappointed that he couldn't play Stump the Rabbi, and his mother was disappointed that she couldn't play *Schtup* the Rabbi. Longing for some fun and games with Rabbi Reuven ran in the family, I thought.

We worked out a schedule for Sam to go to Jeremy and Kimberly's the following weekend and then to stay until New Year's Eve, when the happy honeymooners had a big party to attend and I presumably would be watching the ball drop in my pajamas alone at home. Over two weeks without Sam? It was amazing. Unfathomable really, but I was eager to give it a try.

I wished Jeremy the best and asked him to extend my congratulations to Kimberly. I meant it. Jeremy, handsome as he looked, was just pretty packaging to me now. There was nothing inside I wanted. I no longer craved his attention or needed him to desire me. If Kimberly could rehabilitate him, enjoy him, and fuck him, more power to her.

43

When I didn't see Rob at the gym the next day, I felt concerned. Rob hadn't answered my email of the night before, and that was unlike him. As I sat at my desk scrolling through email, I called the *shul* office and was told that Rob's secretary was out with the flu and that I should email the rabbi directly. Fat lot of good that would do. I decided to call Marjorie. If something was up, she'd know.

"Claire, let me get rid of my mother on the other line," is how Marjorie answered the phone on the fourth ring. Let's hear it for caller ID, I thought.

After a minute or two, Marjorie was back.

"Hi, Marjorie, I was wondering if you would share your chicken soup recipe with me," I said.

"Sure, Claire, the secret is the sweet potatoes. You'll need celery, carrots, onion, peppercorns, and chicken of course. Have you ever made chicken soup from scratch?"

"It's been a while," I replied and added, "I loved it when we had it at your house; you remember, when Rabbi Reuven was there."

Marjorie was off to the races. Interspersed with the preparation instructions, Marjorie talked about Rabbi Reuven. "All the kids were so disappointed that he didn't show up," she told me.

"Does he tend to flake out like that a lot?" I asked with as much innocence as I could muster.

"No, not at all, but Beverly is out of town, and maybe he's a little disoriented. She's super organized and I think she keeps his schedule for him. So be it. I'm sure the kids will play Stump the Rabbi some other time."

"Beverly's out of town?" I asked.

"Yeah, she's on a mission to Israel. She left on Tuesday. She'll be gone at least ten days."

"Really?" I said, not trying to sound too interested. "I need to ask Rabbi Reuven something about Sam," I said. "Do you know how to reach him?"

"He's always on email. Just drop him a line. Beverly and Dena, the synagogue secretary, are the only ones who have his cell number."

I gracelessly extracted myself from Marjorie, assuring her that I had the matzo balls under control, and immediately buzzed my secretary Molly.

"I need two doughnuts and a street address for Beverly Fineberg. She lives in Hudsonville," I said.

"Coming up. Do you want me to run a credit or criminal record check on her?" Molly asked. I was tempted, but declined Molly's offer.

Turns out, Rob lived only a few miles from me. I announced to a surprised Molly that I was going out and would be gone most of the rest of the morning. I was off to do something rash.

44

I saw the trash can on the front lawn along with the empty recycling bins. Trash was picked up on Wednesdays, so this stuff had been sitting in front of the house for two days, along with three newspapers. With Beverly away, Rob was clearly regressing. No big surprise there. But had he gone AWOL entirely?

No one answered my ring or loud knocks on the front door, so I went around the back. The door was unlocked. I entered the kitchen tentatively, at first calling a quiet greeting and eventually yelling "hello" at the top of my voice. Still nothing.

The house was a cavernous ranch. I registered the imposing size and quality of the kitchen—two fridges, two stoves, two dishwashers, two food processors, two mix-masters, all polished to a high gleam. It was the Noah's Ark of kitchens, clearly designed so that everything was available for the dietary requirement of separating milk and meat. Three large bookshelves held more cookbooks than I'd ever seen gathered in one place before.

"Rob?" I called.

I walked through the kitchen to a huge combined living and dining room. A full wall of south-facing windows looked out onto a small but colorful flower garden. The room contained floor-to-ceiling book shelves on the remaining interior walls. Where there weren't books, the shelves held Jewish objets d'art. Apparently Beverly collected Hanukkah menorahs, and there were all types, from traditional, to abstract, to the whimsical. The room's multiple couches and chairs were organized into various conversation clusters. Three separate dining tables (all fully set with different china and stemware) meant that there was enough space to entertain a small army.

Towards the back of the ranch, down a hallway with a Chagall print on the wall, were the bedrooms. One was clearly a study. Another was the master suite with a double bed made up like something out of *House Beautiful*. It was hardly a shock that Beverly was a woman who had mastered the art of pillow placement, but the level of elegance was breathtaking. In addition to the bed and matching ottoman, there was a small antique vanity with perfumes and makeup on a mirrored tray. Everything was in perfect order. I noticed that the door to the walk-in closet was open. I can't say I actually believed Rob was in there, but I couldn't help taking a peek. I saw rows upon rows of color coordinated outfits with matching shoes beneath. The closet was huge and included a three-way mirror. On the upper shelves were carefully organized and artfully stored back issues of *Vogue* magazine.

"Rob," I continued to shout, and looked in the last room. "Rob, are you here?"

No answer, but there he was sprawled on his bed, comforter on the floor and sheets in disarray. Rob's greasy hair was shooting out in all different directions. He had at least a two-day's beard growth. His lips were cracked and something disgusting was oozing out of his right eye.

"Oh my God, Rob, are you OK?" I asked as I rushed over to him.

"Claire?" he croaked in surprise.

"Rob," I said grabbing his hand, "what happened?" I felt his forehead. He was burning up. At least 102 degrees if my mom-o-meter was still accurate.

"I'm sick," he rasped. "Sorry I missed you at the gym."

"Of course, don't worry about it," I assured him, feeling his forehead again. "You're really ill. Have you been taking any medicine?"

He shook his head. "Just resting," he whispered. "Tonight we play Stump the Rabbi. I'll be fine." His voice sounded anything but fine. He could barely get the words out. It obviously hurt him to talk.

"Sorry to barge in on you. I couldn't reach you and I got worried."

"Cell phone out of juice," he said in his pathetic scratchy voice.

"Please don't talk. You sound awful. Just nod your head. Does it hurt to swallow?" He nodded.

"Do you have a headache?" He nodded again. I reached over and felt his glands. "Golf balls," I announced.

"You look like you have the flu. I'm getting you something to reduce your fever and then I want to see you drink."

About ten minutes later, under my firm direction, Rob had taken two ibuprofens and drunk a full glass of water.

"What can I do for you?" I asked.

"Bathroom," he croaked.

"Lean on me, I'll take you there."

Rob was unsteady on his feet, but we got there. His bathroom was functional, but nothing like Beverly's, which had a Jacuzzi and, I shit you not, a fireplace. Rob's bathroom had some pretty tiling, but it was otherwise an unremarkable place to eliminate waste and take a shower. I propped him up against the bathroom cabinet.

"I'm right outside the door. Call me. Don't try to walk on your own."

It was a measure of how sick Rob was that he did call me. I got him back to his room and put him in the armchair while I stripped his bed. I found fresh sheets, made the bed, and plumped his pillows. When everything was ready, Rob stumbled back to bed. He was bathed in sweat and I insisted on changing him out of his smelly pajama top. He was too weak to protest. I tried not to look at his naked chest, but I couldn't help noticing how amazingly hairy he was. It was like his chest was covered in matted bear fur. In all my fantasies of removing Rob's shirt, somehow this particular scenario, with his skin hot to the touch and crusty mucus coming out of his orifices, had never occurred to me. I leaned him against a freshly fluffed pile of pillows and placed a cold, wet washcloth on his forehead.

"You poor man," I exclaimed. "Do you want me to turn on the TV while I get you some tea and toast?"

"You're an angel," he said in a hoarse whisper. "Can you plug in my phone? I want to check my messages." It hurt just to listen to him.

"I'll bring it to you, but you probably have a lot of messages. You've been out for quite a while."

"I've slept all day?"

"Rob, it's 10:00 in the morning. Today is Friday. You must have been sick in bed for a full day."

"Friday?" he squeaked, his eyes darting wildly. "Did you say Friday?"

He looked ghastly. "I missed Stump the Rabbi?" he said, looking like he might cry.

"Everyone will understand. You were sick. It'll be OK. You really need to rest. I'll bring you up something hot to drink and I'll charge your cell. Where's the charger?"

"Office," Rob said as he slumped into his pillows, truly distraught.

Turned out that Rob didn't miss a funeral or anything major other than the Youth Group. There were, however, seven calls from Beverly. It was late afternoon in Israel, and he had to call right away if he wanted to reach her before Shabbes. Despite his lack of voice, this was one call I couldn't possibly help with. I went to the kitchen but I could clearly hear Rob's side of the conversation. He apologized. Repeatedly. Yes, Rob acknowledged, he always answered his phone. It was stupid of him to have let his cell run down. Then came the detailed inquiries about his health.

"I hadn't thought of that," Rob said. Another long silence.

"I'll try, Bev. . . . That's a great suggestion. . . . Yes, I'll call her as soon as I'm off with you." Another pause.

"Come on, Bev, don't cry. I'm so sorry you were worried. *Shabbat Shalom*, Bev. Enjoy *Yerushalayim* . . . I'm really OK . . . I love you too," Rob said as he signed off.

I brought Rob some toast with jam and some tea with lemon and honey. The food revived him a bit.

"This tea is just like what my mom would make when I was sick. Thank you."

In the next half hour I made numerous calls on Rob's behalf, including to a rabbi who was a member of the congregation, asking her if she could fill in for Friday night and Saturday morning services. No one questioned who I was. I guess a woman who announces that she is calling on behalf of Rabbi Reuven Fineberg is just assumed to be his secretary. Rob insisted on writing an email to all the kids in the Youth Group apologizing and explaining his absence the night before.

By 11:00, Rob was ready for more sleep. I told him I'd return in a few hours. I went to the local cooking gear store and bought a large pot. I went to the kosher butcher and bought two chickens and some soup bones. Next, I hit the grocery and bought matzo-meal, eggs, oil, turnips, carrots, parsley, dill, parsnips, celery, and onions. No sweet potatoes. The one thing Bubbe could cook was chicken soup and she had taught me all her secrets.

45

I called Molly to let her know I was ditching the whole day, a first for me. The only time I ever missed work was when I was deathly ill or Sam was sick.

"What's his name, Claire?" Molly asked playfully.

"I'd tell you, but then I'd have to fire you," I said.

Molly snorted. No one had better job security than she did. She knew where every damned body in the whole corporation was buried.

"If he asks, tell Corey I'm trysting with my personal trainer."

"Will do. Train hard," Molly replied with as much exaggerated innuendo as she could muster over the phone.

Come to think of it, that was a good description of Rob. He did serve as my trainer physically, emotionally, and spiritually. However, despite Molly's insinuations, the sight of Rob just then, disgustingly sick, didn't evoke a particularly sexy image, unless one had a very bizarre snot fetish.

Everything in the kitchen was clearly marked and I had no trouble locating the meat dishes and cutlery. The level of organization was astounding, making even Joanie look like a bit of a slacker. The fridge and freezer had individual plates of food labeled for each day Beverly was gone, with detailed instructions for warming everything. Every container was disposable. Beverly didn't trust Rob to wash a dish. The arrangement of each meal on a large Styrofoam plate reminded me of airline food, though I knew from experience it would taste scrumptious.

I read the *New York Times* as the soup cooked and Rob slept. When the soup was done and the matzo balls were bouncing up and down in the fragrant, bubbling liquid, I decided to check up on him again.

He was sitting up in bed watching an old *Star Trek* episode from when William Shatner was, if not exactly svelte, still built like a leading man.

"I've seen every one of these at least five times, but I never tire of them," Rob croaked.

"Don't talk," I commanded. "I have some Jewish penicillin coming your way. I'd administer it intravenously, but the matzo balls might rupture a vein."

I brought up a tray for Rob with two bowls of soup and an acetaminophen chaser. I sat in the armchair and we watched Captain Kirk seduce a gorgeous alien as Rob slurped away.

"This is delish!" Rob said with more enthusiasm than one usually hears from a guy with the flu.

During the commercials Rob checked his email.

"Oy, the Sisterhood ladies are on high alert. I bet Bev called them. I have three offers of chicken soup. Of course I couldn't do better than what I have right here."

I wasn't the least bit surprised that Beverly had sicced her goons on poor Rob. But Beverly was an unmentionable subject. Instead, I accepted the compliment about the soup. "My Bubbe's recipe is the best," I agreed.

"It's not just the food," Rob said. "I'm particularly fond of the service in this restaurant."

"Well it's not every server who will frog-march you to the bathroom," I concurred. "You have to tip big to get that kind of service."

"I owe you," Rob said as he continued to eat the soup greedily. Apparently, the soup pepped him up and soothed his throat. "There's no way I can thank you enough. You're so kind to be here. You must be missing work."

"No big deal. I'm happy to spend time with you. *Bikur cholim* is a big mitzvah," I reminded him.

The last thing he needed was an invasion from the Sisterhood, so I crafted a general email reply from Rob letting everyone know that he had the flu, had everything he needed, and just wanted to rest. The email thanked them for their good wishes and promised that he would contact them if he needed anything.

"This will prevent people from just dropping by the way I did," I explained.

"That's a relief. But," he added quickly, "I'm so happy you came over. With you here, it's almost worth being sick."

During the next round of commercials, after Captain Kirk had saved the alien planet from oblivion and engaged in some clever repartee with Spock and Bones, Rob again checked his messages.

"Hey," he exclaimed, his voice cracking like a bar mitzvah boy's, "I got an email from Sam." Rob passed me the phone. Sam had written:

> Dear Rabbi Reuven,
>
> Sorry to hear u r sick. I knew there had to be a gd reason 4 u 2 miss last nite. Ben & I have some killer questions for Stump the Rabbi. But it can wait til u feel better.
>
> Sincerely,
>
> Sam Schiff

"What a lovely note," Rob said. "The kid's a real *mensch*."

"Well, at least that's one thing Sam and I have in common. We both adore you," I said without thinking. It was quiet in the room. Even the TV seemed to hit a dead zone. Shit, I thought, is it possible that he didn't hear? Maybe his ears were too clogged, I hoped.

"The feeling's mutual, Claireleh," Rob said warmly. Too warmly. Rob's eyes were ablaze. The guy was due for some more meds. He was delirious with fever. What was my excuse?

46

After insisting that Rob rest some more, I was again sitting in the kitchen, eating some of my own, admittedly delicious, soup. I promised Rob more tea and toast as a post-nap treat. I was acting and feeling like a mother, except this time to a kid who was appreciative. I glanced around the kitchen, which was no longer so immaculate now that I'd touched it. How hard did that woman work to keep the place so sparkly? Why couldn't she take off those damn yellow gloves and give some loving kindness to her fabulous husband?

I realized that I had absolutely nothing on my agenda. It was Friday afternoon, work was over for the week, and Sam would be with Jeremy and Kimberly for the next two weeks. There was nothing stopping me from just spending the night caring for Rob. Truthfully, there was no place I would rather be. I'd nothing to feel guilty about in my conduct. We were models of propriety. Yet, the pleasure I felt in his company was positively illicit, and I knew there was no way I could stay past dinner time.

When I went back up, Rob was feeling better still. He drank his tea and toast and asked if I could scramble him up some eggs.

"I'm hungry," he explained, and his voice sounded stronger.

"That's a good sign," I assured him. "I hate to lose a patient."

"I feel that I've been imposing on you."

"Not at all," I reassured him.

"At least tell me what's new with you."

What to tell first? I told Rob that Sam was away until New Year's with Jeremy and Kimberly, and that Kimberly was pregnant.

"How do you feel about it?" he asked.

"Oddly, I'm more OK about the pregnancy than with Sam's going. I'm slowly realizing it will be weird not having him around. How will I remember all of my faults without him there to remind me?"

"I'd be happy to let you know about your faults if I could see any," Rob said. "I'm glad you're OK about the baby. You're a very generous person," Rob continued. "I bet you'll find some way to entertain yourself while Sam's away," he said with a sly smile.

"Why, Rabbi, what are you suggesting?" I said in mock dismay.

"I'm suggesting a vacation."

"I haven't really taken one outside of visits to my father in Florida in years. Since my honeymoon, actually," I said.

"Where did you go for your honeymoon?" Rob asked.

"We went on a Caribbean cruise. I was seasick the entire time. It was the first of many portents that I'd made a dreadful mistake. But as a matter of fact, I'm going back to Florida next week to close up my father's apartment. Even though there's a pool and the weather will be warm, I don't consider it a vacation."

"Of course it's not. That's a hard thing to do. Who's going with you?"

"I'm going alone. I'm just grateful that I won't have a whining Sam on my hands while I pack up the place."

"Claire, that's ridiculous. You shouldn't do this all by yourself. You know," Rob said slowly, "I was thinking of visiting my mom in Boca after Bev returns. Late in December it's kind of slow at the *shul* and it's a good time to go. Bev has to work late every night at the thrift shop."

"Your mother's in Boca Raton? Pop's condo is in West Boca!" I shouldn't have been surprised. Boca Raton is God's waiting room, at least for the Jews. Of course our elderly parents were there.

"Then it's settled. I'm going home to Mom before Christmas—which is a big mitzvah," Rob said with his eyes twinkling, and this time I didn't think it was the flu. "Then I'm going to help you pack up. It'll be fun."

It would be amazing. Just me and Rob for a full day in a totally different zip code. What was he suggesting? Did he realize that we'd be alone in an apartment, out of sight of everyone who knew us, without the protective shield of his disgusting flu? Beneath his child-like enthusiasm was there a grown man's desire?

47

We flew separately and Rob spent two days with his mother at her condo, then arrived at Pop's place the following morning. After lox and bagels, we got to work.

As we sifted through the stuff, I thanked Rob repeatedly for helping me pack up the apartment. I told him if he saw anything that he wanted, to please say so. Most of Pop's stuff was being targeted for the local thrift shop. I'd keep some ties and sweaters for Sam and save Pop's golf clubs for when the boy would entertain his software clients on the green. Rob dismissed my thanks and assured me that he was delighted to help.

"This isn't the sort of job a person should do alone," Rob said, "and besides, you have been so kind to me. I'm glad I can reciprocate."

We began with the breakfront. It didn't have too many tchotchkes; most of its contents consisted of religious objects. I told Rob the story of the silver Hanukkah menorah. Pop's parents had received it before they left Germany. Pop's family had Swiss citizenship and his folks were able to leave Berlin in 1939. If they hadn't, Pop and his family would have perished in the Holocaust. The happy accident of being Swiss saved the whole family. Even as Jews, with their Swiss passports they were able to board the train and leave Nazi Germany. The war was full of deprivation for them in Zurich, but oddly, also full of normal things like ski trips and birthday parties. Before they left Berlin, a man whom none of them knew came to the door and asked to see Pop's father. The man explained that he had heard Pop's family would soon be leaving for Switzerland, and he asked them to take this menorah with them. The man said that if he survived the war, he would come to retrieve it. They never heard from him and the menorah became a family heirloom, one of the few tokens from Pop's life in Europe. The menorah served as a poignant reminder of how lucky we were.

"I collect Hanukkah menorahs," Rob informed me as he admired the piece. "This one was from the Bezalel Academy of Arts and Design in Jerusalem, and was probably fashioned before World War I."

I looked into his face and saw that he was tearing up.

"It's amazing what our people have gone through. This is a real piece of history," he said. "You should treasure it."

I assured him that I would, and we continued sorting Pop's belongings. I was really trying to limit the amount of stuff I was taking home with me. Of course, I took Pop's photos and my parents' wedding album, but there were few other objects of sentimental value. Had I secretly been harboring a hope that Pop saved my kiddy artwork or my handmade gifts? If so, I was disappointed. He had saved very little that belonged to my mother, and there was little among Pop's belongings that held any appeal. Should I have felt more attached to Pop's earthly leftovers?

Rob, on the other hand, acted as if he was digging for (and finding) buried treasure. His enthusiasm when he went through Pop's CD collection was infectious. I reminded him that he should take anything he wanted and Rob was thrilled. "Nat King Cole!" he exclaimed and started to play a track.

As we listened to "Heaven," Rob swept me up and began to dance with me "cheek to cheek," as the song says. Rob sang under his breath and pulled me close. For a guy who looked so awkward on the elliptical machine, he was an awfully graceful dancer. All those years attending bar mitzvah and wedding parties had certainly paid off in the Fred Astaire department. I was more like the broom than like Ginger Rogers, but Rob didn't seem to mind. He guided me around the room and brought me in even closer. Aside from when I was helping Rob when he had the flu, I'd never been in such close proximity to him before. This time he smelled much better. The familiar smell of Rob's sweat mingled with other enticing aromas. His breath smelled like ripe bananas, his neck smelled faintly of shaving cream. Rob's lips grazed my ear as he continued to sing. My heart beat so that I could hardly speak.

As I turned to look into his eyes, Rob's mouth caught mine in what had to be the sweetest kiss of my life. Impassioned, yet gentle. Rob was clearly waiting to see my reaction before going any further.

"If you want me to stop, tell me now." His voice was thick with desire, and he was almost pleading.

Did he want me to tell him to stop? Was I supposed to play the part of designated grown-up, thinking about his wife, worrying about his status as a pillar of the community? And speaking of pillars. . . .

"I want you so badly. I've never wanted anything more in my life." As he said this, he began kissing me in earnest. Clearly if I was going to say something, now was the time. Part of me wanted to sink to the floor and abandon myself to passion. But I knew we needed to talk.

"Slow down," I said, cupping his face in my hands and looking into his eyes. I sat down on the couch and beckoned him to sit near me.

"I can promise you that absolutely no blood is going to my brain right now, so I'm not sure that any action I take will be volitional," he said.

A quick glance at his shorts confirmed my suspicion concerning where all the blood was going. The time for coyness had long since passed.

"I really want to make love with you, but I'm afraid of what will happen to our friendship if we do this," I said.

"I'll still respect you," he said.

"I know that," I said, slightly disconcerted. "I'm worried about how we'll be able to relate to one another. Your friendship is so precious to me. I don't want us to ruin it. Can we do this and go back?"

"I don't see why not," Rob said. "I love you. I know that I'm being selfish; I've nothing honorable to offer you." He paused for a moment and then added with downcast eyes, "You know I can't leave Bev."

"So what happens in Boca Raton stays in Boca Raton?" I asked.

"Making love with you would give me a lifetime of memories," Rob said earnestly. "I know we can't be together, but at least for one night we could be like husband and wife."

The thought was intoxicating. Rob, warm, wonderful, kind Rob would be great to wake up to. But since that could never be, should we compromise our friendship this way? Hadn't I always been scathingly judgmental about women who slept with married men? Did I owe any sisterly solidarity to Beverly? Was it worth just living for the moment and worrying about the consequences later? Tough questions, especially when you're drowning in a whirlpool of desire.

Rob told me again he loved me. That was enough. I took his hand and led him into the bedroom. I shed my clothes and flung them in a corner. Rob, however, was still fully dressed, staring at me with wide eyes and a stunned expression. Surely he had seen a naked woman before, but apparently the sight of my breasts, not small by any measure, had paralyzed the poor guy. He snapped out of it and began, hurriedly, to shed his own clothes. As soon as he was naked, he squirmed under the covers.

I wriggled in next to Rob in Pop's queen size bed. I bet the bed had seen a lot of action: Pop was vigorous until the end and certainly got around. But I doubted that this bed had been witness to much love. The bed Pop shared with Mom had been banished when she died, along with most of her other belongings. Was doing it in Pop's bed disrespectful, or was it a posthumous tribute to the old man?

"It's been a long time," Rob confided to me in a nervous whisper. "I may be kind of rusty."

"Don't worry," I whispered in between kisses. "It's been almost a year since I've slept with anyone."

"Well, it's been six years for me."

"Wow, you're overdue!" I exclaimed. I asked Rob, in what I hoped were sultry tones, to tell me what he'd like. I was willing to do anything as long as it didn't involve weird fetishes, especially of the bathroom variety. I didn't actually state these limitations, but I was pretty confident that after six years he wasn't going to need anything too fancy. Rob was diffident, afraid of insulting me, or letting go, or something. He seemed embarrassed not only by his secret yearnings but by his very sexuality.

It was clear that he had some specific desires in mind but that he was unable or unwilling to communicate them. I would have to pry it out of him. I reminded him that this was our one chance. Paraphrasing from the *Ethics of the Fathers*, I told him that a shy person doesn't get laid, or at least get laid the way he'd really like to. While caressing him, I begged him to tell me what would turn him on, assuring him that I really wanted to know, and that no, I wouldn't find it disrespectful. This was getting to feel a little like work, but I refused to give up.

No one could ever accuse me of being demure in bed, so I started to experiment. Through trial and error I was determined to find out what excited him. My breast grazed his erection, which was literally purple and looked about ready to burst. By his shudder, I knew that I'd hit pay dirt.

"Oh God, Oh God, Oh God," he intoned, sounding like a heartfelt prayer. "You have to stop or I'm going to embarrass myself," he said.

"Don't worry, we have more time. There is nothing to be embarrassed about. Let yourself go. Let my breasts caress your beautiful cock."

I think that it was my description as much as the sensation that sent him over the edge. Talk about Mt. Vesuvius. Well, the guy had been keeping that stuff in storage for quite a while, and when he came he gave, as my Bubbe would say, a real *geshrai*. I hoped that Mrs. Teitelbaum and the other neighbors were deaf, or at least discreetly embarrassed enough not to say anything if we ran into them the next day.

We cuddled and to my distress, Rob began to cry. I think it was a combination of embarrassment, guilt, happiness, and—most of all—drelease, but it was still disconcerting. I comforted him, rubbing his shoulders and neck, kissing his back. Facing away from me, he talked for the first time about his life with Beverly.

48

Haltingly, Rob told me about his relationship with Beverly, things I must have realized at some level. He described the first months of his marriage where sex had been uncomfortable and distressing for Beverly. He told me how disappointed he'd been by the honeymoon—too embarrassed and frustrated to tell anyone about how badly things were going. The well-meaning teasing by his fellow rabbinical students just made him feel worse. Beverly wanted to start a family right away and so submitted to his sexual pestering, particularly when she was ovulating. She measured and charted her vaginal temperature every day. Sex was a chore, but it was one she was going to perform with determination, if not passion. Rob had no illusions that she enjoyed it. Eventually, Rob explained, it became clear that they couldn't have biological children. After consulting a fertility doctor, it turned out that Rob was sterile, apparently because of an illness he had as a child. With all the pain, physical and emotional, there was little point in going through the unpleasant exercise. Basically, Beverly believed in sex for procreative purposes only, and there was no way that was going to happen.

"Didn't you realize that she had a problem with sex when you were dating?"

"I thought she was just modest, saving herself for her husband. I actually liked that about her."

"You mean you didn't sleep together before you got married?" I asked, too incredulous to be tactful. True, Jeremy had lost interest in sex when he became absorbed by work, but we did have our romps in law school. That's one of the reasons I married him.

"I knew I wanted to be a rabbi, and I felt that I had to live a pure and holy life. Set a good example. I wanted to wait until I was married to have relations."

"So Beverly has been your only partner?"

"Yes. I was a virgin on my wedding night—a blushing groom. A mortified groom, actually. Believe me, I've thought many times that if I'd had a little more sexual experience, maybe Bev would have warmed up to the physical side of our relationship."

I doubted very much that anything he could have done would have warmed Bev up short of blasting her with a blow torch, and even that probably wouldn't have defrosted her. But there was no percentage in being nasty about her.

"Why didn't you two adopt?" I asked.

"Bev wouldn't hear of it. She saw no point in raising someone else's kids. I would have loved to adopt some kids, three or four at least, but since I was the one who had created the problem, I didn't feel I could insist."

My heart went out to Rob. The guy missed out on being a dad, something he truly would have treasured and been good at. Beverly couldn't have tolerated the mess and chaos of kids. She couldn't even tolerate the mess and chaos of "relations," for God's sake.

"And you don't sleep with her anymore?" I asked.

"I used to get birthday sex, but even that waned after a while," Rob said.

"Let's pretend it *is* your birthday. And here you are in your birthday suit," I observed. "What do you want for your present?"

He was still too shy to tell me. Instead, he declared: "You. *You're* my present. I envy your uninhibited joy in your body."

I knew this was true. Rob really did envy me. Even now he couldn't fully relax and enjoy the physical sensations. In the past I might have taken such a reaction personally, ascribing it to my fatso appearance and believing that there was something deficient in me that failed to drive my partner wild. With Rob, I had none of those feelings. I had no doubt at all that Rob found me attractive. I was in better shape than I'd been in years, even though no one could mistake me for svelte. I realized that it just didn't matter. He wanted *me*, rolls of fat and all. He wanted *me*, with my stretch marks, jiggly arms, and sagging breasts. He also seemed more than a little bit embarrassed about wanting me.

Rob began caressing me again. It was clear that he didn't have a lot of sexual experience, yet his desire was unmistakable. That's what six years without a woman's touch will do to you, I suppose.

"Tell me, sweetheart, what do you find sexy?"

"If you really want to know," he confided to my surprise, "I imagine that I'm a sultan and a well-endowed, almond-eyed Yemenite beauty from my harem, um . . . services me."

This fantasy was clearly what helped Rob survive the barren years with Beverly.

"Would you settle for a Jewish chick from Westchester who sucks your cock?" I asked.

"What a mouth you have on you!" Rob exclaimed, though he was clearly more turned on than scandalized.

"You're about to find out," I said with a grin.

"Stop," he cried, "I should wash myself. This isn't fair to you," he protested.

I insisted, and finally convinced him that I wanted to taste him just the way he was.

"I can't believe you'd do this for me," Rob said. Heck, if I could do it for David Berman in the tenth grade, I could do it for the most wonderful man I knew.

"It's my pleasure to do as my Sultan has commanded," I informed him, and he moaned, apparently oblivious to how cheesy I was being.

The look of bliss on his face was a sexy sight. He moaned in appreciation with every move I made, understandable since all of his adult sexual experiences were with Beverly, who apparently favored the lie-still-and-think-of-England approach to lovemaking. I was thrilled to be so close to Rob, and giddy that I could offer him so much pleasure. However, I never came, and he never thought to ask me about it. Did he know such things were possible?

We ordered in Chinese food from the kosher take-out place (no need to violate every commandment), and ate it in bed while watching television.

"Are you going to *daven* in the morning?" I asked Rob.

"No," he replied, "I'll skip the morning prayers. I don't think I should call attention to myself with the *kaddosh baruch hu*," Rob whispered in my ear while spooning and cupping my breasts.

As the night wore on, our mood shifted and became imbued with an impending sense of loss. Not regret exactly, but I felt a premonition of the difficulties the morning would bring. We slept from 2:00 a.m. on. Rob cradled me next to his furry chest and I felt wonderfully peaceful lying naked next to him. The next morning, breakfast was a somber affair as we ate quickly so that Rob could be in time for his flight. Dreading our imminent goodbye, I couldn't help wondering if this had been such a good idea.

49

After the cab picked up Rob, I spent the rest of the morning finishing the packing, shipping four boxes back to Hudsonville, and arranging for the rest of Pop's clothes and furniture to be hauled away. I also made a stab at getting Pop's paperwork in order. Pop left me a whole bunch of stock that pretty much guaranteed my retirement. He left Sam a good deal of money too and if Sam managed to stay out of trouble, he could afford to go to the college of his choice and still have money left over to buy a car and put a down-payment on a house. Somehow, the idea of Sam's shaping up to be a normal, upright citizen didn't seem quite as fanciful as it had a few months before.

I made it home late the next day. The plane ride was a breeze despite some turbulence. My thoughts were full of my recent adventure with Rob, and I felt no fear and no need to make resolutions.

I wondered when I would hear from Rob again and what our interaction would be like. I knew he couldn't conduct an affair with me in New York. Being a rabbi was everything to him and was thoroughly incompatible with having an affair with a local divorcee, the mother of a kid in the Youth Group. He couldn't give up his calling, not even for me. Still, I was happy to relive the encounter in my mind, relishing my memory of his deep desire for me.

As it turned out, I didn't have long to wait. The following day there was a message that left no identifying information, but I knew that voice anywhere. "Call me on my phone and I'll call you right back," he said, and he left me the number. Wow, I thought, I've been granted entry into the inner circle. I had Rob's private cell phone number. Was the sex so wonderful for him that he was willing to take a chance and keep things going between us? Did he love me that much? Could I handle a clandestine affair? Did I even want one?

I took the phone into my bedroom and called his number. Two minutes later Rob called me back.

"Hey, Claire."

"Hey," I replied in my best approximation of a lusty yet friendly voice (not a combo that's easy to pull off). "What's up?"

"I'm worried. We didn't use protection," Rob said in a voice tight with anxiety.

"Sweetheart," I said gingerly, "I thought you told me that a child wasn't possible."

"I don't mean protection from pregnancy," he said, "I mean protection from disease. We didn't use a condom, and I could have gotten AIDS."

"How exactly could you get AIDS?"

"AIDS, or herpes, or gonorrhea, or genital warts, or any of scores of sexually transmitted diseases. I could have them because we had unprotected sex."

"But for you to get one of those diseases, I'd have to have it."

"How do you know you don't? Maybe you don't have symptoms, but you could have a disease and not know it. I'm not saying that you'd ever infect me on purpose, but we should have used a condom. I'm going to be punished for this. I know it," Rob fretted.

"Well I'm glad to know that you don't think I would give you a sexually transmitted disease on purpose, which, by the way, is a crime in New York State," I said slowly. Could he hear how ridiculous he was sounding?

"When is the last time you were tested?" he asked.

"The last time I had sex was almost a year ago," I said. "Why would I need to be tested? I'm fine, Rob, and you're fine."

"But that guy could have infected you."

"We used a condom."

"With him you used a condom," Rob muttered.

"We didn't plan for this to happen."

"Are you kidding? I fantasized about it for months. Claire, you're all I've thought about. This was no accident."

A long silence followed.

"OK, you may have used a condom with that guy. . . ."

"Rob. . . ."

". . . but condoms can fail," Rob continued. "I'm a nervous wreck about this."

"Would you like me to get tested?" I offered.

"Would you?" he asked with relief.

"I will," I assured him. "Look, I'll do this if it will make you feel better, but the truth is I think you're just feeling overwhelmed and guilty. Let's face it, we committed adultery—violated one of the top-ten big ones—and I think you're just having a hard time making sense of things. So, instead, you're latching onto something ridiculous to panic about. It will be OK. I want to assure you that I understand that we can't continue now that we're back in New York. And I promise I won't tell a soul."

"It wasn't adultery," Rob snapped. "You're not married and the commandment is against sleeping with your neighbor's wife. So, I didn't really violate the commandment. It was more like a concubine arrangement."

"I beg your pardon," I said.

"Well, technically, you're a *peelegesh*. Concubine is a bad translation. . . ." Rob trailed off. "What I mean to say," he continued, "is that because you're not married, we didn't commit adultery. That's all I'm saying. It's a good thing."

"That's a relief," I said, with as much sarcasm as I could muster.

"Well, I would certainly really appreciate it if you would get tested."

I was torn between anger and pity. The guy couldn't take one day to savor the memory of our hot, loving encounter before immediately imagining how his angry, retributive God was going to punish him. His angry God or his vengeful wife. Bev wouldn't put out, but she was going to make sure that Rob wouldn't get any action from anyone else. Apparently Jehovah was on her side. Who was rooting for the scorned concubine? Probably some pagan goddess.

"I'll do it," I said simply.

"Thanks. I wouldn't bother you, but if I go to get tested, the whole community will hear about it."

"What's his name . . . Seth . . . your cardiologist sure didn't seem discreet," I agreed.

"And Bev is so vigilant about my health, she'd be sure to find out."

"I understand," I said, though I was pretty sure I didn't.

"Call me at this number when you get the tests back."

"That may be weeks. Can't I just give you a thumbs-up at the gym?"

Another long silence followed. I pressed, "Won't I be seeing you at the gym?"

"Um . . . I don't think I'll be going back to the gym."

"Why not?"

"Well, when she came back from Israel, Bev set up a home gym in the basement. She bought a used treadmill, a stepper, mats, and all sorts of weights. It really was a thoughtful gesture."

"Yeah, I bet she put a lot of thought into it," I said.

"Claire, don't be unkind."

"This whole conversation has been unkind. So unlike you, Rob. You're being a jerk. Are you aware of that?"

"I'm sorry, I'm just worried. And about the home gym, what can I do? Bev really does look out for my health," he added.

"Okay, I got it. You fucked me. The mystery is gone. The fantasy is officially over. I'll call you when I have proof that I didn't give you some dreaded but fully deserved sexually transmitted disease," I said in a clipped tone, trying to keep my tears in check.

"I'm sorry. I'm handling this all wrong. Our night together was wonderful and will be a treasured memory."

"One that you can masturbate to?"

Rob gasped. "Claire, please." He was crying. "I love you."

"I love you too, you big dope," I said and ended the call.

50

I couldn't face my own gynecologist with Rob's ridiculous request, so I decided to go to Planned Parenthood. To enter, I had to pass through a gauntlet of anti-abortion protesters.

"Don't kill your baby!" one of them implored.

"Do I look pregnant to you? If so, I'm going to demand my gym membership back," I retorted.

"Ma'am, we can't always tell who's pregnant."

"So you just hassle everyone?" I asked.

"Ma'am, we're trying to save a life. I'm pleading for the unborn," the woman responded.

"I know you're doing this because you think it's right. But ten miles from here there are hungry kids in Yonkers. Why don't you go and do something for the already-born?" I asked.

"I do," the woman replied.

"What do you do for those kids?" I challenged.

"I pray for them," the woman answered, wrapping her arm around a young girl who looked less than thrilled to be there.

"That's nice, but they're still hungry. Do something useful. Go to Grace Church and serve a kid a meal," I retorted angrily, and didn't wait for an answer. My God, was I in a bad mood.

The waiting room was mainly filled with young women, some with partners in tow, some alone like me. I leafed through two back issues of *People* before my name was called. The nurse practitioner, Betsy, was a friendly-looking woman about my age.

I explained the situation. "I don't think these tests are necessary, but the guy I slept with—just once—is now in a panic."

The nurse practitioner rolled her eyes. "Let me guess," she said. "He's convinced he's got AIDS."

"How'd you know?"

"I see this all the time. Is he some sort of religious freak?"

"You could say so."

"They always figure God is punishing them for having a good time."

"At least the sex rated the wrath of God," I observed.

"Glad to hear it," she said with a conspiratorial smile. "I'll need a blood sample and a vaginal swab. As long as we're at it, are you due for a pap smear?"

"Give me the works," I said.

"Any chance that you're pregnant?"

"That ship has sailed," I said.

"I've seen plenty of women our age came back positive. Next to the teenagers, women in their forties have the highest number of unplanned pregnancies," she explained.

"So that's why the protesters accosted me," I said. "Well, I'm confident that there's no chance."

The genital exam went fine but Betsy had trouble finding a vein in my arm. This happens to me a lot. Apparently, the one thin part of me is my vein structure. In frustration, she took off her gloves and felt around for a vein. Clearly Betsy didn't think I had AIDS either. After a couple of uncomfortable false starts, she hit pay dirt and blood started trickling into the vial.

"When will the results be in?" I asked.

"Come back in a week to get them."

"Can't I just call?" I asked.

"Sorry, we worry about giving a bad result over the phone so we require folks to come back in. That way we can be helpful if patients have any questions."

I saw the logic in this, though it did seem a shame to miss another morning at the gym to learn that, surprise, surprise, I didn't have a sexually transmitted disease.

I was happy to see that my desire to go to the gym hadn't diminished even though I knew there was no chance Rob would be there. It certainly wasn't the same, but it was still good, and I was grateful for the time in the morning to organize my thoughts and for the feeling of well-being the exercise generated.

At work, I intended to catch up with lots of paperwork from the few days I'd been gone. "Doughnuts," I instructed Molly as I started to triage through my messages. I saw that Sam's dentist appointment was confirmed and then noticed with some alarm that I had received a message from Officer Arnold, the guy who helped out Teresa. I immediately called him myself rather than have Molly make the call for me. I reached him right away and he thanked me for getting back to him. Officer Arnold reassured me that Duane wasn't being released.

"No ma'am, I didn't mean to worry you on that score. Mr. Williams is being held without bail and isn't going anywhere until his trial, which is currently set for March. I have something entirely different to ask you about, ma'am," he said.

"Shoot," I said, and then realized that might not be the best thing to say to a cop.

"Two of my men went on a domestic violence call the other night, a really bad one. The woman needed multiple stitches, had some broken ribs, and had to be observed in the hospital overnight."

"I'm sorry to hear that."

"Well, it seems that her husband, who bonded out that same night, is going to put up a fight. When she was discharged from the hospital she wouldn't go home with him, though the bastard had the gall to try and pick her up. She went to the shelter instead. He's secured some sort of temporary emergency order keeping the kids from her, saying that she's crazy and a danger to them. Well, the shelter is trying to help, but the guy's some kind of corporate big-shot and has a team of lawyers on the case. This poor woman is totally outgunned. And let me tell you, this isn't the first time we've been called to that home."

"That's outrageous."

"Well, ma'am, I was hoping you might be willing to take this on pro bono."

"I have to make sure that I don't have a conflict of interest, but otherwise, I think I can do it."

"That's great, ma'am. With you on the case, she might have a fair shot."

"Can I ask you a favor, Officer Arnold?"

"Yes, ma'am."

"Call me Claire."

"OK, Claire, if you'll call me Benedict." There was a short pause. "Just joking. My name is Greg."

I didn't know what to make of this guy. From what I remembered, he looked like a stereotypical cop, but our conversation didn't exactly fit my preconceptions. I asked Greg how come he came to me.

"I have to be honest, in my line of work, you don't develop the highest esteem for lawyers. We catch the bad guys and the lawyers just get them off. It can be pretty demoralizing. Most lawyers I meet are clever but basically timid. Now, you, on the other hand, I got to see you in action the night we apprehended Williams. I admired all your careful planning and your behavior on the scene—you were fearless. I'd sure want you on my side in a fight."

What a sweet, if odd, compliment.

"We probably should meet in person to discuss the case," I said.

"Could I drop by later this afternoon?" he asked. "I get off at 3:00. How about 3:30?"

"You're doing this off the clock?"

"What, only fancy-pants attorneys can do pro bono?"

"No, of course not," I said, flustered. "See you at 3:30."

"I'm looking forward to it," he said and hung up.

At 3:30, Molly ushered Greg Arnold into my office.

"I had no trouble getting by your goons," he said flashing a smile at Molly.

"He brought doughnuts," Molly said with approval.

"Don't flatter yourself; a crazed serial killer could get by Molly with a couple of chocolate glazed doughnuts," I said.

I invited Molly and Greg to the conference table. As Molly dispensed Greg's goodies, I gave them both a status report.

"We have no conflict, Greg. The jerk doesn't work here, thank God. Molly has already run criminal records, civil suit, and credit checks. The guy may be rich, but with three prior assault arrests he should be on his last chance with the law. I honestly don't understand why this isn't a criminal matter."

"Well," Greg said, clearly trying to remain calm, "I can't speculate why the prosecutor doesn't pursue him. We assemble the evidence and the prosecutor has to take it from there."

"How frustrating," I said.

"If anyone can get this guy, Claire can," Molly said.

"Thanks, Molly. All I can do is secure a civil order of protection and get her some interim support, but that would be something. And we have to get her access to the kids. There is no way the judge should have granted that order, even as a temporary measure."

"What's the next step?" Greg asked.

"I'll need to interview my client and I'll need her to sign various medical and mental health privacy waivers. Were there any witnesses to the latest attack?"

"Just the kids," Greg said quietly.

"And *he* has them?" Molly asked with alarm.

"Oh, he doesn't touch the kids. The ass-kicking is reserved for the one he promised to love and cherish," Greg said.

"Let's intervene before death parts them," I said.

Greg flashed me a huge smile. "Let's," he said.

We developed an action plan and Greg set up a meeting with my new client.

"That bastard won't know what hit him," Greg said with satisfaction as we said our goodbyes.

"What a nice guy," I observed to Molly after Greg left.

"Nice and beefy," she said. "And he wasn't wearing a ring."

"Don't be ridiculous. Officer Arnold values me for my bulldog lawyering, not as dating material."

"I wouldn't be so sure, Claire."

The next morning, I received a call from Greg that even I had to admit might have some romantic overtones. Not much had happened with our case, so I was surprised to hear from him so soon.

"Anyone listening in?" Greg asked.

"Not unless the feds have tapped my phone," I said.

"What about Molly?"

"We have no secrets."

"So, who should I call to ask you to dinner?"

"There's no need, I'm happy to do this. You don't need to buy me dinner."

"I think you misunderstand," he replied, "I want to buy you dinner. Is seven o'clock on Saturday night good for you?"

"Uh . . . yeah." I was stunned.

"Great, I'll pick you up at home. Wear something sexy." And with that, he hung up the phone.

The day was busy, but every once in a while my mind would wander and the echo of Greg's voice would reverberate. I needed some fashion advice. I asked Molly to summon Teresa, letting her know she was needed in HR immediately.

In the seven weeks since her escape, Teresa had been doing remarkably well. She looked younger and more energetic. She hadn't missed a day of work, and the productivity of her entire department had increased. Teresa would be taking her first airplane flight to spend time with her son in Oregon. I guess there really wasn't much to miss about old Duane, though to her credit, Teresa never spoke ill of him to her kids or anyone else.

When Molly ushered Teresa in, I told her what was up with Officer Arnold and that I needed a sexy outfit, pronto.

"You're right, this is an emergency. But no problem, you've got the curves to pull it off. I've gotta hand it to you. Not many women could find romance at a domestic violence incident."

"I attribute it to my ability to multitask," I told her with a smile.

"I know a great little thrift and vintage place we can try. It would be better than fighting the Christmas crowds at the department stores, and it's open late every day this week."

"I place myself in your capable hands," I told her.

51

After work, Teresa and I met for dinner. Neither one of us could quite adjust to our new-found freedom, and the ability to go out for a last-minute dinner was among the sweetest of them. Teresa had actually gained some weight. She looked softer and less stressed. Although I still had plenty of meat on my bones, I was toned and felt good about my body. I had to admit that much of the credit had to go to Rob, whom I never expected to hear from again, the idiot.

We went out to one of the few local Italian places that Teresa approved of (it was hard to live up to the exacting culinary standards inculcated by her Nonna, and Teresa hated a restaurant meal that she could prepare better in her own kitchen). The place she took me to was one of those unassuming joints with Formica tables, paper napkins, and food to die for.

After dinner, I followed Teresa to the shop she recommended, which I realized only when I parked my car was the Hadassah Thrift and Vintage Shop run by none other than Beverly, Rob's wife.

"Come on, don't be nervous; this will be fun," Teresa encouraged, seeing I was hesitant to get out of the car.

Before I could make up some excuse, Beverly spotted me. This encounter was simply going to have to happen. Doubtless, Rob would think I was stalking his family.

"Claire?" Beverly seemed pleased to see me as I walked into the shop. I was surprised that she remembered my name, but I guess that's a skill that a *rebbetzin* develops, especially an entrepreneurial *rebbetzin*. "I'm so glad you decided to check out the shop. Teresa is one of my best customers," she said as she smiled warmly at Teresa.

I looked around. The place was spotless (no surprise there) and filled, floor to ceiling, with gorgeous clothes, shoes, handbags, and jewelry. The space wasn't particularly large, but every available surface was used to maximum advantage.

"Nothing to donate today," Teresa said, "but we need to outfit Claire for a hot date. I'm thinking something low cut with some high-heeled shoes."

"I never wear heels," I protested.

"Yes, that's why I'm here," Teresa said. "If I let you dress yourself, you would wear a navy suit and flats."

Teresa had my number and I decided that the only rational thing to do was to submit to being her full-sized Dawn doll.

Beverly looked me over carefully, clearly thinking hard. I was braced for some crack about my weight but she was actually quite friendly. "I have this vintage Diane von Furstenberg wrap dress that would look great on you," Beverly said. "And, while you're trying this on," Beverly said, handing me the dress, "Teresa and I will look for accessories."

I've always detested clothes shopping and have done as much of it as possible online. I was bad at choosing the clothes and hated trying things on in the dressing room, wrestling with ill-fitting garments and getting frustrated and sweaty. Clearly, what I'd been missing all along was my own personal shopper. With the expertise and boundless enthusiasm of Beverly and Teresa, this actually felt like fun.

The wrap-around dress looked pretty good. It certainly was low cut, and the brown print pattern camouflaged my still-protruding belly.

"I want to give you a different bra to try," Beverly said.

"A vintage bra?" I asked, imagining something pointy and menacing.

"No, bras we sell new," Beverly replied with a smile.

"What size are you currently wearing?" Beverly asked as she tugged at the straps of the one I was wearing.

"A 40-C," I responded. Apparently, both Finebergs were obsessed with my breasts. Beverly, however, was more clinical and professional. This whole experience was beyond surreal.

"Try a 38-DD. You've got a slender back and need a bit more room in the front."

My back was slender? Well, it could join my veins on the short list of thin things about me. It was nice of Beverly to say so. With the new bra, the dress looked va-va-va-voom. I bought two-inch designer crocodile pumps, jewelry to match, and three bras. As we were checking out, Beverly directed my attention to some handmade soaps.

"They're made by the women at the domestic violence shelter. They're actually great products, all organic and very fragrant."

Beverly was in her element. She was a natural saleswoman who believed in her merchandise. I bought three soaps, one of which I intended to give to Teresa as a thank-you gift. Beverly also provided me with information about donations and volunteer opportunities. Some of my work suits were getting baggy and I would be happy to donate them, but volunteering alongside Beverly was one step too bizarre, even for me.

52

Christmas Day the Jews of Hudsonville all get together to serve dinner to the homeless in the basement at Grace Chapel in Yonkers. I'd agreed to participate months ago, before I could fathom feeling awkward around Rob, who would certainly be there. Also, Sam was coming. I hadn't seen him in over a week—our longest separation ever. Sam would be attending this Christmas event instead of the dinner with Kimberly's family on the Upper East Side of New York. I gathered there was some tension in Kimberly's family over her conversion to Judaism, and bringing a surly Jewish stepson to Christmas dinner was more drama than even she could handle.

Joanie organized the food, which was our synagogue's contribution to the whole shebang. She'd been up early roasting turkeys in the church ovens. Beverly organized the desserts and had sent in a prodigious number of cakes and pies. Tellingly, she'd sent her regrets at the last minute. No big surprise there. Interacting with the homeless just wasn't her scene. There wasn't enough hand sanitizer in the universe.

Bertha Lewis, Dr. Lewis' wife, was in charge of the side dishes. Bertha made the green bean casseroles and salads. She'd assigned Marjorie the task of making the stuffing and delegated the sweet potatoes to me. I was pleased to see that the recipe called for marshmallow fluff.

I found that I actually didn't mind cooking in my newly clean and freshly painted kitchen, though I did get a bit weary of all the potatoes I had to peel. Per my promise to Teresa, I'd hired a cleaning service to come in. They'd already cleaned my house twice and the place looked and smelled a whole lot better. Obviously, the real test would be when Sam came home. But I was hoping that after experiencing the high life at Jeremy and Kimberly's, he might have picked up some good habits.

By the time I got to the church, my stomach was churning and my heart racing at the prospect of facing Rob. I felt a crazy mix of contradictory emotions—deep connection, disappointment, love, and anger. Of course, I was mad at myself too. I should have listened to Lydia. Anyone could have foreseen the looming disaster—anyone, apparently, but Rob and me. Maybe it was inevitable that we had to push the relationship into sexual territory, just as it was inevitable that it would end in farce. It was also inevitable that in a small town like Hudsonville, our paths would have to cross.

I hadn't spotted Rob yet and there was plenty of work to do. With Joanie running the show, the food line moved smoothly and started promptly at ten. The Christmas meal was available from ten in the morning until two in the afternoon. Folks started lining up at nine. I was grateful that it wasn't too cold outside.

Another Hudsonville synagogue had arranged for toys and gifts. Yet a third *shul* was in charge of the decorations. Let's face it, there wasn't much for Jews to do on Christmas Day. How many times can you watch *It's a Wonderful Life*? Rumor had it that a group of my co-religionists was going to hit the Dragon Inn Chinese restaurant after we were through and then light Hanukkah candles.

My first task was to mingle with the patrons, wish them a Merry Christmas, and engage them in conversation. I looked around and saw people of all ages and backgrounds. There were a number of people who were obviously alcoholics and some who smelled as if they hadn't bathed in weeks. Even more disturbing, I saw a lot of parents with young children.

The parents experiencing homelessness were especially excited about the toys, none wrapped. The idea was that these parents could choose a gift and then take it to a wrapping station.

"This is the only gift I have for my daughter," one woman explained as she placed a bow on the wrapping paper. "I'm really glad I won't have to visit her empty-handed."

"Will you get to see your daughter later today?" I asked.

"Yeah, she lives with my sister. I lost my apartment and I didn't have a safe place for my daughter to stay. Now I need permission to go and visit my own daughter," she said bitterly. "My mother and my sister both hate me."

"I'm sorry," I told her. "Maybe this new year will bring you better luck."

"It's not about luck. It's about choices, and I've made some pretty bad ones. At least I'm not drunk at ten in the morning," she said, pointing to a toothless man across the table who reeked of alcohol. The man just smiled sheepishly.

My next job was at the wrapping station, where I was to enforce the one-gift-only rule until we were sure everyone had received something. An older woman with long, graying, unkempt blonde hair, grubby jeans, and too few teeth in her mouth glanced about her furtively then grabbed two items, and ran with them back to her table. I approached her.

"Ma'am, we're asking everyone just to take one gift until we're sure there's enough for everyone."

"I've got kids," she said angrily.

"I see you have a lot of gifts," I said, gesturing to a full garbage bag under the table. "You're welcome to them, but if some more kids come in, I might need to ask you to put some back, so everyone can have something for Christmas."

I returned to the gift table and my duties as Christmas cop and observed the woman leaving with her large garbage bag. The shelter director came up to chat and told me that every year the same few folks grab a ton of stuff and try to sell it to buy alcohol or drugs. Ho! Ho! Ho!

Just then I was startled to see Rob sitting at the piano in the front of the room. I tried not to look his way, but it was hard to ignore him as he started to play and sing his heart out. He clearly knew and, I'd venture to say, enjoyed the entire Christmas hit parade. He had all the kids around the piano singing "Jingle Bells" both in its original and in its subversive "Batman smells" versions.

I continued to circulate and ran into Bertha.

"Gum?" she offered.

"No thanks," I replied. "I'd no idea the rabbi could play so well."

"He never took a lesson," Bertha informed me with pride. "It's all by ear. He also has a lovely singing voice. Our Rabbi Reuven is very talented."

If only Bertha knew how I'd been privy to some of his less well-publicized talents.

Despite serious misgivings and a wildly beating heart, I decided to approach Rob. I couldn't help myself; I was simply drawn to him. I waited until it would be just the two of us at the piano.

"I hear you can play anything by ear."

"Yep, but sometimes my tone is way off," Rob replied as he continued to play "Silent Night." "I can really hit some wrong notes, and things come out sounding horrible, really horrible," he said.

"I bet you feel really sorry when that happens, Rabbi."

"You have no idea how much I regret it," he said.

"Well, everyone hits a few clunkers now and then, especially when they're under a lot of pressure."

"You're a very kind music critic. Very forgiving. Would you consider sitting by me and singing along?"

I wanted to make peace with Rob. He'd been so important to me these last few months of my life. No question, his recent behavior had been ridiculous and hurtful. But Rob wasn't truly a cad. He loved me, in his own screwed-up, repressed way. What the hell? I thought. Let's try to forgive each other.

We began our duet.

"Oh the weather outside is frightful," Rob sang.

"But the fire is so delightful," I rejoined, and we were belting it out, laughing and having a great time. Our voices melded together nicely and the crowd had sort of hushed to listen to us. Joanie came up at the last croon of "let it snow."

"Sorry to interrupt, but I need Claire's help in the kitchen."

There were plenty of people just hanging around; why did Joanie need me? I wondered. Nevertheless, I followed her back to the kitchen.

"I don't know what's going on, but, for God's sake, that's our *rabbi* out there," Joan said in a hushed, angry whisper.

"There's nothing going on. Rob, I mean the rabbi, and I just both went to Jewish day school. We're compensating for our lack of Christmas songs growing up."

Joanie looked at me meaningfully.

"Look," I continued, "we've become friends. I met him while we were caring for you." This was a cruel lie, but I felt desperate. "A rabbi is allowed to have friends."

"I'm just asking you to think about how you're behaving. You're playing with fire here. Rabbi Reuven's reputation has to be above reproach. Any gossip or intrigue will undermine his position."

"Come on, Joanie, I wasn't making out with the guy."

"You might as well have been."

"I think you're overreacting."

"Claire, I know you and he were in Florida at the same time."

"It's a big state, Joanie."

"And you're a bad liar. You know, I'm worried for you, too. This can only lead to heartbreak. I've been holding my tongue, but today, it was just too much."

"I know you have my best interests at heart. I hear you and I promise I'll be more circumspect. I didn't mean to make a spectacle."

"Please, Claire, don't just hide it. Whatever's going on, just put an end to it. For both your sakes."

"I give you my word, there's nothing to worry about. There's absolutely nothing going on."

Joanie gave me a big hug. She was a true friend, the kind who would let you know when you were acting like an idiot.

In my defense, my Clintonesque denial was technically true. Rob and I had nothing going on romantically at that moment, nor would we at any time in the future. Rob and I would never make love again. He couldn't tolerate the stress of infidelity and, if truth be told, he was probably too repressed to fully satisfy me. Sitting next to Rob on the piano bench, I'd finally accepted that we could never sustain an affair. I also accepted that we'd probably tanked our deep friendship that had been teeter-tottering on the edge of romance for months. I'd miss the excitement and sense of possibility that had so permeated our every encounter. But, honestly, I also felt relief. For the first time I was able to feel calm around Rob. How ironic that we got busted after everything fizzled.

I went to join Sam in the serving line. He was dishing out potatoes and stuffing. As I approached the table, I overheard him tell an older gentleman, "I hope you like the sweet potatoes. My mom made them." Was that a note of pride I detected? Was Sam actively associating my name with his rather than pretending he wasn't of woman born (at least this woman)?

"Hey, Sam," I said.

"Hey, Mom," he answered. We were a laconic but not unfriendly pair. I derived a lot of satisfaction from seeing how solicitous Sam was toward the patrons on the food line. He was particularly kind to a small boy, Ryan, who was reveling in his new fire truck. Unwilling to let go of the truck, Ryan couldn't hold his plate. Sam went through the line with him and had Ryan indicate all the food he wanted to eat.

"Nicely done," I said when Sam returned. Although tempted, I didn't recount the story of when Sam, at age four, wouldn't relinquish his police car, even in the bathtub or at bedtime. Would there ever be a time I could wax nostalgic with Sam about those good old days? It would have to suffice that some good new days seemed to be looming on the horizon.

We were getting ready to go.

"Get your coat, Sam."

"My coat's gone," Sam said when he returned a minute later.

"Someone stole your coat?" I asked.

"No. I hung it on the free-coat rack by accident. Somebody already took it. Sorry, Mom."

I laughed. "You hung your new coat on the give-away rack?"

"Do you want me to see if it's still around?"

"No, Sam; whoever took it, needs it. We can't take it back. I'll get you another coat—just not tomorrow when the crowds will be murder."

"You aren't going to yell at me for always losing my shit?" he asked.

"Would yelling help you lose less shit?" I asked.

"No," Sam answered.

"Then there isn't much point in making a fuss about it," I said.

"I can't believe I didn't see the sign," Sam said.

"It's no big deal. It's actually kind of funny. Look, we're lucky we have the money to go and buy another coat. Not everyone has it that good."

Standing next to Sam I could tell that, in the ten days since I'd seen the boy, he'd actually grown taller. Even if he never got neater or more organized, we had much to be thankful for.

53

Greg picked me up promptly at 7:00.

"Wow!" he said. "You look great."

"You can thank Teresa. She took me shopping and picked out my outfit."

"Tell her we're even now. She doesn't owe me a thing for saving her life."

"I thought *I* saved Teresa's life," I protested.

"That's right," Greg conceded, "You saved Teresa, and I saved *you*. How are you planning to repay me?"

"Let's see how the evening goes," I said.

Greg opened the car door for me, something that hasn't happened in, well, ever. As he drove, we listened to Sinatra and chit-chatted about Christmas. I told him about Grace Church and he told me about Christmas Eve dinner at his brother's house with his parents, cousins, and most important of all, his daughter Amy.

Turned out we have kids about the same age, which led to a lively discussion regarding who is more monstrous at age 14, girls or boys. It was an odd conversation because my normally competitive instinct to prove that my kid reigned supreme as the absolute worst was tempered by how improved, if not quite reasonable, Sam had been lately. Also, in the back of my mind I realized that Greg might one day meet Sam, and I didn't want to poison the well. Apparently, Amy was emotional, dramatic, and just plain mean to her dad. Sam, with his role as internet porn procurer for Hudsonville Middle School, clearly could have topped Amy's door-slamming and crying jags, but I didn't press the point.

We arrived at Gino's Steakhouse, a darkly lit, cozy spot with plush red booths and live piano music.

"What would you like to hear?" Greg asked me.

"How about 'Someone to Watch over Me,'" I suggested. It was a song I loved despite its retro message. We all could use a little watching over, I thought as Greg approached the piano player to make the request.

When the waitress came around to take our drink orders, Greg requested soda with lime and I did the same.

"They have a great wine list you can order by the glass. Please don't abstain just because I'm not drinking."

"That's OK. I rarely drink. I just get sleepy when I do."

"So what do you do for vices?"

"Why should I ruin your pleasure of discovery? You can find out the slow, hard way."

"A woman who likes her vices slow and hard," he mused.

"We're talking about ice cream, right?" I asked.

"Of course, what else would we be talking about?" Greg asked, his voice full of faux innocence. He continued, "I know this date is just beginning, but my sense is, it's going well. Before I screw anything up, I'd like to ask you if you're free New Year's Eve."

"I think so," I replied, surprised but happy, "unless, of course, George Clooney calls, in which case I'm ditching."

"He's married now so I'll take that chance," he said, smiling.

The waitress returned and we ordered Caesar salads, spinach, baked potatoes, and rib steaks.

"I'm glad you're not a vegetarian," Greg said.

"You like a woman who can sink her teeth into a juicy piece of meat?" I asked.

"Sure do. Besides, I have a theory that all vegetarians are subconsciously hostile," Greg said. "They secretly want to be cannibals and repress the urge by becoming vegetarians."

"So I passed the first test because I eat meat," I observed.

"No, there are no tests. But if there had been, you would have passed the minute I saw you in that dress," Greg replied.

The food was delicious, and conversation flowed easily. Our talk was convivial and genuine without being overly personal. Neither one of us was compelled by a confessional urge to spill the sorrows of our former relationships. I guess we both figured that we could discuss our failed marriages and poor choices on future dates. This evening was for unadulterated enjoyment. Greg told me about his career on the police force and expressed genuine interest in my job, especially how we handle the occasional violent episode in the workplace. We also spoke about movies and books. Greg was a World War II buff and read every bit of relevant nonfiction out there. Currently, he was reading a biography of FDR's war years. I told him that I was rereading the girls' canon and was on the sixth in the *Little House on the Prairie* series, *The Long Winter*.

"No matter how cold I get this winter, I'll never rival what Laura and Carrie suffered in that long winter in the Dakota territories. There were icicles on the interior nails of their bedroom," I said.

"I used to love reading those books to Amy," Greg said. "I miss those days when the very sound of my voice wasn't automatically irritating to her."

I looked closely at Greg. Although he wasn't classically handsome, he was very attractive to me, with a commanding presence, deep voice, and strong build. As far as I was concerned, head hair was overrated. Greg certainly was opinionated and, I suspected, fairly conservative, but he was also interesting to talk to and very quick to laugh.

I didn't offer to pay or even to leave the tip. It was nice to be treated, and I realized that Greg would be offended if I offered to contribute, especially because I was pretty sure that I earned at least twice as much as he did. This evening would be retro all the way. That air of nostalgia was complemented by Ella on the car's CD player singing "How Long Has This Been Going On?"—one of the sexiest songs I've ever heard.

Greg walked me to the door.

"Do you want to come in?" I asked, not knowing what to expect or even how I wanted the evening to progress.

"Not tonight," he said as he gently wrapped me in his arms, kissing me on my neck, my eyelids, and finally my mouth.

"Are you sure you don't want to come in?" I asked, a little short of breath, feeling chills up my spine, and now quite clear about what I wanted from him as my hands massaged his muscular back.

"It's not from lack of interest," Greg said.

That was for damn sure.

"But I'm not coming in tonight."

His fingers gently stroked my hair. "Do me a favor," he whispered in my ear, "wear the same outfit on New Year's."

"No problem," I replied, and indeed it wasn't, given that it was the only sexy outfit I had.

"Good," he said kissing my ear. "I plan to unwrap you."

With that he gave me a soft kiss on my cheek and returned to his car. Greg waited for me to get safely inside and then drove off.

54

I got a voicemail from the nurse practitioner. "Hi, Claire. This is Betsy from Planned Parenthood. I think you'll be very happy, but not surprised, when you come in to get the results of all your various tests. I know you're very busy and I wanted to let you know as soon as the results were in. Sounds like other folks have wasted enough of your time. Bye."

How kind she was. I especially appreciated that Betsy bent the rules and telegraphed the results, thereby saving me a trip. It was time to contact Rob on his cell. My hands shook as I entered his number, and I was immensely relieved when it went to message.

"Happy to report a positive result," I said and hung up the phone.

Shit. Positive result could be confusing, and Rob did have a hysterical, panicky side. I called again.

"Just to clarify—passed tests with flying colors. No worries. Happy New Year."

There, my ridiculous errand was done.

I headed for the gym and did a brief weight circuit before getting on the elliptical. I'd slowly begun to recognize some of the regulars and we nodded our hellos. I even received a thumbs-up from Kurt. Now that Rob and I weren't talking through the workout, I had started listening to recorded books. I was well into *Bleak House* and loving it.

In the locker room, a tall, stunning twenty-something with flowing red hair was struggling with the zipper on the back of her dress.

"Here, let me help you," I offered.

"Thanks," she said with relief. "This dress is murder to put on, but it has sentimental value. It belonged to my grandmother."

"It's gorgeous," I said. "How nice that it came from your grandmother. I have to tell you there's no way my grandmother could have pulled off a dress like this."

"Yeah, Gran was hot. She had boyfriends into her eighties."

"I could take some lessons from your grandma."

"Me, too, believe me," the woman replied with a smile. "You don't think my stomach sticks out too much? I think Gran always wore a girdle."

"No, you look great. The color is perfect and it really fits you well."

"Really?"

"Absolutely," I assured her.

"Thanks, and thanks for your help! My name is Krista, by the way."

"Hi Krista. Claire. Nice to meet you."

"I'll see you around the gym?"

"I'm sure. I try to come at least four mornings a week. See you," I said as I headed to work in my blue silk blouse, boring suit, flats, and pearl earrings. My hair, which was gathered in a bun at the nape of my neck, was still wet.

As I sat at my desk attending to other work, I reflected on how good I felt. Even though things had ended disastrously with Rob, something about the love and attraction I felt from him had been deeply affirming—almost healing. My healer was a bit screwed up but none of us is perfect. It's amazing how despite all our personal wounds, we human beings can occasionally be of great help to one another.

55

It was Tuesday morning and I was back at the gym, walking on the treadmill. I found myself daydreaming, not even tempted by the book I was listening to on my iPod. I thought about my upcoming date with Greg and relived the thrill of his kisses. He'd certainly been around the block, but far from begrudging Greg his previous experiences, I was delighted to be their beneficiary. And besides, it was immensely satisfying that I had a date for New Year's Eve. When I called to make arrangements, Sam was actually confused about why I wouldn't be home. The idea of Mom on a date didn't compute.

Sam arranged to sleep over at Ben's house on New Year's Eve, and Marjorie allowed the boys to invite a couple of other kids for a small party. For all my griping about the woman, I had to admit that Marjorie had two exceptionally smart, nice kids and was extremely hospitable. True, there were some annoying rules and occasional diatribes, but her heart was in the right place.

Now that my home was no longer a sty, I was planning to purchase some new stuff. In addition to repainting the living room—something that was about five years overdue—I was going to get new carpeting, a new couch, and some comfortable chairs. I was also planning to re-cover the chairs in the dining room. Teresa, it turned out, could outfit a room as well as she outfitted a person, and we'd been having a blast looking at paint chips, carpet samples, and upholstery swatches. She'd painted four different shades of pale sage green on my living room wall in neat squares. My task was to live with them a while, see which one I liked best, and then choose whatever Teresa recommended. The transformation of my kitchen (which she'd painted herself with my negligible help on the Friday after Thanksgiving) dictated that I would be wise just to follow her lead.

Once all the decorating was done, I would start having folks over. I'd begin by inviting Marjorie and the whole Greenberg clan to reciprocate for all their hospitality. Ditto for Joanie and my boss, Corey.

I felt more energetic than I had a few months previously. Certainly part of it was the exercise, but that wasn't the entire story. I felt so much less alone regarding Sam; I don't think I'd fully realized the isolation and shame I'd felt until things began to get better. And it seemed that I'd finally made peace with Jeremy. I wouldn't have credited him with affecting my life at all, but reaching an amicable truce really relieved me of anger and tension I didn't even know I was feeling. Teresa's friendship was remarkable. Her strength and many talents filled me with admiration. Mostly, though, it was just a joy to hang out with her. And as for Rob. . . . Just then my thoughts were interrupted.

"Is this treadmill taken?"

"No," I said without looking over.

"Good," the voice responded, and immediately I knew.

"Rob!"

"Hi, Claire. I was hoping you'd be here."

"Are you coming back to the gym after all?" I asked.

"No, I'm just here one last time to clean out my locker. My membership expires at the end of the month."

We trod on in silence for a minute or two.

"I got your message—messages, I should say. Thanks."

"No problem. I hope you feel a little better now."

"I do. Sorry I was such a basket case," Rob said.

"It's OK."

"No, it's not OK. My behavior was shameful," Rob insisted.

I wondered if we'd agree on which part was shameful.

"Want to go to the Sage Diner for old times' sake?" he asked.

Did I want to go? I didn't think there was enough bacon in the world to get me through a breakfast with Rob, and with our luck, Beverly would happen upon us as we said our last goodbye.

"Probably not a good idea," I said.

Rob looked dejected but said in a soft voice, "I understand."

Again we walked on our parallel tracks, each of us deep in thought.

"There are some things I need to say to you. If we can't go to the diner, can we at least sit at the juice bar?"

This seemed like a reasonable request, though I kind of liked not having to look Rob in the eye. We got off our machines and made our way to the juice bar, where we each ordered a fresh orange juice.

"I feel terrible that I've hurt you," Rob said, placing his hand on mine.

"I'll admit you were a bit of a jerk, but I'm OK."

"Are you sure? I've been feeling so bad about having to let you down. It was a mistake, a terrible mistake, and I hurt you besides."

"I'm fine," I said.

"I hope so. I really hope so."

We sat for a moment in silence and then Rob resumed. "You know, some good did come out of all this. I finally had an honest talk with Bev about the state of our marriage—something that was long overdue."

"Wow," I said.

"I told her that I missed the physical part of our relationship and that I needed it—we both needed it."

"How'd she take it?" I asked, more curious than offended by this turn in the conversation.

"Well, she was surprised. She thought I'd just lost interest. But once she realized that physical closeness was really important to me, she agreed to go to counseling."

"Marriage counseling?" I asked.

"Yes, of course. What other kind?" Rob said, lowering his voice to a whisper. "We're meeting with a woman who specializes in sexual issues. We should have done this years ago, but I was buried in work and Bev always had a million projects. According to the counselor, we started off on the wrong foot. Our focus on making a baby took away all our curiosity and joy."

I had no idea how to respond. "It's good that she's open to working on it, Rob," I finally said.

"Yes, I'm very lucky, and I have you to thank."

Was I supposed to say "You're welcome, I'll be delighted to *schtup* you any time I can inspire a romantic revival in your relationship with your wife"? What if I'd wanted to sleep with him again and was crushed? What if it were painful for me to think of his being sexual with old Bev? I felt furious with him, but it was important to me that this, perhaps our last one-on-one conversation, not end in acrimony. What could I say, I wondered, that was both kind and honest?

"I'll miss our morning conversations," I told him after a long pause. This was unassailably true.

"You know, Sam comes with Kimberly to *shul* every Shabbes. Maybe his mom could come too," Rob suggested with a playful smile.

My God, did he honestly think that hearing him preach to the multitudes would serve as a substitute for our conversations on the treadmill? Was it conceivable that I would want to hang out in *shul* with Sam and his sexy, pregnant step-mama? I'd actually grown to like and respect Kimberly, but horning in on her prayer space seemed like a bit too much togetherness.

One thing was clear, Rob and I could never regain our close friendship. Was it just the prospect of sex that moved us into such intimate conversations? Had it all been one long mind-fuck? I didn't think so. Those moments of connection were real. But they were also really over.

"Don't think so," was all I said.

"Well," Rob said, "you have my cell. Feel free to call me any time."

Fat chance, I thought. I had no interest in being yet another congregant, even if I did get special phone privileges. I looked him straight in the eye. "I'm sorry, Rob. I'm not going to call," I said calmly. With that, I left the juice bar and headed for the locker room.

As angry as I was, I still felt sorry for Rob. He'd lost more than I had. I had a core group of wonderful people with whom I could be genuine and to whom I could expose my true self, warts and all. Rob had only me, and now that friendship was ruined. Who else called him by his one true name? Who else knew his secret longings not just for harem girls, but for children, for warmth?

Walking out the gym door felt liberating, as if, after holding my breath for way too long, I was finally able to exhale. The anxious, adrenaline-filled excitement I'd felt around Rob had completely dissipated. I hoped things would work out for a wild night with Greg, but I knew I'd be OK if they didn't. Whatever happened, I felt poised for a good new year. I would deepen my friendships. I'd try to get along better with my rotten kid. My house would become a home I could feel proud of. And, perhaps for the first time, I would enjoy a sense of comfort and contentment in my own ample skin.

Visit us at *www.quidprobooks.com*.

Proof

51832542R00127

Made in the USA
Charleston, SC
28 January 2016